CW01095201

FORBID

Also by Lucinda Chester in Headline Liaison

Driven by Desire
True Colours
Spring Fever
Vermilion Gates
The Challenge
Portrait in Blue
Course of Pleasure

Forbidden Territory

Lucinda Chester

First published in 1998
by HEADLINE BOOK PUBLISHING

A HEADLINE LIAISON paperback

10 9 8 7 6 5 4 3 2 1

ISBN 0 7472 6044 3

Typeset by CBS, Felixstowe, Suffolk

Printed and bound in Great Britain by
Mackays of Chatham plc, Chatham, Kent

HEADLINE BOOK PUBLISHING
A division of Hodder Headline PLC
338 Euston Road
London NW1 3BH

To Terri, Lee and Lee the ace footballer,
with love

Chapter One

Zoe tucked the bottle of wine under her arm and leant on the intercom. Within seconds, there was an answering buzz. 'Hello?'

'Hi, it's me.'

'Come on up,' Steve said. There was a click; then the front door opened. Zoe made sure that it was closed properly, then headed up to his first-floor flat.

He was waiting for her at the door, smiling; she felt the familiar jolt in her stomach at the look on his face. They weren't officially an item – both of them had other lovers, and they both knew the score – but she'd always found Steve attractive. Right from her first day on *Archetypes*, the archaeology magazine he edited, when she'd been a rookie journalist on a placement in the middle of her college course. The office receptionist had pointed out the tall, slightly scruffy man who stood leaning over the designer's PC; Zoe had wrinkled her nose, wondering whether she'd made a mistake to plump for a placement on the small and obscure magazine whose content she adored, rather than a month's experience on one of the big monthly glossies that she never bought and slightly despised.

He hadn't looked like her idea of an editor: tall and gangling, with longish light brown curly hair and no dress sense to speak of. She'd been expecting someone a bit smarter, someone dynamic who did about six things at the same time. Her heart had been in her mouth as she'd walked over to him, preparing to introduce herself. He'd turned round . . . and she'd been lost. Under that shaggy hair had been one of the nicest-looking men she'd ever seen, with high cheekbones, a beautiful mouth, and soulful hazel eyes.

Within a week, they'd become lovers. And after her course, Zoe had joined the magazine full-time – not because she was sleeping with the editor, but because she loved the magazine's subject and she'd graduated at the top of her class, which made her a natural to join them. She'd had an offer from one of the glossies and turned it down in favour of a much lower salary on *Archetypes*, a fact which made all her friends declare her raving mad, but Zoe knew exactly what she was doing. Working on what she loved was a hell of a lot more important than money.

In the office, Steve and Zoe had always maintained a professional relationship, keeping their personal life precisely that. To see them together at work, no one would have believed that they had an ongoing private competition to see who could introduce the other to the most obscure Classical sexual practice, or that they spent most of their spare time in bed.

Eventually, Zoe had turned freelance and worked silly hours to achieve her dream of a regular weekly column in a quality paper to make her subject more accessible. When she'd spent a year in the States, she and Steve had drifted apart, but they'd always maintained a very close friendship, seeing each other once a week when she was back in the country. A friendship which didn't preclude going to bed together, when the mood took them. Zoe regarded Steve Marwick as one of her very best friends – and one of the sweetest lovers she'd ever had.

Steve enveloped her in a hug. 'Hi. How are you?'

'Fine.' She smiled up at him. 'This is for you.'

He took the bottle as he ushered her into the flat and unwrapped the tissue paper. 'Oh *yes*, Chablis.' He sounded like a little boy who'd just been given the toy he'd wanted for weeks. 'Chilled, too. You spoil me,' he said, grinning.

'Just as much as you spoil me.' Zoe relaxed. It hadn't been one of her better weeks, but tonight was going to change all that. Steve always did manage to make her feel good.

'Sit yourself down, and I'll put this back in the fridge.' At her raised eyebrow, he grinned, slightly shame-faced. 'Sorry, I didn't wait for you. I'm already halfway through a glass.'

'Right.' She grinned back at him and headed for his sitting room, kicking her shoes off in the hall. The minute that she was in his sitting room, she stopped dead, and he almost crashed into her.

'Whoa. You could warn me when you're going to do an emergency stop,' he said, curling his hands round her waist and pulling her back against him.

'What's all this in aid of?' she asked, her green eyes narrowing as she surveyed the room. There were vanilla-scented candles burning on the mantelpiece, and he was playing one of her favourite CDs, a rich bluesy-rock. The bottle of Chablis on the coffee-table, together with the dish of strawberries, deepened her suspicions. 'Steve?'

'You sounded a bit fed up on the phone,' he said. 'I thought you needed cheering up.'

She twisted her head round to look at him. 'And you're just the man to do it, hm?'

In answer, he tilted his pelvis against her, so she could feel his growing erection pressing into the divide of her buttocks. 'Something like that.'

'I should have known that you had an ulterior motive for asking me over tonight.'

He grinned, not contradicting her. 'What are friends for, Zoe? Come on, let's sit down.' He drew her down onto the sheepskin rug, settling her so that her head was pillowed on his lap.

'You're such a cliché, Steve,' she grumbled, teasing him. 'You're the only person I know with a sheepskin rug in front of the fire.'

'I suppose that now you're a regular columnist on one of the Sunday monsters, you mix with people who own imported silk kelims and the like,' he teased back.

'Okay yah,' she quipped.

He leaned forward to kiss the tip of her nose. 'So what's the matter, then? Tell me.'

'Nothing really,' she said honestly. 'Work's going well. I split up with Curtis last week – but that had been on the cards for ages, so I'm not exactly devastated.'

'Especially when you can get sexual consolation elsewhere,' Steve said, starting to unbutton her shirt.

She made no move to push him away. 'Something like that.'

'It's not work and it's not sex, then. Money?'

'Not even with my shopping habits – no. I've been good, lately.'

3

'Your house has developed a raging case of damp or subsidence? The neighbours from hell have just moved next door and they're playing rap at a hundred decibels at three a.m.?'

'No.'

'What, then?'

She sighed. 'That's just it. Nothing's wrong. Oh, I dunno. Maybe I just need a change of scene, a holiday.'

'Sounds to me,' Steve said, 'like you're bored. You're in a luvverly little safe routine – a regular weekly column, the odd bit of work for people like me to remind you what you're not missing in being a wage-slave, and nothing exciting lined up on the horizon.'

'That makes me sound like a spoilt brat,' she told him, raking a hand through her dark curls. 'Like I don't appreciate what I have.'

'Of course you do. You worked hard enough for it, Zoe. If you want my diagnosis, I reckon you're just a bit stir crazy, and you need to get out of London for a few days,' he said. 'Get your column done for the next month, tell everyone you're going incommunicado – and then take yourself off somewhere for a few weeks.' He finished unbuttoning her shirt and drew his fingertip along the lacy edge of her bra. 'In the meantime, you might as well spend this evening enjoying yourself.'

'And what precisely did you have in mind?' Zoe asked.

He grinned. 'I thought you'd never ask.' He reached up to the coffee table, taking the glass and holding it to her lips. 'You could always pretend you're a Roman mistress, being pleasured by one of your slaves.'

'Slave, eh?' She sipped the wine languidly. 'Neither of us is dressed for the part.'

'Or undressed,' he said, putting the glass back on the table. He slid her shirt from her shoulders, then eased his fingers under the cups of her bra, pushing the material down to bare her breasts properly.

Her nipples hardened under his touch. 'So am I supposed to beat you?'

'Only if I don't pleasure you properly, mistress.'

She grinned, pushing his hands away. 'Give over. I came here to moan to my best mate.'

'Moan away,' he said, not in the least put out. He recaptured her breasts and began toying with her nipples, pulling gently at the hard rosy peaks and twisting them.

Zoe arched her back. 'I didn't mean that kind of moan.'

'Well, I do.' He reached up to the bowl of strawberries, selecting a tiny sweet fruit and slipping it into her mouth. 'You talk too much, woman.'

She ate the fruit and didn't answer. Steve took her silence as permission to proceed, and took two more strawberries, squashing one on each nipple and then eating the fruit, licking and sucking it and the juice off her skin.

'Perfect. The only thing missing is the cream,' he murmured against her ear; the way his breath fanned against her skin made her close her eyes with pleasure.

'Indeed, Mr Marwick?' she teased.

'Indeed. And I have just the thing in mind.' He unzipped her jeans; she took her weight on her feet and shoulders, letting him pull her faded denims over her hips, then relaxed back so that he could remove them completely. 'That's better,' he said, stroking her inner thighs. 'Have I ever told you, Zoe, your skin feels like you've just bathed in asses' milk?'

She groaned, picking up on the private shorthand. 'Don't tell me you're doing another article on Cleopatra. You're obsessed with the woman.'

'"Age cannot wither her,"' he quoted, '"nor custom stale her infinite variety".'

Zoe opened her eyes to shoot him a look: a mixture of indulgence and annoyance. 'Honestly. You know that bloody play off by heart.'

'Yup.' He was unabashed. 'Mind you, I think you're as beautiful as she was.' He ruffled her hair. 'All these curls. Beautiful long, heavy hair.' Hair which she'd wrapped round his cock on more than one occasion; by the tremor in his body, Zoe knew that he remembered it.

'Long, heavy hair which would have been extremely uncomfortable, in the desert,' Zoe reminded him. 'That's why most ancient Egyptians were shaven-headed and wore wigs.'

'Indeedy.' He grinned. 'You know what I love most about you, Zoe? The way you can always cap my references.'

She laughed back. 'Not always.'

'Maybe, but at least you understand what I'm talking about. Your mind works on the same wave-length as mine.'

'Which is why we're best mates.'

'And why you're probably the best lover I've ever had, too,' he mused. He squashed another strawberry over her breasts, licking off the juice.

'My bra's going to get sticky, if you keep doing that,' she pointed out.

'What are washing machines for?' he fenced, repeating the action and deliberately spilling drops of red juice on the white lace.

'Don't I get to eat any, then?'

He smiled, popping a fruit into her mouth, then shifted so that he was kneeling between her thighs. 'What we need is some cream,' he repeated.

'What are fridges for?' she mocked, twisting his earlier words.

'Chilling beer. And wine,' he added, giving her a mischievous look. 'I told you, I already have something in mind.'

'Oh, yes?'

'Yes,' he said, his voice soft and velvety. 'Most definitely.' He hooked his thumbs into the waistband of her knickers and tugged at the sheer material; obligingly, Zoe lifted her bottom, letting him remove the garment completely.

Steve smiled at her, his hazel eyes crinkling at the corner; he tossed her knickers to one side and lifted her left leg, drawing her foot up to his mouth. Zoe closed her eyes again, relaxing in the sybaritic feel of the sheepskin rug against her almost-bare skin. She loved it when Steve did this – paid attention to every inch of skin, arousing her thoroughly with his mouth. She shivered as he sucked each of her toes in turn and moved up to caress her instep, then the hollows of her ankle.

She was suddenly glad that she'd had a shower before she'd come over to Steve's. She smiled wryly to herself. As if she hadn't known that they would end up making love. No doubt Steve had heard the slightly plaintive and lonely note in her voice, and known straightaway that she needed something to take her mind off whatever was wrong. Not that anything *was* wrong, really, as she'd explained to him. She just felt strangely restless.

His mouth moved slowly up her leg, lingering over the sensitive spot at the back of her knee; as he reached her inner thigh, Zoe had to force herself not to slide one hand between her legs and start rubbing herself. She moaned slightly, wriggling as he bypassed her quim and started on her other leg, moving slowly downwards.

By the time he'd reached her toes, Zoe felt deliciously fluid; she made no protest as Steve gently bent her knees and set her feet flat on the rug, widening her thighs to give him a better view of her sex.

'Do you know how good you look, like that?' he asked huskily. 'There you are in your demure white bra – except it looks lewd on you, pulled down to expose your beautiful breasts. And then . . . nothing to distract me from the beauty of your skin, the way you look against that rug. The way you curve. Your warm, soft sex – which I knew will feel like wet velvet against my fingers and my mouth and my cock.'

'Promises, promises,' she said lazily.

'Which I intend to keep.' Just to prove it, he eased his hand between her thighs to cup her mons veneris. Zoe gave a sigh of pleasure as he parted her labia with his middle finger, curling it up and then straightening it to rub against her clitoris. He repeated the action again and again, until Zoe pushed against him; then he inserted the tip of his finger in her sex.

'Don't tease,' she warned huskily.

'Would I?' He pushed his finger up to the second knuckle, then eased infinitesimally slowly up to the hilt. He withdrew almost completely, then sank in again; as Zoe started to buck against him, he added a second finger, and a third. He quickened his pace, and she moaned aloud with pleasure; he rotated the pad of his thumb on her clitoris, and suddenly her muscles tautened, her breasts swelling and a familiar rosy mottling covering her face and neck.

He smiled tenderly at her as her internal muscles spasmed hard round his fingers. 'Better?'

'Better,' she agreed, her voice several tones lower than usual.

'Good.' He removed his fingers and picked up another

strawberry, rubbing it across her quim before eating it. Then he pushed another fruit completely inside her, sucking it out. Zoe quivered as she felt the bulbous fruit stretching the narrowest part of her sex; what Steve was doing to her felt deliciously lewd.

He ate a second fruit the same way, pushing it inside her and sucking it out, then squashed the third over her clitoris, sucking the fruit from the hard nub of flesh. 'Strawberries and cream. Just how I like it,' he murmured.

'Oh, Steve.' Zoe was torn between laughing and moaning with delight as he pushed another fruit into her.

He grinned. 'Don't tell me you prefer yours unadulterated.' He pulled the fruit from her quim, then held it to her lips. 'I read about someone doing that with asparagus, once.'

Zoe ate the fruit, delighting in the taste of her own sharp tang against the sweetness of the fruit. 'You would.'

'I thought it sounded rather horrible. Too hot – not to mention being green and thin,' he mused. 'Whereas strawberries – well. They're the right colour and almost the right shape.'

'What are you talking about?'

'If you'd care to divest me of my clothing, Ms Lynton, I'll show you what I mean.'

Zoe stretched and crossed her hands behind her head, 'I don't know if I can be bothered to move. Why don't you strip for me? Give me a show, something to amuse me.'

'Bloody hell, she really is Cleopatra's reincarnation,' he teased. 'The bored Egyptian queen, always wanting some new sensual delight to amuse her.'

'Amuse? Not quite the right word, Marwick. That's red-penned,' Zoe said.

'Smarty-pants. Switch your journo brain off.'

'You obviously have,' she retorted with a grin.

'From where I'm sitting, woman, so would you. I'm looking at the ultimate distraction – and the only language I'm interested in, right now, is body language.' He bent his head to draw his tongue between her bared breasts, then drew a trail of kisses over her abdomen. Zoe arched up, widening the gap between her thighs, but Steve dropped one last kiss on her delta and sat back on his haunches.

8

She looked at him, disappointment written on her face. 'Oh.'

'You told me to strip, I believe. That was a delightful little tangent,' he teased. 'And now I'm back on track.'

Slowly, he removed his clothes; Zoe watched him, liking the way he made a show of it for her, teasing her out of her restless mood. When he'd finished, he held a strawberry next to the swollen tip of his cock. 'See? Same colour, same shape.'

Zoe snorted. 'Like hell!'

'Come a bit closer,' he invited. 'See for yourself.' He knelt down and squashed the fruit on his cock, then tipped his head to one side, looking hopeful.

She smiled. 'If you want me to suck your cock, Steve, all you have to do is ask.'

He fluttered his eyelashes. 'Pretty please with sugar on it?'

'Pretty cock with strawberries on it,' she quipped. In one lithe movement, she was kneeling in front of him; she pushed her hair back, bent down and licked the squashed fruit from his glans. 'What we need is champagne,' she murmured.

'Won't Chablis do?'

'No bubbles,' she said succinctly, and he shivered.

'Oh. That's what you had in mind, you perverse woman.'

She grinned. 'And just who introduced me to that lovely little practice?'

'Yeah, yeah.' The last word was more of a groan as she resumed sucking him, taking just the tip of his cock into her mouth and licking his frenum. When she curled her fingers round his shaft and began to rub him, in direct counterpoint to the movements of her mouth, Steve closed his eyes and rocked back on his haunches.

She continued to suck until he was nearly at the point of orgasm, then sat back and squeezed just below the tip of his cock, delaying his climax. 'Now, now,' she mocked. 'Let's not be too hasty about this.'

'Witch,' he growled, pushing her back onto the rug with mock fierceness. She laughed as he parted her thighs, then wrapped her legs round his waist, tipping her sex towards him; Steve fitted the tip of his cock to her sex and eased in.

'Much better,' Zoe said, arching up towards him as he began to thrust.

'Definitely,' he agreed, bending his head to kiss her.

She shivered as his tongue slid into her mouth, the little stabbing movements echoing the way his cock pushed into her. The hair on his chest was a delicious friction against her nipples; she closed her eyes, moaning into his mouth, and tangled her fingers in his hair, massaging his scalp to urge him on.

Her restlessness forgotten, she moved in perfect synchronization with him, pushing up as he thrust down and moving away from him as he withdrew, her movements increasing the friction to give them both greater pleasure. She bucked and writhed beneath him; he took his weight on his knees and one hand, sliding the other between their bodies to that he could rub the pad of his thumb over her clitoris.

Pleasure lanced through her as he played with the little nub of flesh, alternately circling it and rubbing it back and forth, varying the pace and pressure until she was driven crazy with desire. All the time, he kissed her – her mouth, with his tongue probing her deeply, or her throat, taking tiny nips at her skin to arouse her still further.

She'd almost forgotten how skilled he was, how well he knew her body; everything he did was calculated to drive her to fever pitch, and then some. 'Oh, yes,' she murmured as he licked the sensitive spot at the side of her throat. 'Yes, yes, yes.'

In one fluid movement, Steve withdrew, flipped her over onto her stomach, guided her to her hands and knees and pushed his cock back into her sex, filling her to the hilt. He pressed down gently on her shoulders, so that she dipped her face to the rug; the angle allowed him deeper penetration, and she groaned into the sheepskin as he continued to thrust, setting up a rapid pace that had her at the brink of a climax within seconds.

Just as she thought she could take no more, he moved one hand up to his mouth; then she felt his spit-slicked thumb pressing against the hard nub of her clitoris.

'Oh, God,' she moaned, her voice muffled by the rug, as her flesh throbbed beneath him. Steve worked in perfect synchronization, pacing the thrusts of his cock with the way his thumb moved against the hard little bud of pleasure.

Zoe almost howled in pleasure as she felt his balls slapping against her quim, sensitising her sex even further.

He didn't let up the pace, even when the first explosive tremors shook her body; he rode her through the first climax and into a second, adding another dimension to her pleasure by sneaking his other hand round her waist and sliding it up her midriff to caress her breasts, pulling gently at the rosy peaks of her nipples.

Zoe came again and again; only when her whole body was shaking did he release his own control, pumping into her and pressing his cheek affectionately to her back. They remained locked together until their heartbeats had slowed to normal; then, slowly, Steve withdrew and flopped on his back beside her, pulling her into the curve of his body and curling his arm round her.

They lay there for a while, listening to the music – which Zoe suddenly realised was on continuous loop – and relaxing together.

'Your rug's going to be in a mess,' she murmured.

'So?' he said, not caring. 'There's a dry-cleaner down the road.' He paused, stroking her buttocks. 'You know,' he said, 'I reckon I've got the solution.'

'To what?'

'To your bout of stir craziness,' he told her.

Zoe sat up, catching the note in his voice. 'This was your ulterior motive, wasn't it? Not just spending the evening in bed with you.'

'The night, and it's on a rug, at the moment,' he corrected, pushing her back down onto the rug. 'You obviously changed before you came over here, and you don't have an office to watch the clock for you, so you can spend tonight here, can't you?'

In his king-size bed. Between cool, smooth cotton sheets. Warmed by the heat of his body. She smiled. 'I reckon so. So what's this solution of yours, then?'

He beamed at her. 'Put it this way, Zoe, it's straight out of your dreams.'

'Steve, don't be elliptical. My brain isn't functioning.' He'd just inserted a finger into her moist sex, and was busy teasing her again. 'Tell me.'

'Okay. How do you fancy a few days in Norfolk?'

'Norfolk?' She frowned. 'What's in Norfolk? I mean, I know they found the Roman villa at Holt – it's meant to be spectacular – and there's the excavation of RAF Lakenheath where they found that warrior actually buried with his horse, though that isn't quite in Norfolk . . . but you've already featured both of them in *Archetypes*. Surely you don't want me to cover old ground?'

'This is something else,' Steve told her. 'Something that could be even better.'

'Ohhh.' Zoe's moan was more in response to what he was doing to her than what he was saying.

'What would you say if I told you someone found Boudicca's grave?'

'No way.'

'Yes, way,' he corrected.

As his words penetrated her sex-befuddled brain, Zoe pushed his hand away and sat bolt upright. She'd long been interested in Roman Britain, and she'd identified with Boudicca ever since she'd been a schoolgirl and read about the way the warrior queen had sacked Colchester, nearly beating the Roman army. 'You're kidding. Where?'

'Well – it isn't official, yet,' he warned. 'And it might not be true.'

'I thought it sounded too good.' The flicker of excitement in her eyes died.

'But supposing it *is* true, Zoe? Supposing we were about to unearth the find of the millennium?'

The suppressed excitement in his voice told her that Steve had some hard facts, some sort of proof which meant it probably was true. 'Tell me what you know.'

'There's a guy called Jack Mitchell. He's a farmer – retired – who lives in Norfolk, somewhere near Diss. He was out metal-detecting, and he found some Roman coins on his land.'

Zoe nodded. 'That's pretty common around those parts. There was a mint at Thetford, remember.'

'I know, but it's right in the middle of Boudicca country. The centre of Iceni tribelands. There's a village legend about her, too, something to do with a ghost. A warrior queen with red hair, on horseback.'

'So how do you know about it?'

12

'One of our readers sent in some local press cuttings.'
Steve shrugged. 'It might be just an old man's dream, but I
rang him, the other day, and he sounds like he knows what
he's talking about. He's done a fair bit of research.' He
paused. 'This might be what you need, Zoe. The chance to
be in on something really big, right from the start – and it
just happens to be your favourite subject.'

She still had misgivings. 'It sounds too good to be true.'

'It probably is – but you can be the judge of that. And
who better than my best-ever journo—' At her cough, he
grinned. 'You might have escaped from the staff, but you're
still the best, Zoe. Anyway, it's a nice part of the world. Full
of medieval churches. You can spend a few days indulging
yourself.' Zoe's other passion, well known at the *Archetypes*
office, was for *mementi mori*, the grim poetry usually
accompanying a skull and crossbones in ancient churches,
to warn whoever read it that 'so I am, so shall ye be'. He
smiled at her. 'So what do you think? Are you up for it?'

She nodded. 'Yes. I need some more information first, of
course. Background. And directions to wherever this place
is.'

'Your wish is my command.' He stood up and left the
room, uncaring that he was stark naked; he returned a couple
of minutes later with a thin cardboard wallet file.
'Everything's in here. A copy of the readers' correspondence
and local paper clippings, an ordnance survey map with the
relevant area marked with a yellow highlighter pen, notes of
my conversations with Jack – and directions to Whiteacres.
That's his farm,' Steve explained. 'He's expecting you the
day after tomorrow.'

Zoe's mouth thinned. 'You were taking a hell of a lot on
trust, Marwick, making an appointment for an interview
before you'd even asked me if I'd do it.'

'Was I, hell.' He grinned. 'This is going to be the hottest
story in archaeology for years. I knew you wouldn't pass up
the chance to be involved – especially as it's all to do with
your pet queen. And don't pull that face, Zoe. You're worse
about Boudicca than I am about Cleopatra. Obsessive.'

'The day after tomorrow.' She frowned. 'I'm not sure if I
can make it. I've got—'

'Whatever you've got,' Steve cut in, 'you can either beg a

few days' grace or think about it on the A12, write it up in your hotel bedroom and fax it through your laptop. Or email it. With modern technology, you can do things where the hell you like.'

She sighed. 'You've got an answer for everything.'

'Except the answer I want you to supply. Is Boudicca really buried in the middle of an obscure Norfolk village, or not?'

'Right.'

He pulled her to her feet. 'But you can't do anything until you're in Norfolk and talking to Jack Mitchell, so I suggest we retire somewhere more comfortable – with the rest of the wine . . .'

Chapter Two

The next morning saw Zoe at her most efficient. She left Steve's early, before the rush-hour, and had already packed before her usual contacts were due in at their respective offices. She spent the morning and the first half of the afternoon working intensively and rapidly on her outstanding work, making sure that she had the next few weeks' deadlines in hand, and faxed the copy through to her editors.

Three phone-calls and six emails later – including one to her other closest friend, Alicia, to let her know where she was going – Zoe was ready to leave.

Steve had been right, she knew. She needed some time out of London. And this was just the kind of diversion to suit her: a quest into the past. Steve had also been right when he'd said that she'd never pass up the chance to be involved. She'd even specialised in Roman Britain, for her Classics degree. Something about the period appealed to her. Not for her the refined gentility of the Victorian view of Greece and Rome; she liked the raw power struggles of Roman Britain, the defiant and hot-blooded spirit of the Britons. Even her wildest sexual fantasies involved Roman centurions; and Steve had once indulged her, taking her to a New Year's fancy dress party as a Roman centurion, with her as his British slave. They'd acted out their parts later that night, too, in bed . . .

She shivered, switched on her burglar alarm, locked her house and headed for her car. Steve had her spare key, and had promised to keep an eye on the place while she was away; the best part about the trip was that it could take anything from a day to a couple of weeks, depending on what she discovered. And, she thought with a grin, how many old churches she pottered round. Norfolk had two of the thickest Pevsner volumes, proving that it was rich in beautiful architecture. She needed a holiday, and the idea of just travelling round the county, stopping wherever took her fancy, was more than appealing.

Two hours later, she'd left the A12 and A140 behind, and was driving through narrow country lanes in South Norfolk. Eventually, she found Lower Yareham, the small village where Jack Mitchell lived; she was half tempted to drive to the farm, but remembered that Steve had already arranged an appointment for the following day. Time to find a bed for the night, she thought. And something to eat.

Halfway through the village, she saw a pub sign: *The Feathers. Free house. Bar meals, beer garden, accommodation.* It looked a pleasant enough place: a long low thatched building painted white, with window-boxes and hanging baskets. Late seventeenth century, she thought. The kind of place she'd enjoy staying.

Inside was even better. The walls inside the bar were creamy-white, and old maps and framed sketches and photographs of the village hung on the walls. The large inglenook fireplace had several brasses hanging on the bressumer beam, and there was a wicker basket full of logs and kindling on the pamment tiles, proof that the fire in the grate was real rather than a clever gas coal-effect one. Pleased with what she'd found, she walked over to the bar.

The pretty young blonde barmaid smiled at her. 'Good evening. What can I get you?'

Zoe smiled back. 'I wondered if you had any rooms free?'

'I'll just ask Mum. I won't be a minute.' The barmaid disappeared, returning with a middle-aged woman who was unmistakably her mother. They shared the same bone structure and the same warm, welcoming smile.

'Hello, I'm Betty Fielding. Sam tells me that you're looking for a room.'

Zoe nodded. 'That's right.'

'We only have doubles, if that's all right?'

'That's fine, thanks.'

Betty paused. 'Do you know how long you want to stay?'

'I'm not sure, yet,' Zoe said honestly. 'It all depends on how things go.'

'You're on business in the area, then?'

'Partly. I'm a journalist,' Zoe explained. 'I work with a

16

magazine in London, and we heard about Jack Mitchell's find. So I've come to interview him.'

Sam whistled. 'I hope you've got thick skin, then.'

'Why?' Zoe was interested.

Betty nudged her daughter. 'Stop gossiping.' She smiled at Zoe. 'Don't listen to Sam. You'll be fine with old Jack.'

'It wasn't Jack I was thinking about,' Sam muttered, but she went over to the other end of the bar to serve a customer, leaving her mother with an intrigued Zoe.

'Come with me,' Betty said, 'and I'll take you up to your room.'

Later that evening, when Zoe had settled in and eaten her fill of Betty's excellent chicken provençale and an even better apple pie, she went over to the bar where Sam was serving. She had a feeling that the young barmaid would be a good source of background information – more so than her very pleasant but very discreet mother, who had resisted Zoe's best attempts at finding out just what would be so hard about seeing Jack Mitchell. 'Hi.'

Sam returned her smile. 'Settled in okay?'

'Yes, thanks.'

'So what can I get you?'

'A spritzer, please. And one for yourself.'

'Cheers.' Sam made Zoe a spritzer, and poured an orange juice for herself. 'Well, I hope you enjoy your stay.'

Zoe glanced at the other end of the bar. Betty was busy; this was her chance. 'I hope so, too. But I'm a bit concerned.'

'Oh?'

'It's what you said earlier – that it might be difficult to interview Jack.'

Sam shrugged. 'Jack Mitchell's a sweetie.'

'Then what's the problem, Sam?'

Sam winced. 'Mum'll kill me if she hears me gossiping. Especially if any of it ends up in the papers.'

Zoe chuckled. 'I'm researching an article for an archaeology magazine. I promise you, anything you tell me won't make the front page of the tabloids, or even the local paper.'

Sam gave a quick glance towards her mother, then nodded. 'Okay. The problem's Brandon.'

'Brandon?'

'Jack's grandson. He runs the estate.'

'And he and Jack have had a row?'

'Sort of. Jack has this bee in his bonnet about Boudicca's grave being on their land. He reckons he's found proof – it even made half a page in the local daily paper.'

'And Brandon doesn't like people invading his privacy?' Zoe guessed.

'I suppose not – and he has other ideas about that particular field.'

'Like what?'

'He wants to build some houses on it.'

'I see.' Time to tread carefully, Zoe thought.

'It's caused quite a stir in the village. Half the people are in favour of the development, because they think that it'll create a few jobs; the others are behind Jack, and they want the land left as it is.'

'So they're at each other's throats, then?'

'Only over that subject,' Sam admitted. 'Brandon's parents died when he was very young, and Jack brought him up. They're very close – except where those fields are concerned. Brandon thinks that Jack's fantasising about the grave, and Jack thinks that Brandon doesn't care about the past.'

Zoe nodded. 'Difficult.'

'Yes.' Sam paused, and a smile crossed her face. 'Brandon's nice-looking, too.'

'Just your type, hm?' Zoe teased.

Sam grinned. 'Not just mine. Half the women in the village have lustful dreams about Brandon Mitchell. Obviously you haven't met him.'

'Not yet.'

'Well, he's got these gorgeous slate-blue eyes and a bone structure to die for – I suppose he's your typical tall, dark and handsome man. But he's not the "good-looking and I know it" sort. He's really nice, as well as being sex on legs.' Sam sighed. 'It's just a pity that he's mixed up with Mark.'

'Who's Mark?' Zoe probed.

'Mark Burroughs. He's Brandon's business partner on the development.'

'And you don't like him.'

18

Sam wrinkled her nose. 'He's very charming, when he wants to be, but . . .' She grimaced. 'Most people in the village think he's a snake, and don't trust him – Jack hates him. And as for his daughter, Helena . . .'

'What about her?'

Sam rolled her eyes. 'She's a typical spoilt bitch, if you ask me. Daddy's little girl, used to getting anything she wants within seconds – and that includes Brandon. It's pretty obvious she's after him – and more than just an affair, too. She's got her eyes on a wedding ring and the money from the development and the farm.' She smiled wryly. 'She's very attractive, if you like that sort. Half the men around here would give a lot to get into her knickers.'

'Sam, I told you to stop gossiping – and I don't expect catty remarks behind this bar.' Betty came up behind them, overhearing her daughter's last words.

Sam winced. 'Sorry, Mum.'

'It's my fault,' Zoe cut in swiftly. 'I asked Sam to tell me a bit more about this Boudicca business. I read the article in the local paper – that's why I came here in the first place – and it always helps to have some local background.'

'Yes.' Betty looked faintly disapproving. 'Though quite what Helena Burroughs has to do with Jack Mitchell finding a few Roman coins is beyond me.'

'Sorry.' Both Sam and Zoe flushed, giving each other a complicit look.

'Well. Least said, soonest mended. Remember that, Sam.'

'Yes, Mum.'

'And I can't work the whole bar on my own, love.' Betty nodded to a customer who had just walked in.

'I know. Sorry. I'll see you later, Zoe.'

'Okay.' Zoe smiled apologetically at Betty. 'I'm sorry. I'm the one who kept Sam talking.'

'She doesn't take much holding up, believe me.' Betty's smile was equally rueful. 'I was the same, at her age. I think she misses the bright lights a bit.'

'Probably. I'll – er – let you get on.'

'I hope you don't think I'm being rude.'

Zoe shook her head. 'Not at all. I can see you're busy.'

'Well, if you need anything, you know where I am.'

'Thanks.' Zoe went over to a corner by the fire, and sat

nursing her drink, thinking about her planned interview tomorrow. It was obvious that she'd have problems, if Brandon was around. Attractive but moody, by the sound of things. She'd just have to hope that she could get Jack on his own. And if she couldn't – well, she'd have to try another tack.

A few minutes later, she was aware that someone was standing next to her table and was saying something.

'I'm sorry, I was miles away.' She smiled up at the stranger, and as soon as she met his eyes, she felt that familiar jolt of arousal in the pit of her stomach. Whoever he was, he was just the type she went for: floppy blond hair, small round glasses, and deep soulful brown eyes. He couldn't be Brandon Mitchell, then; she remembered Sam saying that Brandon had blue eyes.

'I was just asking if you were on your own, and if you'd like some company,' he repeated. He held out his hand. 'Dale MacKenzie. I'm the village doctor.'

His handshake was firm; Zoe smiled approvingly at him. 'I'd be delighted if you joined me. Zoe Lynton. I'm a journalist.'

'Are you new to the village, or a tourist?' he asked as he sat down.

'A tourist. Though I'm here to work, too.'

'Work? The only news around here is . . .' His voice faded. 'Ah. Jack Mitchell's find, right?'

'Right.'

Dale grinned. 'He's quite a character. Have you met him, yet?'

'No. I've got an appointment to see him tomorrow – but I gather that I have to get past his guard-dog, first.'

'Something like that.' He chuckled at the teasing light in Zoe's eyes. 'How long are you staying?'

'I don't really know. Once I've finished looking into the background of the Boudicca story, my time's my own. I was planning to spend a few days in the area, just pottering around.' She spread her hands. 'According to my friends, I'm nearly as bad as a train-spotter. I can't resist old churches.'

'Graveyards or architecture?'

'A bit of both,' Zoe admitted. 'One day, I wouldn't mind

writing a book about English country churches.'

'So that's your specialty?'

'More or less. Churches, digs, that sort of thing. I always wanted to be an archaeologist, when I was a child. I suppose that being a journalist who specialises in archaeology is the next best thing.'

'Yes.'

They continued chatting, and Zoe discovered that Dale MacKenzie had been the village GP for the past eight years, since he'd finished his medical training in London and taken a holiday on the Broads, falling in love with Norfolk and deciding to stay there. He'd joined a practice in Diss, then taken the opportunity to move into the village. He hadn't lost that much of his native Edinburgh accent, though, and he told her that he'd always be known around here as the Scottish Doctor.

In turn, Zoe told him how she'd worked on *Archetypes* and had turned freelance, giving her the chance to work on projects which really interested her.

He looked at her glass. 'Can I get you another?'

She shook her head. 'My round.'

Dale chuckled. 'Why do I suddenly feel suspicious?'

Zoe grinned. 'It might have something to do with the reputation of journalists. And they do say that there's no such thing as a free lunch, let alone a free drink. As you're the village doctor, I imagine you must know quite a bit about the village.'

'Yes. But I can't answer any questions about my patients,' he reminded her.

'I'm after background, not medical details,' she said. 'I just want to know more about the village itself.'

'Well, most of what I know, I learnt from Jack, so I suppose it's a bit biased.'

Zoe spread her hands. 'All background is useful,' she said. 'What are you having?'

'A pint, please.' He named some beer she'd never heard of, grinning at her surprised face. 'It's made by the local brewery.'

She went to the bar. Sam served her, and aimed a meaningful nod at Dale. 'Drinking with the dashing Dr MacKenzie, eh?' she teased. 'He's the most eligible bachelor in the village. Except Brandon, who's sort of spoken for, if Helena could get her way.'

'Thanks for the tip,' Zoe grinned back. It was good to know that Dale was unattached. She'd found him attractive – she'd always had a soft spot for deep brown eyes, ever since Steve – and she could tell that it was mutual. She could also tell that something was going to happen between them, and very soon: her sixth sense was very strong when it came to sex. The first time she met someone she would make love with, at some time in the future, she always had an odd tingly feeling in the tips of her fingers – almost like a rush of adrenaline. Exactly the same feeling that she had, right now.

She rejoined Dale at their table. 'One pint, as requested.'

'Thank you.' He lifted his glass in a toast. 'OK, Lois Lane, what do you want to know about the village, then?'

'Have there been many finds of Roman coins and the like, since you've worked around here?'

'One or two. Though Jack believes there's a lot more to it than the couple of coins he found. He's pretty sure that there's evidence of a grave.'

'Without a proper survey? Come on, Dale. There has to be more to it than that. From what I hear, half the village is behind him on this.'

'And the other half is behind Brandon.' Dale glanced at the bar. 'I take it that young Sam has been filling you in on the details?'

'About the development, you mean? Yes.' Zoe paused. Was Dale trying to tell her that Sam wasn't a reliable source of information? 'She seems pretty straightforward.'

'She is. She's a nice kid,' Dale said.

'So basically, would you say that the reason people are supporting Jack is because they don't want the housing development, or do they really think that he's found something important?'

'A bit of both, I'd say.'

'And where do you stand, Dr MacKenzie?'

He lifted his hands in mock surrender. 'On the Hippocratic oath.'

Zoe laughed. 'That's cheating.'

'I can't be seen to take sides, Zoe. I'm the village doctor.

I have to remain impartial – believe me, once you get involved in village politics, you store up all kinds of problems for yourself. I'm staying neutral.'

'Off the record, then.' At his doubtful look, she smiled. 'Brownies' honour, I won't use what you say in any article. I just want to know for me.'

'To be honest, I don't know,' Dale said. 'There's a legend about Boudicca leaving Colchester after she was defeated and drinking poison. We're not so far from Colchester.'

'But why here?'

'Maybe she was born around here. Historians don't know that much about her, do they?' he asked.

'Not that much,' she admitted. 'And no-one knows for sure where she was buried. This is Iceni territory, so it could well be around here.'

'There's more to the village legend than just her death. Apparently, a tall woman with red hair is seen wrapped in a cloak and riding a black horse, on certain nights of the year, riding across the Mitchells' land.'

'And if you see her, you're likely to have a death in the family before the end of the year,' Zoe finished.

He smiled wryly. 'Something like that. Have you heard it before?'

'No – but it's a pretty standard tale, along with headless horsemen, black carriages with horses driven by a red-eyed man, and Old Shuck, the black dog which haunts most of the east coast,' she told him.

'I've never seen the woman with red hair, myself,' Dale said. 'Or any other ghost, come to that. But there's often a nugget of truth in old legends.'

Zoe thought about it. 'If Jack is right and the grave is in those fields, it will change the whole village. The area will become a national site, and bring a lot of tourist trade here. The whole character of the village would be altered – and probably not for the better. Tacky souvenir shops and over-priced tea-shops: I can just see it now.'

'On the other hand, if the fields are developed instead, the new housing estate will change the character of the village. It'll become a dormitory town for London commuters, as we're so close to Diss station.'

'So either way, life won't be the same, this time next year.'

23

She eyed Dale thoughtfully. 'Dale, can I ask you something personal?'

'That depends.'

'What do you think of Brandon?'

'Brandon Mitchell?' He frowned. 'Why?'

'Because from what Sam says, I'll have to persuade him to let me anywhere near Jack; and I think you'll give me a less biased view than Sam. Being male, I mean.'

Dale grinned. 'Most of the single women in the village are a bit in love with Brandon. So are half the married ones – not that they'll admit it, if their husbands are around.'

'So he's a bit of a lady-killer, then?'

'He has nice manners,' Dale said simply. 'Women respond well to him . . . around here, anyway,' he added quickly.

Zoe chuckled. 'Don't worry, I'm not about to hit you with a feminist diatribe. I just wondered what you thought of him.'

'He's a decent guy. He cares a lot about his grandfather, and he's done a lot of good in the village. He's given jobs to some of the village boys who really didn't stand a chance elsewhere, having left school with virtually no qualifications and a bad reputation, and he's worked wonders with them.'

'I see.' Half saint, half devil, by the sound of things. Meeting Brandon Mitchell was going to be very interesting, she thought.

He finished his pint. 'Another?'

'Unless you feel like showing me round the village. Is the field near here? The one with the grave in – allegedly – I mean?'

'Not really. It's on Whiteacres – that's the Mitchell farm – and it's a good half-hour walk from here.'

'Right. How about the church, then?'

He glanced at her. 'You do realise that if you leave here with me, half the village will know by tomorrow morning, and they'll all assume that I took you back to my cottage?'

She grinned. 'I can live with that . . . if you can.'

The slightly smoky timbre of her voice made his pupils dilate. 'I think I can,' he said, his voice growing husky.

'Good. Then lay on, MacKenzie,' she misquoted deliberately.

He chuckled as he ushered her out of The Feathers. 'That could be taken two ways.'

'Indeed.'

'As a doctor—'

She cut him off, placing a finger on his lips. 'I'm not talking to Dr MacKenzie. I'm with my new friend Dale. Okay?'

'Okay.'

They walked through the village together, with Dale telling her more about Lower Yareham; when they reached the church, she stifled a feeling of disappointment. It looked very plain from the outside: built of traditional Norfolk knapped flint, but with a square tower where a round tower should have been. Lower Yareham church, she decided, had been very badly restored at some time in the past. The interior was probably plain, with all the stained glass replaced by new plain glass, bare wooden pews and rough stone flooring.

When Dale opened the heavy studded door for her, her eyes widened. 'My God! You could have warned me.'

'Definitely not. It looks a mess, from the outside,' he said, 'but that only makes the inside look better.'

It was what Zoe thought of as a proper country church, with rich stained glass windows – some of them obviously Victorian commissions, with one looking suspiciously like a Burne-Jones – and richly carved dark oak pews, the sides adorned with tiny harvest animals. There were brasses set in the floor and, to her delight, a *memento mori* in a niche in one wall. Her gaze travelled up towards the altar, and her eyes widened still further. 'Original wall paintings?'

'Yes. There was a problem with damp, so the villagers raised enough money to get it repaired. When the plasterers scraped away the first layer, they found the paintings; it took about three years to uncover them properly.' He looked at her. 'I'm surprised you haven't heard about them, with your interest in old churches.'

'It must be a well-kept secret,' she said wryly. 'They're beautiful, Dale.'

'St Edmund the Martyr. The church is dedicated to him, too,' he informed her.

They stayed for a while in the church, then wandered

around the graveyard, looking at the inscriptions. 'It's terribly morbid,' Zoe admitted, 'but I find it fascinating.'

'Me, too.' He paused, and took her hand. 'Would you like a coffee?'

'And scandalise the village?' she teased.

His lips twitched. 'Oh, I can do more than that to scandalise them.' Without warning, he spun her round to face him, and lowered his face to hers, kissing her lightly on the mouth. Zoe found herself responding, winding her arms round his neck and opening her lips under his; the kiss deepened, and Dale pulled her closer, stroking her buttocks and moulding her to him so that she could feel his erect cock pressed against her belly.

When the kiss broke, Zoe's eyes were pure emerald. 'I think you're in need of treatment, Doctor.'

'Yes. And I know exactly what I'd prescribe.' His eyes glittered. 'Although it's very tempting to ask for it here, I think it might be better if we dispensed it in private.'

Zoe's eye was caught by a flat sepulchre, its inscription worn away by time and the top weathered smooth. 'It's very convenient,' she said, nodding at it.

Dale followed her gaze, then laughed. 'Now that really would scandalise the whole of Lower Yareham! Besides, it's not very comfortable.'

She couldn't help grinning. 'Know from experience, do you?'

He bent to whisper in her ear. 'Yes, from when I was a mad student. Not here, though – in a graveyard in Walthamstow. Spooky, scratchy, and not sexy at all.'

Zoe chuckled. 'You didn't!'

'I did.' He licked his lower lip. 'I'd prescribe a comfortable yet firm mattress – good for the back – and cotton sheets. Followed by freshly-squeezed orange juice, to aid rehydration.'

'You're on,' she said.

They walked back to Dale's cottage hand-in-hand, in near silence; with every second that passed, Zoe felt her arousal growing. By the time he unlocked his front door and ushered her inside, she was decidedly wet.

She couldn't wait for niceties. As he closed the door again, she spun round to face him and slid her hands round his neck, drawing his face down to hers. She kissed him hard, nipping at his lower lip so that he opened his mouth, then sliding her tongue inside, exploring him. She pressed his body back against the door, tilting her hips against his and massaging his cock through his trousers with her pubic bone; his arms came round her, stroking her back, and she arched against him.

Dale broke the kiss. 'I'm too old to take you on the hall floor,' he said.

'Old?' she scoffed. 'You're only a couple of years older than me – and they say that your mid-thirties are your best time.'

'For women, yes. So you've got it all to come.'

She grinned. 'Dale. Just shut up and take me to bed, will you?'

He grinned back. 'Seeing as you put it so nicely . . .' He took her hand, leading her up the stairs. She was pleased to notice that his bed was a king-size rather than a double: more comfortable, she thought. Not that she was intending to stay the night.

He kissed her again in the bedroom doorway, then slowly walked her backwards across the room until the edge of the mattress nudged at her knees. He broke the kiss for long enough to remove his glasses, placing them on the pine bedside cabinet next to what Zoe recognised as the cover of a best-selling and very gory thriller, then started to undo the buttons of her shirt, kissing every inch of skin as he revealed it. His fingers slid to the waistband of her jeans, undoing the button and then the zip; she wriggled slightly, helping him ease the soft denim down over her hips.

Dale dropped to his knees before her, lifting one foot and then the other so that he could remove her jeans and her shoes; then he worked his way up her legs, kissing and licking the sensitive spots. By the time he reached the apex of her thighs, Zoe was almost coming. She closed her eyes in anticipation, widening her stance slightly as she felt him slide one finger under the edge of her lacy knickers. He stroked the length of her quim with one fingertip, teasing her; she was unable to stifle a groan of impatience, and she felt him laugh against her skin as he bent his head.

He pushed his tongue against her knickers, teasing her

clitoris through the thin material, and she pushed her hands into his hair, the pressure of her fingertips urging him on. He continued to tease her, until she was thrusting her pelvis towards him, desperate to feel his mouth on her sex; and then, at long last, he pushed the gusset of her knickers to one side and replaced his hand with his mouth. The tip of his tongue probed the musky furrow of her sex; as he found her clitoris, Zoe cried out, her internal muscles spasming. Dale took no notice and flicked his tongue rapidly over the sensitive bud of flesh, pushing her climax to a higher peak.

Her orgasm seemed to go on for ever, with Dale's skilful tongue alternately working on her clitoris and pushing as deeply as possible inside her; finally, her legs gave way, and she fell back on the bed.

'My God,' she murmured, when she was finally able to speak. 'I . . .'

'Sh.'

At some point – probably while she'd been coming down from cloud nine, she thought – he'd removed his clothes and had joined her on the bed. He pulled her on top of him; and it felt good to be lying against him, she thought, skin to skin.

He fiddled briefly with the clasp of her bra, then eased the material away, lifting her slightly and nuzzling the soft creamy globes of her breasts. Her nipples were still erect, the rosy tips betraying the extent of her arousal; he caressed her for a moment, then rolled her gently onto her back again, kneeling over her and taking one dark crest into his mouth, sucking hard.

Zoe wriggled against the cool cotton of his duvet. 'Mm. Dale.' Her voice was heavy with arousal. 'That was good.'

He lifted his head. 'I haven't finished, yet,' he told her, his eyes glinting. 'Not by a long way.'

'I'm glad to hear it.' She couldn't help a soft moan as he removed her knickers. 'Dale . . . No strings, though.'

'If that's the way you want it.' He rubbed the tip of his nose against hers.

'It is. I'm my own woman, and I like it that way. No one to demand things from me, expect me to fit into his way of life.'

'Warning heeded. In the meantime, I think we have some

unfinished business.' He drew her hand down to his cock, curling her fingers around the thick shaft.

'Definitely.' Zoe smiled at him. 'You believe in living dangerously, Doctor.'

He shook his head. 'Not completely.' He turned away from her for a moment, reaching over the drawer of his bedside cabinet and extracting a condom.

Zoe sat up as he opened the little foil packet, and took the rubber disc from him. 'Let me,' she said huskily, fitting it over the tip of his cock and using her mouth to unroll it. It was Dale's turn to gasp as she started to fellate him through the thin latex, her dark hair brushing against his thighs and one hand ringing his shaft, the other cupping and caressing his balls.

When he was on the point of climax, she stopped, squeezing him just below the frenum; Dale grinned. 'That's a good trick,' he said.

His accent had become thicker, in passion; Zoe found it incredibly sexy. 'Mm. I know a better one,' she told him softly, pushing the duvet aside and patting the sheet.

He took the hint, shifting to lie on the mattress; he slid his hands behind his head, watching her as she straddled him. 'I was hoping you were going to do this,' he said.

'Don't think you're just going to lie back and enjoy it,' she warned him, her eyes glinting with a mixture of affection and lust. 'I have other ideas.'

'Just tell me what you want me to do.'

She grinned. 'I'd rather show you.' She lifted herself, positioning his cock at her entrance and sinking down on him, then leaned forward, pulling his hands from the pillow and placing them on her breasts. She guided his fingers with her own, so that he was alternately stroking the soft underside of her breasts and plucking at the hard and aching tips of her nipples; when she was satisfied with his rhythm, she leaned back slightly and placed her hands on the sheet so that her breasts thrust towards him. Then she began to move, lifting and lowering herself onto his cock.

Dale made a small noise of pleasure in the back of his throat; as his fingers grew less gentle, responding to her rising needs, her rhythm quickened. She rode him hard, rocking her pelvis as she pushed down, so that her already sensitised clitoris rubbed against the root of his sex.

She felt her orgasm building within her, a slow simmering in her veins that suddenly became a rolling boil and erupted, shocking her with its intensity. She spasmed round him, taking him over the edge of his own climax, and he cried out her name; then, drained, she slumped forward, burying her face in his shoulder. His arms wrapped round her tightly, and he held her close. Neither of them said anything; they didn't need to, their bodies were so in tune.

When Dale felt himself slipping from her, he slid his hand between their bodies, taking care of the condom; while he went to the bathroom, Zoe stretched luxuriously against the sheets. Yes. It had been good. And it was only going to get better . . .

Chapter Three

The next morning, Zoe woke in her large bed at The Feathers; she blinked at the unaccustomed silence, then remembered where she was. She smiled, and stretched again. She'd slept well. She always did, after good sex – and it had been very good with Dale MacKenzie. They'd made love twice more, before she'd regretfully taken her leave of him; they'd agreed that it would be better for her to go back to her room at the pub rather than staying overnight at his cottage. The last thing she wanted was for Betty Fielding to label her a tart and start being unhelpful or even coldly polite. Depending on the outcome of her meeting with Jack Mitchell, she might need to spend a few days in the village, and The Feathers was convenient – as well as a potentially good source of information.

Besides, she didn't want to start another relationship, even with someone as attractive as Dale. As she'd told him, she liked having the freedom to do what she wanted, when she wanted. That had been half the problem with Curtis: he'd wanted to control her life, and she wasn't looking for that kind of relationship.

She stretched again, took a leisurely shower, and sauntered downstairs for breakfast. Then she drove to Whiteacres, after checking Steve's directions with Betty. The house was a typical Norfolk farmhouse, wide and sprawling. It was painted white, with large sash windows, a terracotta tiled roof, and ivy climbing up one wall. The type of ivy that would turn a glorious flaming red in autumn, she thought.

She climbed out of her car, taking her briefcase from the back seat and locking the car door behind her, then crunched across the gravel to the front door and rang the bell. There was an immediate cacophony of barking, and Zoe grinned. It was like a scene out of *All Creatures Great and Small*, she thought; no doubt there were half a dozen assorted farm dogs bouncing around the place.

When the front door was opened by a stout middle-aged woman, a couple of minutes later, Zoe discovered that there were in fact only two dogs responsible for the din. Golden Labradors, who pattered impatiently on the stone flags, barking and wagging their tails.

The woman's pale blue eyes regarded Zoe thoughtfully. 'Can I help you?'

Obviously Mrs Mitchell, Zoe thought. She smiled at the older woman. 'Hello, I'm Zoe Lynton. I have a meeting with Mr Mitchell.'

The woman frowned. 'He didn't say anything to me about that. Anyway, he's not here. He's probably in the farm office.'

'Oh.' Zoe flushed. She'd expected Jack to be at the house: didn't his grandson run the farm? 'Sorry. I didn't think.' She bit her lip. 'Could you tell me where the farm office is, please?'

The woman was about to give Zoe directions when she was joined at the door by a tall, thin elderly man. The dogs immediately stopped barking and sat on his feet; he stooped to fondle their ears. 'Miss Lynton?' he asked.

'Yes.'

He smiled, his slate blue eyes crinkling at the corners. 'It's all right, Eileen. I was expecting her.'

The older woman rolled her eyes. 'And there was I thinking that she wanted Brandon. Why you don't tell me things, Jack Mitchell, is beyond me.' She gave Zoe a conspiratorial look that quite clearly said *Men!* 'Would you like some tea, Miss Lynton?'

'Zoe, please,' Zoe said quickly. 'And yes, I would, thank you.'

'We can do the introductions inside, in comfort.' Jack Mitchell's eyes twinkled kindly at her. 'Tell me, Miss Lynton – Zoe – do you mind dogs?'

'Not at all. I grew up with them,' Zoe replied honestly. She put her briefcase on the floor, then crouched down and extended one hand. The dogs rushed towards her, sniffed her hands and then licked her to show their approval. 'What are their names?' she asked.

'Candy and Belle,' Jack told her. 'And you've met with

their approval, so come in, come in.' He turned to Eileen. 'Put the kettle on, Eileen. And if there's any of your Victoria sponge left, we'll have some of that, too.'

'Yes, sir.' Zoe half-expected her to add, 'What did your last servant die of?'

'We'll be in the sitting room. Join us, if you like. Zoe's here to talk about my finds.'

'I see.' Eileen's stern face softened slightly. 'Tea coming up. Unless you'd prefer coffee, Zoe?'

'Tea would be lovely, thanks.' Zoe followed Jack and Eileen down the hall. Jack ushered her through to the sitting room; Zoe sat on one of the battered armchairs, and the dogs settled at her feet.

'I'm sorry if I upset your wife,' Zoe said.

Jack hooted. 'My wife? Eileen, you mean?'

'Er – yes.' Zoe flushed, conscious of putting her foot in it.

'Eileen Walters is my housekeeper,' Jack explained. 'She's been with us for thirty years. And she's a confirmed spinster, although half the men in the village over fifty would marry her tomorrow, on the strength of her stew and dumplings.'

'Oh.' Zoe's embarrassment grew.

'You weren't to know,' he said kindly. 'I was married, but my wife died fifteen years ago.'

'I'm sorry.'

'From old age,' Jack told her succinctly.

'And then there are wicked old devils like you, who'll live until you're a hundred,' Eileen said tartly, coming in with a tray of tea and overhearing the last couple of sentences. 'Help yourself to tea and cake, Zoe.'

'Thank you, Miss Walters.'

'Eileen,' the housekeeper corrected with a smile.

'Aren't you joining us?' Jack asked.

Eileen shook her head. 'I've got better things to do than listen to old fools babble on about Roman queens.' The affection in her voice was obvious, making her words sound teasing rather than critical. 'I'll be getting on. You know where I'll be if you want me.'

'In the kitchen, I know.' Jack nodded. 'Thanks, Eileen.'

The housekeeper smiled back at him, her face softening

33

for an instant, then left the room. Jack poured the tea. 'Milk and sugar?'

'Just milk, please.'

'And do have some cake.'

'Thanks.' Zoe accepted the large slice with pleasure. The dogs shifted, each putting a head on her knee; Zoe looked down at the two pairs of soulful brown eyes, and grinned. 'As if I couldn't guess what you two want. You're as bad as Bill and Ben.'

'Bill and Ben?' Jack asked.

'My parents' dogs. They adore cake, and they're not above begging,' she enlightened him.

'Neither are these two. Just ignore them,' Jack told her, laughing.

'All right. Would you mind if I taped our conversation?' Zoe asked.

'Taped it?' His surprise showed on his face.

'It'll be easier than having to read back my rusty shorthand,' she said with a grin, 'and it means that I have a proper record of everything you've told me, rather than relying on my notes. I can make a copy of the tape for you, too, of course.'

He smiled at her. 'No, there's no need for that. Go ahead; use whatever you need.'

'Thank you.' Zoe took the small tape recorder from her briefcase, switched it on, and tested that it was working properly. Then she looked up at Jack again. 'So tell me about these things you've found, Mr Mitchell.'

'Jack,' he corrected.

'Jack.'

'Well, local legend has it that Boudicca was buried in the village. There have been one or two finds of coins and the like around here, and it's a real haunt for metal-detecting fans. But there have never really been any digs or anything around here.'

'Lack of money?' Zoe suggested wryly.

Jack nodded. 'It's short-sighted, in my view, but who's going to listen to me? Anyway, I don't run the farm any more. I leave that to my grandson, Brandon. So I can spend my time more or less doing what I liked. I've always been interested in Roman history. Eileen laughs at me, saying that I'm a silly old fool, and I know Brandon thinks the same – but I wanted to know if it was true, if Boudicca really was buried round here. I spent a fair amount of time last summer in the local library. I even got Eileen to drive me into Norwich.' He spread his hands disarmingly. 'Too old to drive myself, I suppose, and the two of them would only worry about me if I took off on my own in the car. Anyway, it gave Eileen a chance to do some shopping.'

'Indeed.'

He grinned. 'I spent my time poring over maps and the like, and the more I thought about it, the more I was sure that the grave was somewhere on our farm. So I borrowed a metal detector. I narrowed it down to three fields, which just so happened to be fallow—'

'Just so happened?' Zoe asked, seeing the look on his face.

He smiled. 'All right. They're the three I've always thought the most likely, and I persuaded Brandon that we ought to let them lie fallow this year.'

'So that you could have a look at them?'

'Yes.'

Something in his face made her think that it wasn't the only reason why the fields were fallow. Would a hard-headed businessman really indulge his grandfather and not care about losing money on three fields – fields which could have been sown very profitably with crops? Jack was keeping something back from her, she was sure.

'Anyway, I walked them all – every inch.' He smiled. 'In a way, it was almost like farming in the old times, when you used to walk behind the horses. I know, things have to progress, and you have the farm the most efficient way, nowadays, if you want to stay in business – but you were somehow more part of the land, then, just you and the horse and the plough.' His eyes grew dreamy. Then he shook himself. 'Sorry, Zoe. I was supposed to be telling you about my find. Like I said, I walked the fields with a metal detector. I must have spent the best part of a week searching. Then I struck lucky. I found the coins.' He stood up and walked over to a cabinet on the other side of the room, opening one of the drawers and taking out a small velvet pouch.

Zoe's eyes widened. Surely Jack Mitchell wouldn't keep

his Roman coins here? They'd be safer—

'In the bank?' Jack finished, his lips twitching.

Zoe flushed. Her thoughts had obviously been written across her face. 'Well, yes.'

'Maybe.' Jack shrugged. 'But there's a security alarm here – not to mention the dogs. Anyone who tried to break in would have to deal with Candy and Belle, first.'

'Yes.'

'Anyway.' He handed her the pouch. 'See what you think.'

Adrenalin made Zoe's fingers tingle as she opened the pouch and tipped the contents into her hand. Roman coins. Half a dozen silver coins, the edges rough and the raised pattern on them betraying their origin. 'My God,' she breathed.

'My thoughts exactly. I couldn't believe it, either.' He smiled at her. 'At first, I thought that there might be just the one. But there were half a dozen. I'm sure there are other things buried there, too.'

'Have you done any more digging?'

'No. I'm an amateur, Zoe, and I've read enough to know how much damage I could do if I just dug around willy-nilly.'

'How about the local council, or the university? Have you spoken to them, asked them if they wanted to excavate?'

He shook his head. 'There aren't any funds.'

'What about other local people? There must be some experts who'd do it for love.'

'I don't think so.'

For a moment, Zoe thought that he looked slightly shifty; then she was cross with herself for imagining things. Of course Jack Mitchell wasn't being shifty. He was just disappointed that he couldn't take his dream any further, that was all. 'Maybe I can help, there,' she said.

'How?'

'Through *Archetypes*. If you can give me enough evidence, either we can fund some excavations ourselves, or put an appeal in the magazine and raise the money that way.'

Jack's face brightened. 'You really think so?'

She nodded. 'Boudicca's grave is something most archaeologists dream about finding. What I need is a bit more background from you, like why you think that

Boudicca's buried here rather than near Colchester.'

He smiled at her. 'Prepare to be convinced, young lady.'

Brandon's forehead creased as he drove up to the farmhouse. He didn't recognise the small red Peugeot parked outside. It certainly didn't belong to Dale MacKenzie – unless Dale was on holiday and it belonged to a locum who'd called in to visit his grandfather. His breath caught, and he braked sharply, wrenching the keys from the ignition and striding swiftly into the farmhouse. He could hear voices in the sitting room; he was about to open the door and ask what was wrong when he heard what they were talking about. Boudicca.

'Oh, Christ, not again,' he muttered. Who was it, this time? Some reporter from the local paper, needing to make up the news pages? A student archaeologist? Whoever it was, this would have to stop, he thought. Apart from the fact that his grandfather just wasn't strong enough to cope with the excitement, it could cause him greater problems. The last thing he needed now was for his plans to be held up. Particularly after his meeting at the bank.

He pushed the door open, and stopped dead. By the look of the briefcase and the small tape-recorder, the woman was a journalist. Not the usual hard-bitten type, either; this one had a softer look about her. Attractive, with those long dark curls flowing over her shoulders, small round glasses hiding intense green eyes, and a generous mouth. A mouth that he could easily imagine working its way down his body, arousing him to the limits of pleasure before she took him deep into her mouth and started to . . .

He shook himself. Now wasn't the time to let his libido get the better of him, either. He had to get this woman away from Jack, before she started making things difficult.

'Hello, Brandon.' Jack smiled. 'This is Zoe Lynton. Zoe, this is Brandon Mitchell, my grandson.'

Zoe looked up at the man who'd just walked in and caught her breath. Sam had been right. Brandon Mitchell was gorgeous. No wonder the women in the village lusted after him. He was tall, just over six feet, with broad shoulders and slate-blue eyes. His hair was dark and thick, curling into his collar; although he was wearing a suit and tie, he would have looked equally at home in a working farmer's faded jeans, a checked shirt and a worn green wax jacket. And she could all too easily imagine him naked on silk sheets, his body hard against hers as he drove into her . . .

Trouble, Zoe thought, with a capital T. Not only did he look far from pleased to see her – and she already knew why that was, thanks to Dale and Sam – but she also felt that familiar rush of adrenalin. Something was going to happen between them, at some point in the future; but if she didn't watch her libido, she could blow the Boudicca story. The chance to find her own dreams, as well as Jack's.

'Pleased to meet you,' she said, standing up and holding out her hand.

Brandon took it, shaking it firmly, but he didn't reply.

Zoe's fingers tingled. God. If such a neutral contact as this could have this effect on her, what would happen if he touched her more intimately? *When* he touched her, she thought with a little shiver; her intuition was never wrong where sex was concerned. It wouldn't be slow and sensual, as it had been between her and Dale; it would be urgent and rough and incredibly arousing.

'Zoe's come to help me with Boudicca,' Jack said. 'She's writing an article about it.'

'Indeed.' Brandon's eyes sparked briefly with anger. 'Miss Lynton, perhaps you wouldn't mind continuing this another day? I need to talk to my grandfather. Family business. I'm sure you understand.' His voice was polite, but cold and very definite. She wasn't welcome, here – at least, not in his eyes.

'Of course.' Zoe had already switched off her tape-recorder, the minute that Brandon had entered the room; quickly, she packed it away and stood up. 'Well, Jack, it was good to meet you. I'll see you again soon.' She took a card from her briefcase, giving it to him. 'Here's my number, give me a call on my mobile when you're ready to finish our chat. Or you can contact me at The Feathers.' She stopped to fondle the dogs' heads. 'See you later, you two. Bye, Jack.'

'I'll show you out,' Brandon said, ushering her from the room.

'Brandon—' Jack began, but the younger man ignored

him, closing the sitting room door and virtually marching Zoe down the hall.

'Ms Lynton, I don't know what my grandfather's been saying to you, but I advise you not to bother with the article. Finds of Roman coins are quite common around here.'

'Oh?'

'Yes. There was a mint at Thetford, which is only about twenty miles from here. Coins are always turning up in the fields.'

Zoe was silent. She'd already had that argument with Steve.

'My grandfather just happened to find a couple of coins. It doesn't prove a thing about this grave he thinks is there.'

'Perhaps you'll let an archaeologist be the judge of that.'

He sighed. 'Look, my grandfather's eighty-five.'

'And completely *compos mentis*,' Zoe said. 'So don't try to tell me that he's losing his marbles or doesn't know what he's talking about.'

Brandon rolled his eyes impatiently. 'I wasn't going to say anything of the sort. But he's not as well as he looks. I don't want him upset or over-excited, Ms Lynton. This fantasy about Boudicca is just that, a dream, and it's upsetting him. To be honest, I thought your car was the doctor's, and that's why I rushed into the room.'

Very commendable, Zoe thought. Genuine, too, up to a point – but she knew about the housing development. That was what was really rattling his cage. Fear that she'd find out the truth, and his plans to make a pile of money would hit the dust. 'I see,' she commented neutrally.

'Ms Lynton, I'd prefer it if you went back to wherever you came from.' Under the nearest stone, by the look on his face, Zoe thought. 'Please don't bother my grandfather again.' Unfailingly polite, but with a hint of steel in those beautiful eyes.

And something else.

Her stomach kicked. He felt that same rush of sexual adrenalin as she had – and he was fighting it as much as she was, for the same reasons. Part of her felt like being reckless and reaching up to kiss him; but the rational side of her brain kept control. Just. Until they'd resolved this matter about Boudicca's grave, there was no way she could go to bed with Brandon Mitchell. It would complicate the issue far too much. She needed to keep a cool head and gather the evidence. Maybe she could persuade Steve to fund some aerial reconnaissance or geophysics, once she'd talked to Jack a bit more and seen his notes. If Steve couldn't find the money, she could set up a joint initiative between *Archetypes* and the national paper which ran her *Dry Bones* column.

'Goodbye, Ms Lynton,' Brandon said pointedly, opening the door.

'Goodbye.' For the moment, at least. Zoe knew that it wouldn't be their last meeting. Not by a long way.

She realised that she was shaking as she drove back to The Feathers. Not from fear – she didn't think that Brandon Mitchell was the sort to hit a woman, and she could hold her own in an argument – but from excitement. A mixture of relish at the thought of the fight to come. She smiled wryly. Not just the fight, either. What would come afterwards. Or at some time in between: their bodies fusing in desire.

God. Brandon Mitchell was forbidden territory, at least until she'd sorted out this Boudicca business. She didn't mix work and pleasure, with the exception of Steve Marwick. But she couldn't help thinking about Brandon. Imagining what it would be like to have him peel her clothes off, very slowly. And then he'd cover her body with kisses, starting at her shoulders and working downwards. He'd nuzzle the valley between her breasts, tracing her curves with the tip of his tongue, and finally taking one hardened nipple into his mouth, sucking on it until she gasped and thrust her hands into his hair.

Then he'd withdraw slightly, blowing on her skin in a way that would make her whole body ripple with desire; then he'd continue his path downwards, caressing the soft undersides of her breasts with his mouth, down over her ribcage, her abdomen. He'd drop to his knees before her, sliding his hands between her thighs and urging her silently to part her legs for him; and then, at long last, he'd bury his face in her quim, licking and lapping, savouring the taste of her arousal and exploring her most intimate furls and hollows.

His mouth would find her clitoris and skate over it, teasing her with the tip of his tongue, then pressing flat and hard against the little bud of flesh, using long slow deep strokes that would make her cry out and mash her sex against his mouth. He'd slide a finger into her to ease the ache, and concentrate on her clitoris, driving her to the peak and beyond, until her musky juices filled his mouth. And then, when her breathing had slowed to near-normal, he'd stand up, lift her and carry her to his bed. A large king-size wrought-iron bed, with a firm deep mattress and thick feather pillows. And perfectly ironed smooth cotton sheets that would be a rumpled mass in the morning, after they'd spent the whole night making love . . .

By the time Zoe pulled into the car park at The Feathers, her sex was tingling and her breasts were swollen with desire. To her relief, neither Betty nor Sam was at the bar; she headed upstairs, knowing that there was only one way to clear her head. Part of her was furious with herself – Brandon Mitchell was an arrogant bastard who didn't want her spoiling his plans to make a fast buck, and she despised him utterly – but she couldn't help herself.

'It's pheromones,' she told herself sharply as she let herself into her room and closed the door behind her. 'Get a grip, Lynton.' But her brain wasn't listening. Her body needed release.

She pulled the curtains, stripped swiftly, and pulled the sheets back from the bed. She couldn't wait any longer: her whole body was tingling and aching. Her nipples were so hard that they hurt, desperate for the touch of Brandon's mouth and fingers; and her quim was decidedly wet.

She closed her eyes, pushing her head back into the pillows, and slid her hands down her body. She cupped her breasts, squeezing them gently, and rubbed the pads of her thumbs over her aching nipples. Is that how Brandon would touch her? she wondered. Would he be gentle, coaxing a response from her body, bringing her slowly to a peak? Or would he be rougher, pinching her and shocking her body into response?

That sensuous mouth belonged to a seasoned lover, she was sure. A man who knew instinctively what his lover wanted, and would match her mood. But then again, if he was arrogant in business, surely he'd be equally arrogant in

41

bed? He'd do whatever he wanted to her, expecting her to like it . . .

She smiled wryly. No. Brandon would insist on submission – but he'd know that bullying wasn't the way to get it. She'd caught him on the hop, that was all. He'd been telling the truth when he'd talked of his fears for his grandfather's health. He'd wanted her off the premises and out of his way, to give him time to think, to weigh up how to deal with the situation. And, as a lover, she was sure that he'd be the same. He'd think about it, first, make her wait. Talk to her. Use all his senses to work out what she wanted. And then he'd move.

Oh, yes. He'd touch her in just the way she liked. In just the way she was touching herself. He'd make sure that she was comfortable against the pillows, touch her face in a tender gesture, then bend down to kiss her. His mouth would be soft and coaxing; his kiss would only grow demanding when she opened her mouth under his and touched the tip of her tongue to his, taking the initiative.

She could almost savour him now, the clean sweet taste of his mouth, the soft sweetness of his lips. And his hands – strong, firm hands, used to work and yet not rough and callused. She could almost feel them stroking her body instead of her own. They were his hands touching her breasts, rubbing her nipples and pinching them gently. It was his hand sliding down over her abdomen, parting her thighs and cupping her mons veneris. It was his finger sliding over the moist furrow, parting her labia and finding her clitoris.

Oh, yes. She almost purred as she began to rub the hard bud of flesh, slicking her fingers with juice and then working harder on her clitoris, rubbing in the figure-of-eight pattern she liked so much. She changed position slightly, using her thumb to rub her clitoris and pushing her middle finger deep inside her.

It felt good, so good. But Brandon would be better. He'd tease her, bringing her almost to the peak and then withdrawing, delaying her climax. He'd do it again and again until she was moaning, begging him to put his cock inside her. Somewhere between undressing her and stroking her sex, he'd remove his own clothes, and she'd feel him skin to skin with her as he knelt between her thighs. He'd stoop

42

down to kiss her delta, a touch of affection – and then he'd fit the tip of his cock to her sex.

He'd ease in slowly, so slowly, letting her body grow used to his size. Because Brandon, of course, would be endowed with quantity as well as quality. His cock would be long and thick, perfectly proportioned to give her the most pleasure – and he'd know exactly how to use it. He'd move millimetre by millimetre, until his cock was embedded to the hilt; and then he'd start to thrust, moving with long deep slow strokes, pulling almost all the way out and then easing back in.

It would be too much for her. After the way he'd aroused her with his mouth and his fingers, she wouldn't be able to wait to take it slowly. She'd wrap her legs round his waist, using her heels on his buttocks to pull him deeper into her. Then he'd laugh softly – with pleasure, not triumph – and change his rhythm, moving with short sharp strokes to stimulate the narrowest part of her sex.

She'd feel the familiar dizzy spiral of her climax starting, and he'd slow again, letting her body ripple round his cock; but he wouldn't stop. Just as her climax began to ebb, he'd take her to another peak – and another. She'd be bucking crazily against him, her teeth bared and her eyes squeezed tightly shut, her whole senses centred in her sex as she came again and again and again . . .

Zoe slumped back against the pillows, her sex still spasming round her fingers. Bloody hell. It had been a long time since thoughts of a man had caused her to masturbate like that. And why did it have to be an ambitious bastard like Brandon? Annoyed with herself and unable to relax in the pleasure she'd just given her body, she headed for the en suite and turned the shower on at its coldest setting. Just what she needed to get her brain in order, she thought crossly.

Brandon Mitchell would not be good for her. Yes, they'd end up having sex – she knew instinctively that he shared the passionate side of her nature. It would be good sex, too. But that would be all it was. Sex. No ties. No resolution to the conflict between them.

She sighed. God. Trust her to get the hots for someone like him. A self-centred, arrogant man who wouldn't take kindly to the idea of anyone interfering in his money-making

43

schemes. Well, that was it. Her mouth thinned. Even without the evidence, she'd already decided whose side to take. Jack's. She'd help him all she could – and she'd teach his grandson a lesson, at the same time.

Chapter Four

After her shower, Zoe's head had cleared sufficiently to let her transcribe her notes from her conversation with Jack. As she read through her notes on the laptop, she grew thoughtful. There really could be something there, something more than the hopes and dreams of an old man.

She glanced at her watch. There was a good chance that Steve would still be in the office. Alone – he didn't expect his staff to put in the hours for show, preferring them to work a shorter but more productive week. On impulse, she rang *Archetypes*.

Two rings, three: then the answerphone kicked in. 'Hello, this is *Archetypes*. I'm afraid there's no one to take your call at the moment. Please leave your name, number and a brief message after the tone, or alternatively send a fax after the long tone.'

She waited for the tone. 'Steve. It's Zoe. Sorry I missed you. I'll try and catch you in—'

The phone clicked. 'Zoe. Hi. I was wondering when you'd check in.'

She chuckled. 'You weren't call-screening, were you?'

'No. I was in the middle of something, and I didn't feel like breaking off to talk to anyone.'

'So how come you're talking to me?'

'Because, sweetheart, you're not just anyone, and you could be more interesting than what I was doing.'

'Definitely.' She coughed. 'I saw Jack Mitchell, today.'

'How did it go?'

'Pretty well.' She decided not to mention Brandon. 'I haven't inspected the site myself, but I've got a good interview, and Jack has a sheaf of notes. I'm going into Norwich tomorrow, to do some research.'

'Gut feel?'

She and Steve knew the way each other's mind worked so well that they often conversed in shorthand. 'Geophysics.'

'Not cheap.'

'We can get the money.'

'Don't say the Lottery fund,' Steven warned. 'They've turned us down on four projects already.'

'An article in *Archetypes*,' Zoe said succinctly.

'We won't raise that much.'

'We will, Steve. It's big enough.' She paused. 'There are people out there who would love to be involved in this. They'll pay for the sheer privilege of being in on the discovery of the century, having their name as a benefactor on the displays in the British Museum – that sort of thing. If you won't do it, I'll put it in *Dry Bones*.'

'You wouldn't.'

'Try me.'

Steve sighed. 'Okay. Just do some research, first. I'll sort the budget.'

'And the geophys?'

'I'll call in some favours,' he promised. 'Once I know you're sure.'

'Gut feel, Steve.'

'As a journo?'

'As a Classicist, too.'

'Sure you're not letting your fantasies run away with you?'

Zoe rolled her eyes. She knew that he was teasing. Steve trusted her enough not to question her judgement. 'There's another article here, too. Wall paintings.'

Steve groaned. 'I might have guessed that you'd spend your time poking round churches.'

'Seriously – they're Edward the Martyr, and they're good. I won't do justice to the photographs.'

'So you want a photographer from me, as well?'

'Two stories for one visit. Boudicca and some extremely well-preserved frescoes. Bargain.'

He chuckled. 'Okay, okay. Sold.' He coughed slightly. 'Where are you?'

'The village pub.'

'Downstairs?'

'Nope.'

'So you're calling from your mobile.'

She laughed. 'Listen, Steve, the whole village is divided on this issue. Having a telephone conversation about it in the bar wouldn't be very clever.'

'There isn't a phone in your room, then?'

'Steve, it's a village pub, not an hotel.'

'Right.' He paused. 'How much battery power do you have left?'

Zoe checked the front of her phone. 'About half.'

'Half.'

She recognised the smoky note in his voice. 'And you're on your own, too?'

'Yup. Zoe . . .'

'Yes?'

'You really think that Boudicca's there?'

'Maybe.'

'All your fantasies come true.'

'Not quite.' She grinned to herself. 'You're working on Cleopatra again, aren't you?'

'What gives you that idea?' he fenced.

'Because it always makes you as randy as hell, and I can hear it in your voice.'

'How well you know me, Ms Lynton.'

It was a game they'd played before, many times. 'Indeed.'

'You were talking about your fantasies. About Romans.'

Actually, he'd been the one to raise the subject, but Zoe didn't bother to correct him. 'Yes. Especially now I'm in the middle of Iceni country. I can see it all so much more clearly, *in situ*.'

'Tell me all about it,' he invited.

'I'm a queen,' she said. 'Royal blood on both sides of my family, married to a king – a king who died fighting for us. So I'm head of the tribe.' She didn't need to specify which tribe. Both she and Steve knew exactly which one she meant. 'We hate being under Roman rule, obeying their laws and unable to guide our people. Except . . . there's one. One in particular. I've noticed him looking at me. Under my law, his look would be forbidden; under their law, I have no choice but to suffer his gaze.'

'How does he look at you?'

'He wants to have me. I can see it in his eyes.'

'What does he look like?'

Zoe stretched out on the bed and closed her eyes. 'He's tall. Broad-shouldered, from his time in the Roman army: strong thighs, flat stomach. Good muscles. Dark hair, curling into the nape of his neck. Sensitive mouth. High cheekbones. Slate-blue eyes.' She realised with sudden shock that she'd more or less described Brandon Mitchell; but she couldn't stop now. Her imagination was running riot and her sex was growing hot and wet.

'And you're attracted to him.'

'Yes. Though my people would never forgive me if I made love with the enemy. I can do nothing about it.'

'Mutual attraction, held apart by war.'

'Yes.' Her voice sank to a whisper. 'I dream about him at night. I touch myself, pretend he's the one touching me.'

'Why can't he sneak into your quarters, at night?'

'It's too difficult. Too many obstacles to overcome.' She smiled. 'I didn't tell you. He's their commander.'

'Ah.' Steve paused. 'So he could command you to submit to his will.'

'But he doesn't want to risk an uprising. My people will revolt if he takes me by force.'

'Unless you transgress their law. They'd understand that.'

'Exactly,' she said. 'So that's what I do. Something minor – but enough to give him the chance to teach me humility.'

'Nice,' Steve breathed. 'So what does he do?'

'He calls a gathering of the whole tribe – and his troops, too. He challenges me with my crime. I admit to it. And then he tells me what the punishment will be. He pulls down the front of my dress, exposing my breasts. I can't help myself: the excitement of what he's going to do to me makes my breasts swell and my nipples harden. I know I look good, the creamy flesh and the rose-dark areolae; and he can't help a sharp intake of breath when he sees me for the first time. I know he's hard for me, just from this. And it's only going to get better.'

'What then?'

'He touches me. Very, very lightly. It sends a shiver through my body, the way his fingertips brush my flesh; my sex is wet by the time he's finished, and I'm sure he can smell my arousal. And so can everyone else. His troops, my people. They all know: but none dare challenge me. Or him.'

48

She paused, unzipping her jeans and pushing them down to her knees with her knickers in one swift movement. 'And then he makes me go down on my knees before him. He releases his cock from his clothing; I was right. He's hard for me. He looks good. His cock is long and thick, swollen with desire for me, and the tip is plum-coloured. He thrusts a hand into my hair and pushes my head down; I make a show of resistance, because my people expect it – and so do his – but we both know that I want to do this.

'I take the tip of his cock into my mouth, swirling my tongue round his glans; I make my tongue into a hard point and flick it against his frenum until he's shuddering. Then I take him as deeply as I can into my mouth, sucking hard; his hand is in my hair, and he's pressing hard against my scalp, wanting me. He can't help rocking slightly, pushing it into my mouth; I cup his balls, stroking them and the soft silky skin just behind them, and it makes him even harder. I can taste the salty-sweet tang of his arousal; I know that the eye of his cock is weeping clear fluid for me.'

'Oh, yes.' Steve's voice left Zoe in no doubt of what he was doing. She knew that he was leaning back in his office chair, his jeans unzipped and his cock freed; his fingers were curled round his shaft and he was stroking himself gently, imagining himself in the position of Zoe's Roman commander. Just as she had one hand working between her legs, stoking her own desire.

'And then he stops me; I know that this time, this first time, he wants to make it as long drawn-out as he can. He wants everything – in case it's the last time. Although we both know that after this, he will be able to come to my quarters when he likes, as of right. He commands two of his foot-soldiers to bring a bench; he places it before me, and makes me kneel over it. To the tribe, it looks like he's pushing me into a position of indignity; I know that he's doing it to support me, because my knees will give when he finally enters me.

'Then he pulls up my skirts, flinging them up to bare my bottom. He commands me to part my legs, and I know that everyone can see my sex. Everyone can see how swollen and wet it is; everyone will know of my desire. And yet it doesn't matter. Somehow, it is permitted – because this is a show of mastery by the Romans. If it was rape – well, my tribe would revolt, and there would be bloodshed. But this – this is ritual enough to satisfy both the Romans and my tribe.'

Steve groaned softly. 'Oh, yes. Zoe, yes.'

Zoe's voice cracked slightly as she continued. 'He draws one finger the full length of my sex, and holds it up. Everyone can see my juices glistening there. He licks the finger clean, as though he's eating honey; and then he kneels down behind me. He places his hands on my buttocks, squeezing them gently, and then he nuzzles me, breathing in the scent of my quim. I'm almost screaming with anticipation. I can feel his breath warm against my skin, and I want to feel his tongue, his fingers, his cock. I want him to fill me and fuck me. Stretch me. I want him to rut with me, like some splendid animal, showing off in front of my people and his. I don't care about the audience. I just want him.

'He makes me wait. He warns me in a low voice not to move – I cannot be seen to enjoy my humiliation. I must just submit proudly and in silence, like the queen I am. It's almost as if he already knows that I'm a noisy lover, that I like to cry out my pleasure and demands. And I have waited so long for this, so long. I have worked myself to fever pitch every night with my hand, squeezing my nipples and rubbing my clitoris hard, pushing three fingers deep into me; and I know he's done the same, rubbing his shaft and pressing down on his solar plexus as he comes. How can we be restrained? But we must.

'Then, so slowly, I feel his tongue move the full length of my slit, top to bottom and back again. He flicks his tongue over my clitoris, teasing me. Then he presses his tongue into my sex; I dig my nails into the ground to stop myself writhing against him and pushing back. And then I feel his tongue slide back, press against my puckered rosebud. I can imagine him doing darker things, there, entering me and giving me new sensations. Forbidden ground. It makes my sex weep harder, just thinking about what I want him to do to me.'

Again, Steven groaned. Zoe could picture him at the same time as her Roman leader, the same expression on their faces. Steve and the Roman. Steve and Brandon – no matter that the Romans traditionally had dark eyes, not blue. Brandon. Brandon kneeling behind her, touching and tasting her sex, teasing her . . . She shivered, and her hand worked harder.

'What then?'

'Then I feel his finger penetrating my sex. He moves deep inside me, sensitising me and making me desperate to be filled properly. It's agony, lying still and pretending to be regal and haughty. I want to scream out like a servant maid. He pushes my skirts up still further, flipping them over my head to cover my face, and I'm grateful. He knows that my face will be too expressive, that I won't be able to hold out, and he's giving me a chance to cover myself. The Romans and my tribe will take it as a sign of mastery, but I know the truth. It's mercy, giving me some privacy.'

'Oh, yes. So your sex is bared to everyone?'

'Everyone,' Zoe acknowledged.

'And what are they doing?'

'Just watching. Maybe touching themselves, maybe just thinking it, wishing themselves in my place – or his. I don't know. I can't see them any more, and they don't matter. All that matters is the way he's touching me, the way he's rubbing my clitoris and pistoning his finger in and out of me. He's determined to make me come at least once before he enters me properly. And I do. I can feel the heavy swell starting in the soles of my feet, a warm rolling sensation that gathers pace as it sweeps up my calves, making my thighs tremble, then roaring into the pit of my stomach. I come, my internal muscles clutching at him; he bends over me, seemingly to whisper an order, and I feel his lips brush the back of my neck, a light caress of desire and affection.

'Later, in private, I know that he will kiss me all over. He will have me kneeling again – but this time on soft lambskins, by the flickering light of an oil-lamp and completely naked, so that he can worship my body with his lips and tongue. For now, we will make do with a more restrained coupling – because he, too, must show no emotion. He is merely doing his duty, showing a subject queen that he is master, as if he were scolding a slave or a dog.

'I can hear him licking his fingers, savouring my juices. And then, at long last, I feel the tip of his cock pressing against my sex. It feels as good as I'd hoped; he eases it into me, very slowly, and I almost come again. He fills me completely, he's so long and thick. He stays there for a moment, letting my body grow used to the feel of his; then he begins to thrust. I know he has stamina, from his time with the Roman army. This will last as long as he chooses.

'A wicked impulse fills me, and I flex my internal muscles, tightening them as he withdraws and then relaxing as he pushes back into me. He knows what I am doing, that I am trying to make him lose control, and he has his revenge. I feel something pressing against my anus – it's the tip of his finger, spit-slicked to make things easier. He presses it into me, and I nearly scream out, it feels so good. Had it not been for my covering skirts, the whole of my tribe would see my face, realise what this is – a mutual coupling, performed in public as though it were penance, when it's really for the pleasure of both me and the Roman commander. I would be seen as a collaborator, a traitor to the memory of my husband; but this way, I retain my noble standing. I am merely submitting to our overlords, to save my people from punishment.

'I long to push back against him; but I cannot be seen to do this. All I can do is let him dictate the pace. Fast, bringing me close to the point of crisis: then slow again, bringing me down and soothing me. Fast again, and that penetration of that forbidden place, making me pant beneath my covering; and slow, slow, easing me into it.

'Just when I think I can take no more, I feel his cock throbbing deep inside me, the rushing warmth of his emission. And then he withdraws without ceremony, restoring order to his own dress and leaving me exposed. I am to remain there until he dictates otherwise. My quim is bare, and they can see that I have not come: my sex-flesh is still dark and puffy, and there are none of those helpless quivers of after-shock.

'His seed runs from me; finally, he pulls my skirts back down and helps me to my feet. In his eyes is one word: *later*. And we both know that later, he will continue where he left off, but he'll take it to the full conclusion, let me climax, with my quim rippling round his cock. And my cries will be buried in the lambskin – or in his shoulder, as we couple face-to-face. Because tonight, he will take me in every position I know, and every position I have not yet dreamed about . . .'

As Zoe finished her tale, her quim contracted sharply round her fingers; from Steve's breathing, she could tell that he'd just come, too.

'Like it?' she whispered huskily.

'You know I did.' His voice was equally hoarse.

'Tell me what you were doing.'

'Guess.'

'Tell me.'

'I was imagining myself as your Roman,' Steve said.

'And?'

'And I'm alone in the office. No one can see in. I unzipped my jeans and stroked myself. The more you told me, the harder and hornier I got,' he said simply.

'And you just came?'

'Mm. Lucky I had a handkerchief in my pocket – or I'd have had some cleaning up to do.' He paused. 'And you?'

'Guess,' she teased back.

'Knowing you, you're not wearing a skirt – so I'd say either your jeans or your leggings are at your knees, and your hand is between your legs,' he said.

'Was,' she corrected.

He chuckled. 'You're one wanton woman, Zoe Lynton.'

'You started it.'

'I know.' He paused. 'So what's the plan, then?'

'Back to business? Already?' she teased.

'Just thinking of your mobile phone bill. If you're still in peak rate time . . .'

'Then you'll cough up half the cost, won't you? As this was your idea.'

He laughed. 'That goes without saying. Anyway. Plan A is?'

'I'm going to check out what I know from Jack.' She paused. 'There might be a complication.'

'Such as?'

'A housing development – right in the same field that Jack says contains the grave.' She paused. 'I'm not sure how far planning permission's progressed. I'm going to check that out first, before I head into Norwich. Then I'm going to check out Jack's notes. I'll call you tomorrow night, to let you know what I've found out.'

'Good.' Steve paused. 'This development – do you know who the proposers are?'

'Yes.' Zoe rubbed her jaw. If she told Steve who their opponents were, he'd think twice about mobilising help. He'd think the problem was that Jack didn't want part of the farm turned into a housing estate, rather than that the old man had really found something. 'I don't want to get involved in village politics, though.'

'Why do I get the feeling you already are?'

She smiled wryly. 'How well you know me, Mr Marwick.'

'And you're on Jack's side.' His voice was rueful. 'Zoe, don't let your heart rule your head on this one. I know you want it to be true, just as much as Jack does.'

'That's why I'm suggesting geophysics,' she pointed out. 'So we have physical evidence, too. Or we could do aerial reconnaissance, if you want to be old-fashioned.'

'Just how many favours do you want me to call in?'

'You're the one who sent me here,' she reminded him. 'It was your idea in the first place. You knew how I'd react.'

'Yeah, I know,' he admitted. 'Well – take care, Zoe. And be careful. Village politics can be – well, I don't want you hurt.'

'Sticks and stones, Steve,, sticks and stones,' she said casually. 'I'll check my facts.'

'You do that, sweetheart. Sleep well.' He paused. 'And, Zoe?'

'Yes?'

'I . . . ah, nothing.'

She had the feeling that he'd been about to say that he missed her, but they'd agreed a no-strings approach to their relationship, a long time before. 'Take care,' she said softly. 'I'll call you with an update tomorrow.'

Chapter Five

The next morning, Zoe had a leisurely breakfast, eating two helpings of croissants and Betty's home-made raspberry jam. Betty had already told her that there wasn't much point in heading into the city at the crack of dawn. The council offices were on her way in, so she might as well visit them first, and avoid the rush-hour traffic.

She drove into Long Stratton, and spent half an hour inspecting the proposed site development at Lower Yareham. She had been expecting an executive-style development, with large five-bedroomed houses and their double garages crammed on top of each other; she was surprised to discover that the houses were no more than three-bedroomed, with large gardens. Brandon could have made a lot more money by targeting the executive market and packing them in tightly, in common with most new developments.

A few more enquiries of the pleasant clerk in the planning section, and she learnt that Mark Burroughs was actually the prime developer, and Brandon was the sponsor. Mark had several other developments in the pipeline; Zoe asked to see the plans of those, and they were more like she'd expected the Lower Yareham site to look.

Something, she thought, didn't quite add up. Why was Lower Yareham so different? Further enquiries drew a blank; the clerk didn't know much about a Roman site in the area, other than what she'd read in the local paper.

Thoughtfully, Zoe took the A140 to Norwich, hardly noticing the gently undulating cornfields flanking the road. When she reached the city, she followed Betty's directions to the car park nearest to where the reference library was temporarily housed, and spent the rest of the morning poring over books and manuscripts, checking Jack's sources.

She took a quick lunch in a tiny French patisserie, unable

to resist a *tarte aux fraises* after her baguette and the superb coffee, then headed for the offices of the local newspaper. She'd already made a phone call before leaving The Feathers, arranging to meet Shannon Lewis, the journalist who had worked on the original story; over a drink in a nearby pub, she learnt more about the history of the area. Shannon was just as interested as she was in finding Boudicca's grave, and was more than happy to promise coverage, if Zoe wanted to run a campaign – an offer which Zoe was quick to take up.

Pleased with her day's work, Zoe headed back to Lower Yareham.

'Good day?' Sam asked as Zoe walked through the bar.

'Yes, thanks.' Zoe coughed. 'Though I got caught in the rush hour traffic.'

'Yeah. It's murder,' Sam said. 'If you're stuck behind a tractor, it'll take you an hour and a half to get to Ipswich from the city. They're always on about making the road dual carriageway and bypassing some of the bottle-neck villages, but then the plans always get set back again.' She shrugged. 'I dunno. Mum says it keeps the county's character, having slow roads instead of speed-tracks, but maybe that's her generation.'

'I heard that,' Betty Fielding said, coming into the bar and giving her daughter a playful cuff. 'And I'm sure Zoe doesn't want to hear about local politics.'

'Normally, I would,' Zoe said, seeing the crushed look on the younger girl's face, 'but it's been quite a long day. And I still have to work up my notes.' She yawned. 'After a shower.'

Betty chuckled. 'It looks like you're starting to feel the effects of Norfolk air.'

Zoe was mystified. 'How do you mean?'

'People – especially from London – say that they sleep more and eat more up here. It's something to do with the air.'

Zoe smiled. 'You could be right. I'll see you later, then.' She returned to her room and showered quickly, turning the water to its coldest setting to wake her up again, then rang Steve to update him on her research.

'So it's a goer, then,' Steve mused.

'Yes. Did you manage to sort the geophys?'

'Yes. In a couple of days,' Steve said.

'Right. I'll let Shannon know. The more publicity we get, the better.'

'And if there turns out to be nothing there?' Steve cautioned.

'There will be. Gut feel,' Zoe said. 'I'm going to ring Jack tomorrow, and have a look at the place.'

'You mean, you haven't seen it yet? And I've—'

Zoe cut him short. 'Steve, stop worrying. You trust me, don't you?'

'We-ell . . . Yes, you know I do.'

'Exactly. Just relax. Have a nice evening.'

'What are you up to, then?'

'A solitary dinner – and catching up with my notes.' Unless, perhaps, Dale was free and fancied having dinner with her.

'Don't overdo things. You're supposed to be taking a break, as well,' he reminded her.

'Yeah. I know.'

'Mind you, you already sound a hundred per cent happier than the last time I saw you. I reckon I was right. You were just bored.'

'Maybe.' Zoe paused. 'Take care. I'll ring you tomorrow, when I've seen the field.'

Zoe was just about to start putting her notes into order when her mobile rang. 'Hello. Zoe Lynton,' she said.

'Ms Lynton. It's Brandon Mitchell.'

She almost dropped the phone in shock. Why the hell was Brandon ringing her? Particularly as his voice wasn't in the slightest bit aggressive. Unless . . . 'Is Jack all right?' she asked, suddenly concerned for the old man.

'He's fine. A whole Roman army couldn't stop him, believe me.' There was a tinge of amusement in Brandon's voice. 'Look, I wondered if we could have dinner tonight? If you're not busy, that is.'

'I . . .' Zoe usually thought on her feet – it was one of the reasons she'd been successful as a journalist – but this was so completely unexpected that it threw her. 'Why?' The word was out before she could stop it.

'Because I was rude to you, yesterday. My grandfather's given me a lecture about bad manners, and I'd like to make it up to you.'

That would square with Sam's assessment of him as a nice guy – and Dale's – but there was no way that a hard-headed businessman who was on the opposite side to her would ask her out to dinner, just like that. Not without an ulterior motive. 'I . . .'

'If you're washing your hair, I understand,' he said.

God, why did he have to have such a sexy voice? 'No. But I was . . .' No. She couldn't pass up an opportunity like this. If he was intending to use dinner as a means of extracting information from her, she could do the same. 'I mean, I'd like to. But I haven't brought any dressy clothes with me. This is more or less a working trip,' she told him.

'We can eat at The Feathers, if you like. Betty's cooking is just as good as some of the city restaurants – if not better. Shall we meet in the bar at half past seven?'

'I . . . Okay.'

'I'll look forward to it.'

Zoe stared at the phone after he'd cut the connection. This was the last thing she'd been expecting. Brandon being nice to her. It sent a shiver of desire down her spine. After the way she'd fantasised about him, the previous day, she wasn't really sure that she could handle dinner with him. It would be hard to meet his eyes; she had a nasty feeling that he'd be able to guess her thoughts.

But supposing he did, an insidious voice whispered in her ear, and he shared them? The way he'd reacted to her in Whiteacres, it was obvious that he'd felt that same sexual charge. He'd fought it, yes; but he'd felt it, too . . .

She forced herself to concentrate on work, until seven o'clock; then she changed into a pair of summery trousers and a loose white cotton shirt. She left her hair loose and tumbled round her shoulders. A touch of make-up to widen her green eyes and emphasise her full mouth, and she was ready. She left her glasses on her bedside cabinet and headed downstairs, intending to be early and catch him unawares, but he'd already beaten her to it.

What was worse was how good he looked. She'd seen him in a suit, and he'd been ravishing. Dressed casually in jeans and a collarless black shirt, he looked even better. Incredibly sexy.

'Ms Lynton.'

'Zoe,' she said automatically.

'Zoe.' He smiled at her, and her stomach did a somersault.

The logical side of her brain knew that Brandon wasn't really here to apologise for being rude to her. He was setting out to charm her into dropping the Boudicca story. Hence the offer of dinner, and that gorgeous smile. It meant no more than that.

Her libido thought otherwise, and went into overdrive; Zoe was horribly aware that her nipples were erect, and Brandon could probably see them through her shirt. She wished fervently that she'd worn a dark and patterned shirt instead, something that would have covered her body's reaction to him.

'I asked Betty to reserve us a table. Would you like a drink, first, or shall we eat?'

Mr Charming himself. 'Er – I don't mind,' she said.

His eyes sparkled with mischief; he knew exactly what he was doing to her. That she wasn't the indecisive, weak little girly type: that she usually handled herself much better. 'Let's eat, then.'

She followed him into the separate restaurant, and they sat down. Brandon handed her a menu, and smiled at her. 'My bill – to make up for my rudeness yesterday.'

Zoe thought about arguing with him, insisting that they go Dutch, but knew that that was precisely what he was expecting. She could play games as well as he could. 'Thank you,' she said, giving him her most charming smile. 'Do you recommend anything in particular?'

His eyes met hers. 'It's all good. But I can order for you, if you wish.'

There was a tingle at the base of her spine. They were both talking normally, having a completely neutral conversation – but that was only on the surface. Her body was totally aware of his. He wasn't even touching her, but she knew virtually to the millimetre how far his skin was from hers. All he had to do was stretch out one long leg,

59

and he could nudge his knee between hers. Or, even worse, he could pretend to drop a napkin, and feather light caresses along her bare ankle, slipping her foot from her shoe and placing it in his lap as he sat up again. She'd be able to feel his cock swelling against the sole of her foot; and then he'd start to caress her, his fingertips brushing the sensitive spot just below her ankle-bone . . .

Brandon looked at her, and cursed himself mentally. He'd thought he was being so clever, asking her out for dinner as a peace offering. Spending some time on neutral ground would give them the chance to talk, and he could put his side of the case to her. He'd made enough enquiries about Zoe Lynton to know that she was well respected in the business, not a muckraker or a sensationalist. She'd give him a fair hearing.

What he hadn't bargained for was the way his body reacted to her. Right from the first moment he'd seen her, he'd had to force himself to keep his libido in check. Being this close to her was a bad idea. He could hardly think straight. She was dressed very simply, but he could imagine all too easily how it would feel to undo that soft cotton shirt. How soft her skin would be, how sweet it would taste as he followed the path of his fingers with his lips. Her hair was loose; he could imagine her sitting in his bed, that glorious dark curly hair spread over her shoulders, in such sharp contrast to her creamy skin. And her nipples . . . He'd seen the way she'd reacted when she'd met him in the bar. He hadn't been able to help looking at her breasts; and her areolae had definitely darkened. Her nipples had hardened, peaking against her loose shirt, and he'd wanted to touch her, taste her.

He shifted slightly in his seat. Even sitting with her made him hard. He wondered whether she was feeling the same as he was, imagining what it would be like to be somewhere more intimate with her. Whether her sex was growing warm and soft and wet and welcoming. It made him want to slide his hands between her thighs, to cup her delta and feel the warmth of her sex through those soft cotton trousers.

She wasn't wearing much make-up: just enough to highlight her eyes – this time, not hidden behind her glasses – and that beautiful kissable mouth. Eyes that were darkening with desire, and a mouth that was growing more and more bee-stung, the lower lip full and inviting. Inciting. Part of him itched to reach over and kiss her, taste the sweetness of her mouth; particularly as she looked lost in the same erotic dream as he was.

He made no effort to pull himself into the present. 'Zoe?'

She flushed deeply. 'Sorry. You were saying?'

I want to go to bed with you. Right now. I want to take you upstairs and explore every inch of your body. He smiled, keeping his voice carefully neutral. His self-control had made him an excellent businessman, and he wasn't going to lose it now. 'I was saying, everything's so good, it's difficult to choose. I could order for you, if you like.'

'Thank you.'

'Are you vegetarian?'

'No.'

He smiled to himself. She hadn't expected him to be that thoughtful, that much was obvious. God. In other circumstances, he would have liked to get to know Zoe better. He had a feeling that things would have worked between them. But as it was, with her chasing Jack's unfulfillable dream and believing him to be the bad guy . . . He'd just have to settle for a truce.

Betty came over to take their order; Brandon ordered smoked salmon mousse, chicken with asparagus and Betty's Chocolate Surprise, teaming it with a bottle of Chablis.

'Sorry?' Zoe was horribly aware that he'd been talking to her – and she'd been so lost in her erotic fantasy of Brandon taking a shower with her and soaping her all over, she hadn't been paying attention.

'I was just asking what you thought of the area.' Brandon tipped his head to one side. 'You look tired.'

'Yes.' She was surprised by the sympathy in his voice. 'I've been knee-deep in papers all day.'

'Checking my grandfather's research.'

'Yes.'

'And?'

She shook her head. 'I'm sorry, Brandon. I don't want to discuss that with you.'

61

'Fair enough.'

She was surprised again by his response, and fought to hide it. This was crazy. She knew that he was just playing up to her. And yet she couldn't help a growing liking for the man. To say nothing of her attraction to him. 'You were talking about the area. It's beautiful around here. I thought Norfolk was all flat and full of windmills.'

He grinned. 'That's more the east of the county, around Yarmouth and the Broads. Mid-Norfolk's full of little folds and hollows and churches.'

'And your church is a real surprise.' Zoe found herself talking to him about her love of medieval architecture and her plans to write a guidebook, one day; Brandon listened as though he really were interested.

He, in turn, told her more about Lower Yareham, how he'd gone away to college but decided to join Jack in the farm, unable to turn his back on the place he loved. Zoe wondered how a man who obviously adored his surroundings could even consider the idea of turning part of it into a housing estate; it just didn't add up. Something was going on – but what?

Neither of them really noticed the food they ate, although it was excellent; eventually, Brandon sighed. 'Zoe, we need to talk. But we can't do it here. We're right in the middle of the village gossip zone.'

'Betty Fielding's very discreet. She wouldn't tell me anything.'

He grinned. 'Betty's a one-off. I'm talking about the rest of The Feathers. They might look as if they're engrossed in their own meals and their own conversations but, believe me, their antennae are tuned in to us. Look, can we go for a walk?'

'So dinner wasn't an apology, then.'

'Yes and no. And you didn't accept just to make overtures of friendship.'

'Yes and no,' she echoed ruefully.

'Come on. There's going to be gossip, whatever we do, but I'd rather have some of our conversation in private.'

Zoe's nipples tingled, and she took a deep breath, unwilling to meet his eyes. All sorts of crazy ideas, fuelled by her libido, were running through her brain. Brandon wanting a private, intimate conversation, in a private, intimate place . . . 'All right,' she said, once she was sure that her voice would remain steady.

Brandon paid the bill, then ushered her out of The Feathers. They took the same path that she had taken with Dale, towards the churchyard; Zoe remarked on this, and Brandon gave her a thoughtful look. 'Dale's taken you sightseeing?'

'Sort of.' Zoe's skin heated. She certainly wasn't going to tell Brandon that part of the tour had included Dale's bedroom. And although it had been a pleasant interlude, it was nothing compared to the way her body reacted to Brandon. She could see now why half the women in the village were in love with the man. He was sexual dynamite. The younger ones would fantasise about an older man; and the older ones would either fantasise about having him as their toy-boy, or meeting him when they were much younger.

He made no comment; she risked a quick glance at him as they walked into the churchyard, wondering what he was thinking. He was doing exactly the same; he grinned ruefully. 'The two lions circled, sizing each other up?'

'Something like that,' Zoe admitted. Though it was less to do with their opposition on the Boudicca issue than a sheer longing to feel his body against hers. Particularly as she'd just noticed the gravestone she'd pointed out to Dale, the previous evening, and he'd told her wickedly that he'd made love on a similar stone in Walthamstow churchyard. The idea of making love, combined with Brandon's presence, was one hell of a cocktail.

'Zoe.' She noticed that his voice had dropped a register. 'We don't have to be enemies.'

'I know.'

He drew her round the side of the churchyard, where they wouldn't be overlooked. 'I'm being presumptuous, but . . . Oh, hell.' He lowered his head and touched his lips very lightly to hers.

At the first touch, Zoe was lost. She couldn't help sliding her hands round his neck and responding, opening her mouth beneath his and letting him explore her with his tongue. It was as though they'd both lit a fuse: Brandon pulled her closer, stroking her back and her buttocks, moulding her against him. She could feel his erection pressing against her pubis, and she knew he could feel the hard peaks of her nipples against his chest.

He broke the kiss so that he could look into her eyes; his own were almost black with desire, his pupils had expanded so much. 'Zoe. I need to touch you, to taste you . . .'

She didn't care that they were in a public place. She felt the same urgent need: to touch and be touched, taste and be tasted. His gaze held hers for a moment; in reply, she stroked his face, feeling the faint rasp of stubble against her fingertips.

He caught her hand, drawing it to his mouth, and sucked each finger in turn; Zoe gasped, imagining his mouth working on more intimate parts of her body, and he smiled at her. 'This is half the problem. I can't think straight when I'm with you, Zoe. I can hardly hold a conversation – I keep thinking of what else we could be doing.'

'Me too,' she admitted.

'We need to talk – but I can't do that right now. All I can think of is . . .' His gaze dropped to the open neck of her shirt. 'I want you, Zoe. I want you so badly.'

She pulled her hand away; with shaking fingers, she unbuttoned her shirt. Their surroundings were forgotten: all she could concentrate on was Brandon. His eyes, his mouth, his body. She didn't care who might see them, who might talk. She knew that he wanted her just as much as she wanted him, and that was all that mattered.

Brandon's eyes widened; slowly, he pushed her hair back and slid the soft white cotton off her shoulders. 'You're as beautiful as I imagined,' he said softly. 'All through dinner, I kept wondering just what you looked like, beneath that demure shirt. Though it wasn't *that* demure. When you walked into the bar, I saw your nipples harden and change colour.'

Zoe blushed. 'I . . .'

'It's nothing to be ashamed of. You're beautiful, and it made me hard as a stone in seconds,' he said, sliding the straps of her bra off her shoulders. 'Your skin's so soft, so tempting . . .' He bent his head, licking the sensitive spot at the side of her neck and trailing his mouth along her shoulder. Zoe arched her back, closing her eyes, and she

64

felt him unclasp her bra, gently removing the garment. She had no idea what he did with it and, as he cupped her swollen breasts, she didn't care.

She gave a sharp intake of breath as she felt his mouth close over one nipple, his tongue lapping at the puckered skin of her areolae; then he grazed the sensitive tissue with his teeth, lightly enough to keep on the right side of the pain-pleasure barrier, and her sex grew wet. 'Brandon. Oh, yes. Do it,' she said huskily.

He needed no second bidding. He dropped to his knees before her and hooked his thumbs into the waistband of her loose trousers, pulling the material down. Zoe kicked her shoes off and stepped out of the garment as the soft cotton pooled around her feet; all the while, Brandon kissed and caressed her breasts, teasing her nipples and making her writhe against his clever fingers.

She tilted her pelvis towards him; his mouth tracked down her abdomen, lingering round her navel, to tease her, then sliding down further, towards her delta. 'Please,' she begged as he slid one finger under the elastic of her knickers. 'Please. Touch me. Taste me.'

He probed her soft curls, then let his finger drift along the full length of her musky furrow. Zoe squeezed her eyes tightly shut and wound her fingers in his hair, urging him on. She wanted him to touch her, to taste her. She wanted to feel his tongue pushing deep inside her; she wanted to feel his lips against her clitoris, nipping the sensitive nubbin and then sucking hard, bringing her to the edge of pleasure.

He pushed the gusset of her knickers aside and pressed the flat of his palms against her thighs, urging her to widen her stance. She gave a small moan of pleasure as he breathed on her quim, then began to lap her in earnest, varying the pace and pressure, his tongue sometimes soft and smooth and licking her from the top to the bottom of her slit, and sometimes hard and tormenting and flicking rapidly across one spot of pleasure. He lapped and sucked, nipped and soothed, probed and explored and savoured the taste of her arousal; Zoe began to move her lips, pressing hard against him, wanting more and more and more.

She could feel her climax building, a silver wire linking her clitoris with her nipples and pulling tighter, tighter, growing hotter and hotter, and finally splintering into a million white-hot pieces; her sex pulsed against him, and she cried out.

He held her tightly until her pulse had slowed, then pulled her down on top of him, lying back so that she was straddling him in a kneeling position. 'Zoe, Zoe.' He kissed her hard; she could taste herself on his mouth, the sweet-salt musk of her climax.

He stroked her back, his fingertips warm against her cooling skin, and she shivered, suddenly remembering where they were. She was almost completely naked – apart from her knickers, which he'd left in place – and he was fully clothed. 'Brandon, I . . .'

'Shh. No one can see us. This area of the churchyard isn't overlooked by the village.'

She looked suspiciously at him. 'How do you know?'

'I grew up here,' he told her simply. 'If you're a teenager in Lower Yareham, you know about this place.'

The glint of mischief in his eyes won her over. Her lips twitched. 'And I can imagine just how often you came here.'

'In more than one sense of the word,' he murmured huskily. His eyes had darkened again. 'Zoe. I wanted the first time to be for you.'

She could feel his erection pressing against her, and smiled. 'I think you'd better be wearing a bit less, before we go any further.'

'You're in charge,' he told her.

Zoe bent her head to kiss him; his mouth opened beneath hers, and she kissed him hard, exploring him as he'd explored her, touching the tip of her tongue to his and kissing him thoroughly. At the same time, she unbuttoned his shirt, pulling the material apart to bare his chest; she ran her fingers through the light covering of dark hair, discovering that his flat button nipples were as hard as her own. She leant forward, brushing her nipples against his chest; the friction was delicious.

He murmured something against her mouth, and tipped his pelvis up; Zoe pressed herself against him, and he groaned. She broke the kiss, grinning. 'Tut, tut. Patience is a business asset.'

'And a virtue. I'm not feeling virtuous,' he informed her.

His voice was slightly slurred; she knew that it owed less to the bottle of wine they'd shared than to her proximity and his need for her. She smiled, secure in her power over him, and reached between their bodies to undo the button of his jeans. She slid the zip slowly downwards, and urged him to lift his buttocks so that she could slide both his underpants and his jeans down to his knees, in one smooth movement.

He'd felt good against her; she couldn't resist looking down, and gave a small gasp of pleasure at the sight. His cock reared from a thick cloud of dark hair, the tip purple and shiny with clear fluid. She curled her hand round the shaft, squeezing gently, and was rewarded with a soft moan.

'Yes, Zoe, yes. I want to be inside you. I want to feel your sex wrapped round my cock, warm and silky and wet, gripping me tight. Do it, Zoe. Do it.' It was more of a plea than a command; hadn't he already said that she was in charge?

And it was exactly what she wanted to do. She lifted herself up still further, pulling her knickers to one side and fitting the tip of his cock against her sex. Then, very slowly, she eased herself onto the rigid column of flesh. She paused when the tip was halfway into her; he felt so good, stretching her like that. Then she slammed down, hard, grinding her pubis against his. Her clitoris was still swollen and sensitive, and she moaned as she rocked against him, stimulating the little bundle of nerves at the same time as she flexed her internal muscles round his hard rod of flesh.

He reached up to cup her breasts, stroking and squeezing them; she leant backwards, arching her body and changing the angle of his penetration, and began to move her hips, rocking back and forth, pushing down on him until he filled her to the hilt, then pulling up so that he was almost out of her.

It seemed to go on for ever; then, finally, Brandon raised his upper body from the grass, pulling her towards him and kissing her hard. He lay flat again, drawing her down with him, and jerked his pelvis upwards; at the same time as her own inner sparkling began again, she felt his cock throb deep inside her. He wrapped his arms round her, holding her close and burying his face in her hair; neither of them said a word until his cock slipped from her.

He kissed her lightly. 'Thank you,' he said softly. 'I think we both needed that.'

'Yes.' Though her head still wasn't clear. She could still taste him, smell his scent. If anything, making love with him had made things worse; now that it had happened, her fantasies had something concrete to use as a base, and would be even more intense.

He stroked her face. 'Time to get up. Though I could stay here all night with you, making love under the stars, watching them reflected in your eyes, seeing your skin bathed in moonlight.'

She smiled wryly. 'Poet as well as farmer?'

'No. Just your effect on me, I guess.' He rubbed his nose against hers. 'Better clean you up.' She climbed off him; he shifted to his knees, and cleaned her with his mouth. Zoe shivered. She'd never known anyone do that before; even Steve had preferred her to use a handkerchief or something on the couple of occasions when they'd made love outside.

She shivered as she realised that he'd aroused her again – and that he knew it, too, because he continued lapping her after he'd cleaned the pearly tang of his semen from her, until her body convulsed again and flooded his mouth with nectar. Then he stood up, gathering her clothes at the same time, and dressed her carefully before restoring order to his own clothes.

'I can't believe what we've just done,' she said, as reality returned. 'In a churchyard, of all places.'

'Merely reaffirming life,' Brandon told her with a grin, tidying her hair with his fingers. 'It's not morbid at all.'

'No. I suppose not.' Her lips twitched. 'Though I have to admit, I have a fascination for these places. That's part of the reason why Steve gave me the story – because this area is so rich in *mementi mori*.'

'Yes. There's one in Norwich Cathedral – worth a visit, if you get the chance.'

'I'll remember that.'

'I know what you mean about churchyards, though. There's something about gravestones – epitaphs and the like.'

'And there's something even more fascinating about older

graves,' Zoe said. 'Older burials.'

Brandon's face twisted. 'Boudicca. Come on, Zoe. We've already been through all that. It doesn't exist.'

'Jack thinks it does.'

'He's dreaming, Zoe. It's an old man's fantasy. One I used to share, when I was a kid – but this is the real world. Archaeologists would have found it by now, if it existed.'

'Not necessarily.'

'I think we both know better. Look, Zoe, just stop interfering, will you? I've already told you, Jack might look like he's ten years younger than he is, but his health isn't brilliant. I don't want him over-excited and then disappointed.'

'He won't be.'

'He will be, if you stir him up like this. I know you spent the day in Norwich, looking at the records. Why don't you tell him that you found nothing?'

'Because it wouldn't be true. I think he has a valid point, and it needs checking carefully. God knows how many things have been lost in the past, thanks to greedy farmers selling out to developers who couldn't care less.'

'Now you're being unfair.' There was a hard edge to his voice.

'And you're not?'

'No. I'm thinking of my grandfather. Zoe, if you won't drop it, I'll have to look at other options.'

Her eyes widened. 'If you're threatening me, Brandon, it's because you've got something to hide.'

'*What?*' He looked at her in disbelief. 'I came to see you tonight because I thought you'd give me a fair hearing. But you're just like any other journalist on her hobby-horse, aren't you? Not prepared to listen to anything except your version of the truth.' His mouth twisted in disgust. 'I'm just sorry that I was so wrong about you.' His fists clenched. 'But believe me, if anything happens to Gramps, I'll hold you responsible.' Turning on his heel, he strode off.

Zoe watched his retreating back in shock. Not ten minutes before, they'd been skin to skin, their bodies melting into each other. Now, they were back to being sworn enemies, the surge of desire between them forgotten.

She clenched her jaw. Well, there certainly wouldn't be a

next time. It would be a cold day in hell before Brandon Mitchell touched her again. She stomped back towards The Feathers. She'd prove Jack right – and the first thing she'd do was ring Shannon.

Chapter Six

'Have you seen this morning's local paper?'

Brandon recognised his business partner's voice, and frowned. Mark Burroughs was known for being unflappable. Yet he sounded as if he were pacing up and down his office in a temper, no doubt shouting at anyone unfortunate enough to be in the way. 'No. It hasn't been delivered, yet – anyway, Gramps usually reads it first.'

'Well, go and get yourself a bloody copy. No, on second thoughts, I'll fax it to you.'

'The whole paper?'

'The front page – and that's more than enough. Bloody, bloody hell. This could ruin everything.'

'What could?'

'The article. Your precious grandfather's been mobilising the troops.'

Brandon's eyes widened. 'What?'

'There were some people sniffing round the site, yesterday. I saw them. I thought you'd got it covered?'

'No. I was in Cambridge all day, yesterday, on farm business.'

'Well, why didn't you have the site guarded?'

'Calm down, Mark. Apart from anything else, there's a bridle-path along one side. If I cordon off the field, I'll have the Ramblers' Association down on me like a ton of bricks – to say nothing of Jenny, for stuffing up one of her hacking routes.' Jenny Sorenson was the owner of the local riding stables, whose land was next to Whiteacres, and a string of her ponies, topped by delighted children, was often seen along the bridle-paths in the area.

'There weren't any horses in sight, and they were right in the middle of the field. They were people with what looked like metal detectors.'

'Did you say anything to them?'

'No. I was on my way to a client. I can't do everything, you know.' Mark was huffy.

'Calm down, and fax me the article. I'll sort it out.'

'You'd better do. I've got a lot invested in this site. You know that.'

'Okay, okay.' Brandon soothed his partner's ruffled feathers, then put the phone down. A few seconds later, his fax machine beeped; he waited for the paper to finish printing, then picked it up and read it. His face creased into a frown. Zoe had obviously been talking to the local paper – and more than just talking. The people Mark had seen hadn't been using metal detectors. They'd been using very sophisticated geophysics equipment, which had revealed traces of what could be an archaeological site.

He took a deep breath, and left his office, heading for the kitchen. His grandfather was there, drinking tea and chatting to Eileen, surreptitiously feeding toast to Belle and Candy.

'Brandon! Come and have a cup of tea,' Jack said, pulling out the chair beside him. 'And don't tell me that you're busy working. You've already done at least an hour, so you deserve a break.'

Brandon's smile was rueful. He couldn't stay angry with his grandfather for long. 'All right,' he said. 'Morning, Eileen.'

'Morning, Brandon.' The housekeeper poured him a mug of strong tea, sliding it in front of him. 'And you'll have some toast. I know you – you didn't have any breakfast.'

He couldn't help laughing. 'Oh, you two. You will insist on treating me like a naughty little boy.'

'That's because we remember you as one,' Eileen teased.

'Yeah, well. I'm not the only one around here – eh, Gramps?' Brandon passed the article to his grandfather. 'I've just had this faxed through to me. Something you want to tell me, is there?'

'Ah.' Jack scratched his nose. 'I wondered if it'd be in today.'

'Front page, no less. Look, Gramps, I thought we'd agreed to let it be?'

'I didn't think it'd make the front page.'

'News like this? Come on.' Brandon tipped his head to one side. 'What's the story?'

'Zoe has . . . well, contacts in London. They came down for the day, yesterday, to do a quick survey of the site. Fascinating machines, Brandon. It's amazing. The kind they use underwater, too. One of these days, they'll find Nessie with it.'

Brandon was torn between laughter and anger. 'Nessie's as much a myth as . . . Well. Why didn't you tell me about it?'

'Didn't see the point. We agreed not to argue, didn't we? And if I'd told you about it . . .' Jack shrugged, and drank some more tea. 'I didn't want a fight.'

'Looks like we've got one, now.' Brandon sighed and lifted his hands in a gesture of submission, as Eileen cleared her throat. 'Not in your kitchen, Eileen, and not with Gramps. I know who's behind this, and I'll have a word with her. Or maybe Mark will.' He didn't trust himself around Zoe. He could still remember what had happened between them when he'd last tried talking to her. He hadn't been able to get it out of his head, ever since: her scent, her taste, the feel of her skin against his. 'I just wish you hadn't blown it out of proportion.'

'It proves there's something there, though,' Jack said smugly. 'I told you so.'

'And you'll find it's just an ancient midden or something like that.'

'To have a midden, you need a castle,' Jack fenced.

'Boys, boys. Shut up,' Eileen told them.

'All right.' Brandon drained his tea. 'But I need to make some phone calls. See you later.'

'What about your . . .?' Eileen looked resignedly at the plate of toast as Brandon left the room without a backward glance. 'Well looks like you and the hounds will be getting seconds, you old reprobate,' she told Jack. 'I wish you wouldn't wind him up.'

'Whose side are you on?'

'Neither,' Eileen told him briskly. 'And if you had any sense . . .'

Jack grinned. 'That's the privilege of old age,' he told her, unrepentant. 'You can chase your dreams.'

'Zoe Lynton,' Mark mused.

'Yes. She's a freelance journalist – she specialises in archaeology. She saw the original article, and she's teamed up with my grandfather.'

'That's just what we don't need. Get rid of her, Brandon.'

'I had a word with her, the other day. Obviously it didn't work.'

'I'll do it, then.' Mark sighed. 'What's her number?'

'She's staying at The Feathers.' Brandon decided not to give Mark her mobile phone number. 'Be nice to her, though.'

'Nice is my middle name.'

'I mean it. Turn stroppy with her, and she'll use it against you.'

'I have dealt with journalists before, you know.'

Brandon sighed. 'Sorry. I'm just . . . Well, I've got things on my mind.' Like Zoe's legs straddling his body, her beautiful breasts naked and ripe in his hands. Like the feel of her quim as his cock sank into her. Like—

'All right. I'll turn on the charm, persuade her that there's nothing to be found around here. I had the place surveyed before we applied for permission, you know. There really isn't anything there.'

'I know.'

'It's an old man's dream, that's all.'

'You're preaching to the converted – otherwise I wouldn't have agreed to the development. It's my land, remember?'

'Yeah. Okay, I'll give her a call. I'll take her to lunch somewhere nice, talk her round.'

'You do that.' When Brandon replaced the receiver, he was surprised to see that his knuckles were white. Even the thought of Mark in close proximity to Zoe . . . He grimaced. No. He and Zoe were on opposite sides; although their bodies were more than compatible, their minds weren't. It wouldn't work. Even so, he was shocked to find how jealous he felt, even at the thought of Mark having lunch with her. When Mark decided to be charming, he could charm the knickers off any woman – literally.

He swore, and turned to the accounts. That would keep

his mind off everything else – particularly thoughts of Zoe and Mark together . . .

'For me?' Zoe was surprised. All the people she would have expected to phone her had her mobile number. Who could be calling her at The Feathers?

Betty sniffed. 'Mark Burroughs.'

'I see.' Zoe had expected Brandon to confront her about the article; obviously he'd decided to leave it to his business partner. And it looked like even the usually cheerful and tactful Betty was another non-member of the Mark Burroughs Appreciation Society; Zoe's curiosity was roused. What kind of a man was Mark Burroughs, to make everyone dislike him so much?

She followed Betty downstairs to the bar, and picked up the phone. 'Hello? Zoe Lynton speaking.'

'Miss Lynton.'

The voice on the other end of the line immediately annoyed her. This was a smoothie – and, worse than that, a man who thought himself exceptionally smooth and sophisticated. It also annoyed her that he immediately assumed that she was a 'Miss'. She was half tempted to tell him that actually, it was 'Mrs', but stopped herself just in time. 'And to whom do I have the pleasure of speaking?' she purred instead.

'Mark Burroughs. I'm Brandon Mitchell's business partner. I saw the article in the paper, this morning, and I think we need to talk.'

'I don't think there's anything to say, Mr Burroughs.'

'Mark, please. I prefer doing business on first-name terms – don't you, Zoe? So much more . . . intimate.'

Mark Burroughs could have looked like a cross between Antonio Banderas and David Duchovny, and she still would have found him repulsive, she thought. There was something in his manner that made her hackles rise. Well, two could play at that game. 'Yes, Mark, I quite agree.' She just stopped herself from adding, 'sweetie, luvvie, darling.' 'First-name terms are so much better. But we still don't really have anything to say.'

'Even about my survey of the area?'

'Your survey?'

'Yes. I thought perhaps we could discuss it over a long lunch – if you can fit me into your schedule, of course. I know how busy you journalists are.'

Implying that she was easily bought – with a free lunch – and that busy was nothing of the kind. 'I'll just check my diary,' she said, playing along. She wasn't planning anything until the excavation, at the weekend – and she had a feeling that Jack hadn't told Brandon about that, yet, so she certainly wouldn't be breathing a word about it. 'Yes, I think I can fit you in. Twelve o'clock.'

'I'll be there,' he said, injecting a wickedly sexy note to his voice. 'I'll have a reservation at a restaurant in Norwich – unless you'd rather take advantage of the weather and have a picnic?'

'A restaurant is fine.' At least in a restaurant, she could excuse herself every time he became too irritating. A little voice inside her head added that if Brandon had made the offer of a picnic, she would have leapt it at it . . . But they hadn't spoken since that unforgettable night in the churchyard. She'd been careful to avoid him, and it looked like he'd been doing the same. 'See you at twelve.'

She grimaced as she replaced the receiver. 'Is Mark Burroughs as oily as his voice?'

'That's not for me to say,' Betty said diplomatically.

Zoe grinned. 'You don't have to. Your face just did it for you.'

When Mark turned up at twelve – at least unpunctuality wasn't one of his bad points, Zoe thought – he turned out to be charming. He had the slightly floppy blond hair and small round glasses that had always attracted Zoe to a man; his suit was designer, a beautifully cut sober grey affair. The only thing about his appearance that jarred was his tie: a bright yellow patterned silk thing that marked him out as a man in financial services who wanted to look flamboyant and trendy.

'Miss Lynton. Zoe. Delighted to meet you.' He took her hand, drawing it to his mouth and kissing the backs of her fingers.

Zoe couldn't exactly say likewise. Not after the veiled comments she'd had from too many people in Lower

Yareham over the past few days, when she'd chatted casually in the bar to judge the groundswell of local opinion about the site. But there was no point in being rude to him and creating a row, just for the sake of it. She decided to be just as charming to him; maybe it would make him drop his guard more quickly and they could get to the point. 'Mr Burroughs. Mark,' she purred.

'Shall we go?'

He was driving a top of the range BMW; she smiled wryly to herself. Mark Burroughs obviously believed in impressing his clients. And who wouldn't entrust their funds to a man who dressed in designer suits, drove a flash car, and listened to classical music in his car? Even if it was only *The Four Seasons*, one of the most commonly known pieces: the meaner side of her couldn't help wondering if Mark would recognise anything more obscure.

He kept the conversation light as they drove to Norwich, concentrating on her and her interests and avoiding the subject of Boudicca's grave; Zoe found herself responding, and was impressed by his easy charm. She could see just how he'd achieved his client base, quickly finding out his clients' tastes and interests and indulging them. At the same time, she didn't trust him at all, and was careful not to give too much away.

Lunch was superb, at a tiny and obviously exclusive restaurant in one of the narrow cobbled streets in the old part of Norwich: an expensive place, she thought, noting that the prices were not displayed on the menu handed to her. She chose a light meal of quail's egg tartlet followed by sole meunière, and accepted Mark's offer of Sancerre.

'I honestly didn't expect you to be like this,' Mark told her as they ate. 'I know it's a cliché, but I suppose I've always expected journalists to be chain-smoking, hard-drinking and scruffy. But you . . . Has anyone told you how stunning your hair is? Like that famous Rossetti painting.'

Zoe couldn't resist testing him. '*Beata Beatrix*, you mean?'

He clicked his fingers. 'Yes, that's the one.'

Zoe forbore to tell him that the model in that particular painting had red hair; but it made her smile inwardly. Mark was obviously adopting the tactic of charming her into giving

77

up the Boudicca story – after bedding her – and had decided that she was the cultured type who would appreciate being compared with the great beauties of art. Such a pity that he didn't know enough about the subject; if she hadn't, either, his smooth manner would have fooled her into thinking him genuinely cultured. As it was, she'd caught him out, very early on, and her opinion of him dropped even lower. 'That's very sweet of you to say so.'

'And your eyes . . . such a beautiful green. If I were a painter, I'd love to paint you – capture the tones of your hair and your eyes and your skin, so beautifully creamy.' He spread his hands ruefully. 'Alas, I can't draw a straight line with a ruler.'

'Me, neither.'

'But you're still beautiful. I love the way your mouth curves.'

'Thank you.' Zoe wasn't sure whether he was expecting her to compliment him back, or merely to melt into his arms. She continued to eat, playing it cool.

He gave her another charming smile. 'If we weren't in the middle of a restaurant, I'd be tempted to kiss you, you know.'

'Oh.' She raised an eyebrow. Time to change tack. 'Even though I'm on the opposite side to you, over the development?'

He waved an expansive hand. 'That's nothing. Well, I suppose it's part of the reason why I wanted to see you, to talk to you. I've already had the site surveyed, and there's nothing there. I had a couple of archaeologists out to search the place.'

'Perhaps they were looking in the wrong field,' Zoe said. 'Because we have geophysical evidence.'

'Modern technology's a wonderful thing. But it isn't always reliable, you know. Like metal detectors – just when you think you've found a hoard of coins, you dig up a heap of ring-pulls. You're wasting your time and money, you know. There's nothing interesting in that field.'

'Perhaps we can agree to differ.'

'Perhaps.' Mark gave her a rueful – and practised, Zoe thought – smile. 'I was intending to have a real fight with you, you know. Until I met you. Then your smile drove every

78

thought straight out of my head.'

Zoe sipped her wine, suppressing the temptation to throw the contents of her glass over him. His ingratiating smile was fine for a financial adviser, smooth and charming – but his manner was beginning to grate on her. She could see, now, why so many people in the village disliked him. 'Oh.'

His smile grew warmer. 'I have a private office, not far from here. Perhaps we could have our coffee there, in more, ah – ' he paused ' – comfort.'

'I'm not sure that's a good idea.'

'Zoe. You must know that I'm attracted to you. And I think it's mutual. Maybe if we get to know each other a bit better . . .' He took her hand, his thumb stroking her palm. 'I think we'd make a good team. We'd be good for each other, Zoe. I like a woman with brains as well as beauty – and I've always found brunettes far more striking than blondes. Perhaps we—'

She withdrew her hand. 'I think not, Mr Burroughs.'

'Mark, please.' He gave her a hurtful look – again, something he'd practised on a lot of clients, she thought. 'I thought we were friends, Zoe? And we could be even better friends.'

She shook her head. 'You missed one thing off your description of a typical hack journo. And I don't sleep around.' It wasn't strictly true, she thought: she'd already made love with Dale and Brandon. The difference was that it had been a no-strings arrangement, based on mutual attraction. And the more time she spent with Mark Burroughs, the more he irritated her.

'Of course not. I wasn't suggesting that we should go all the way, today. No, when we make love for the first time, I want it to be in a four-poster bed, on crisp white sheets, with a bottle of champagne beside our bed. Maybe in Paris, Rome – somewhere romantic.'

'I think you'll be disappointed.'

'In your beautiful body? Never.'

She smiled thinly. She couldn't keep up the pretence of being charming, any longer. 'In that your fantasy won't happen. You're not my type; and I'm not that easily deflected from my work. Thank you for lunch, Mark. I'll find my own way back.'

He shook his head. 'My God, you really are a hard bitch, aren't you?'

'No. I'm direct and to the point. Goodbye,' she said sweetly, turning on her heel and leaving him sitting there with his mouth open.

She called in at the newspaper offices to see Shannon and update her on the latest developments. Mark's reaction to the article smacked of panic. If he'd had a survey done, which she doubted, he'd lied about the results. Then she caught a taxi back to Lower Yareham. On the way, she couldn't help wondering what Brandon had told his partner – and why a man like Brandon Mitchell would team up with his complete opposite. Mark Burroughs wouldn't recognise sincerity if it hit him in the face.

She sighed. Had Brandon suggested that Mark try to charm her into bed, to take her mind off the Boudicca story? Or had that been Mark's own idea? Whatever: Brandon Mitchell was going to find out that she wouldn't budge that easily.

The phone rang; Brandon scowled at it, saved his file, and picked up the receiver. 'Brandon Mitchell.'

'It's Mark.'

'How did you get on with Zoe?'

'You didn't tell me that she was so beautiful.'

Brandon's stomach clenched. 'Beautiful?'

'Yes. Like bloody Medusa. I took her to Gabriel's, thinking that we could discuss business over lunch and I could talk her out of that story.'

'And?'

'She walked out on me.'

'I told you to be nice to her.'

'I *was*. Very nice.' Brandon had to stifle a grin at his partner's disgruntled tone. Obviously Mark had tried the famed Burroughs charm on Zoe, and it hadn't worked.

'Well. She can't do that much damage.'

'Yes, she bloody can. I told her I'd had a survey done. Look, just deal with her, will you? The longer she's around, the more likely she is to ruin everything.'

'Okay, okay. I'll talk to her,' Brandon soothed. Maybe if he did talk to her, this time, and tell her the reason why he

80

was setting up the development, she'd understand.

'Let me know how you get on.'

The line went dead; Brandon cleared it, and dialled Zoe's mobile number.

'Zoe Lynton.'

'Hello. It's Brandon Mitchell. Jack's grandson.'

Zoe shivered. As if he'd needed to state who he was. She'd recognised his voice instantly. 'What can I do for you?'

'I wondered if I could see you, later this evening – to talk.'

'Is there anything to say?'

'I think so. Would it be possible to come to your room?'

The slight wobble in his voice sent shivers down her spine. Whatever their differences on the Boudicca front, the attraction between them was still there – and he felt it as strongly as she did. Sincerely, too: he didn't bother with any of Mark's honey-tongued smoothness. 'I . . .' Brandon, in her room. The two of them, near a bed. It would be just too tempting. But then again, they were more likely to have a fully-fledged fight than to make love. That needed a bit more privacy. 'All right. Eight o'clock.'

'That's fine.'

She cut the connection with shaking hands, and tried to concentrate on the article she was outlining. But every time she started to type, she found herself mixing up letters and spaces. 'Oh, hell,' she said, after deleting a paragraph for the sixth time. There was only one way to clear her mind enough to work. She switched off her laptop and walked over to the curtains, closing them, then made sure that her door was locked. She stripped swiftly, pulled down the covers, and climbed onto the bed.

She closed her eyes, remembering the way Brandon had touched her in the churchyard; she stroked her swelling breasts, teasing her hardening nipples and plucking at them. She licked her suddenly dry lower lip, letting her right hand drift over her abdomen, lightly brushing the skin; she cupped her mons veneris, parting her legs, and sighed with pleasure as she slid one finger between her labia.

Her clitoris pulsed beneath her questing fingers; she began to run herself hard, still stroking her breasts with her free hand. All the time, she had Brandon's face in her mind: the voluptuous curve of his lower lip, those beautiful slate blue eyes, the way his eyes crinkled at the corners as he smiled. And the way he'd bared his teeth in pleasure as she sank onto his cock.

Moaning softly, she widened her stance and brought her left hand down to work between her legs, sliding one finger into her warm wet depths and adding a second and a third. She began to piston her hand back and forth, bucking her hips and pretending that Brandon's body was on top of hers, driving in deeply.

She opened her mouth in a groan of pleasure, pushing back hard against the pillows and squeezing her eyes tightly shut as her climax approached: then she felt the flooding relief in the pit of her belly as her internal muscles contracted sharply. She lay there for a moment, her hands still buried in her sex; when her pulse rate had slowed, she headed for the en suite bathroom on shaky legs, showering briskly. Then she dressed, restored order to the bedclothes, and spent the rest of the afternoon working.

Betty forbore to ask her how she got on with Mark; Zoe was impressed by the landlady's discretion, and respected it enough not to ask for more information on Mark Burroughs. Instead, she ate her evening meal, then told Betty that she was expecting Brandon to call in to see her on business, asking her to send him up to her room when he arrived.

Again, Betty displayed her amazing tact, making no comment; Zoe knew that it certainly wouldn't be talked about in the bar at The Feathers, that evening, unless she or Brandon said something about it.

She continued working on her file, with one eye on the clock. At eight precisely, there was a knock on the door.

'Come in. It's open,' she called.

Brandon walked into the room and closed the door behind him. 'Thank you for agreeing to see me.'

She inclined her head in acknowledgement. 'Do sit down.' She saved her file and switched off the laptop. 'So what can I do for you, Mr Mitchell?'

He smiled ruefully, as if disappointed that she'd switched back to formality with him – particularly after what they'd shared. 'I think you know.' He sat down on the bed.

Zoe shivered. God. This had been a bad idea. She should have offered to go to the farm, or if he didn't want Jack involved, even meet him in his office. Seeing him on that wide double bed was doing crazy things to her imagination and her libido. 'I . . .' She swallowed, moistening her lower lip. 'Look, I'm sorry if Jack didn't tell you about the geophysics. But sending your business partner round to charm me into giving up – well.'

'Not the best of moves,' Brandon admitted wryly. 'I don't want to fight with you, Ms Lynton.'

Zoe cursed the sudden wetness between her thighs. God, why did he have to be so attractive? And why did her body keep remembering the way he'd touched her, the feel of his skin against hers, when she was trying to keep a clear head? 'I don't want to fight with you, either.'

'So we're agreed on one thing.'

'Yes.'

Their eyes met, and both of them were starkly aware of their surroundings. How Brandon was sitting on the wide double bed, and Zoe was sitting on a chair within arm's reach. All he had to do was reach towards her . . .

Zoe fought for control; she could see by the set of Brandon's jaw that he was having equal difficulty. It would be so easy for them both to give in, for her to stand up and take that one small step to him and for him to meet her halfway, pulling her onto his lap – but it wouldn't solve the real problem. Boudicca.

Brandon pushed a hand through his hair; Zoe realised with shock that he was shaking, and that she desperately wanted to run her own fingers through that beautiful thick mane of hair. 'Ms Lynton – Zoe. Can we be honest with each other?'

She nodded. 'I think so.' Brandon, unlike his business partner, had integrity. She trusted him.

'So far, you've only heard Jack's side of the story: that he thinks there's a Roman grave on our land. Boudicca's grave, to be precise.'

'The geophysics results bear it out.'

'There might be something there,' Brandon admitted, 'but it isn't necessarily Boudicca's grave – and Mark has had a survey done. He says that there's nothing there.'

'And you believe him?'

'He's my business partner. I trust him.'

More fool you, Zoe thought, but said nothing. Antagonising Brandon now wouldn't help matters. 'So what are you trying to tell me?'

'My side of the story. Why I want to build a housing estate. I grew up in Lower Yareham,' Brandon said. 'You're a journalist, and I assume you've already done enough research to know that my parents died in a car crash when I was ten, and my grandfather brought me up on the farm. Like I told you the other day, I went to university, and I was going to be some hotshot in business – but when it came down to it, I couldn't leave my roots. I love this place, Zoe. I love the whole character of this village.'

He was speaking the truth: his body language matched his words, and his eyes were sincere. 'What I hate is the way it's changed over the past ten years. It's become almost a dormitory village. People who work in the city, maybe in London or Colchester or Ipswich, decide that they want to live in the country and commute. Property prices around here are low – so they buy it, and the prices rise quickly.'

Zoe forbore to comment that she was already conversant with the economics of the property market; Brandon must have seen it in his face, because he smiled ruefully. 'Sorry. I'm preaching. Basically, people who grew up here can't afford a house; so they end up going to live on a modern estate – the kind that's virtually a village in itself, the development's so huge. The kind that, once you've bought a house there, you're stuck – because no one wants to buy yours, when they can buy a brand new one just down the block, with special deals of carpets and curtains of their choice and deposits paid. Meanwhile, the houses that their families once lived in are weekend retreats for rich city businessmen or dormitories for a childless couple who work all the hours God sent, and then some – so they don't have time to be involved with Lower Yareham.' He sighed. 'It's taken the life out of the village. I hate to see the village spirit dying – and that's why I want to build this development. Low cost housing for local people; and with decent-sized plots, not a tiny square of land hemmed in on all sides.'

'Right,' Zoe said slowly. So that was why the houses had seemed so widely spaced on the plans – and why they hadn't been executive-sized four- and five-bedroomed detached places.

'I want to keep the village spirit alive, Zoe. And that's far more important than chasing a ghost who doesn't exist.'

Chapter Seven

Zoe looked at him. Brandon was sincere about it – she could see it in his face – but it still didn't add up. Why would a reptile like Mark Burroughs, a man who was phoney and glib even down to his compliments, be involved in a scheme like that? Mark wasn't the altruistic type. He was a money-maker. So somewhere, someone wasn't being completely honest.

'I don't believe you,' she said softly.

Brandon's eyes widened. 'Zoe, I'm telling you the truth. I'll bring you my prospectus in the morning, if you like – you can see for yourself. The prices are low, but the condition is that anyone who buys a house must have lived in the area for at least five years, and can't sell it again for at least two years. That stops people just making a fast buck and turning the place into just another dormitory estate.' He raked a hand through his hair, narrowing his eyes. 'What do I have to do to convince you? I know you've done the geophysics and it's shown something on the land, but it's not Boudicca's grave. You're chasing a dream, Zoe, something that doesn't exist. Mark's already had the site surveyed by archaeologists. He knew how Gramps felt about that site, and there's too much money invested in that land to take stupid risks.'

That was more like it; but Zoe still couldn't believe it. 'In that case,' she said quietly, 'you won't mind if my friends do a small excavation before any work starts on the site.'

'You're wasting your time – and your money,' he warned her.

'I don't think so.'

'Zoe Lynton, you are the most pig-headed, stubborn—'

He cut off sharply and stood up.

Zoe, too, stood up. She knew that she was probably making a huge mistake, but she placed her hand on his arm.

86

'Brandon. I understand how you feel.'

'Do you? I wonder, do you? Living in your – wherever it is in London, with your bright lights surrounding you and your parties and your friends. You have no idea what it's like to live in a village, with real community spirit – and watch all that die, watch people become strangers and suspicion move in. When I grew up, people didn't even lock their doors; nowadays, the pensioners daren't even leave their weekly paper money on the doorstep, because it'll be stolen.' He glared at her, daring her to tell him that he sounded like an old man whining for the past.

'I grew up in the outskirts of Bristol, so I've always lived in a city,' Zoe admitted, 'but that doesn't mean I can't appreciate how you feel.' In more than one sense; the pads of her fingers tingled just at the contact of his shirt. She could feel the warmth of his skin through it and it made her want to touch him skin to skin. 'I can understand why you want this development.'

'So why are you doing your damnedest to obstruct it?'

'Because I think that there's something more important on that site. Isn't there another field you could use instead?'

He glared at her. 'Don't you think I've already explored all the options? That's the best site for the development, Zoe.'

'In whose view? Yours, or your business partner's?' Her mouth twisted. 'And thanks for telling him I was an easy lay.'

His eyes widened. 'I did nothing of the kind.'

'So he usually tries to charm the knickers off any female in the vicinity?'

Brandon's lips twitched. 'Yes. He said you walked out on him.'

So they had discussed her. In just how much depth? she wondered. She dropped her hand. 'I don't know why I'm bothering. I'd like you to leave, please. I don't think we have anything else to say to each other.'

'You're probably right.'

They stared at each other for a long moment; he moved slightly, and Zoe thought that he was about to kiss her. It was written all over his face: that he remembered what had happened between them in the churchyard, and he was aware of just how near her bed was. How easy it would be to break the deadlock between them, by switching off their minds and letting their bodies do the talking for them . . .

And he knew that she felt the same way.

But it wouldn't change anything. They'd still be on opposing sides of the development afterwards. 'Just go, please,' she repeated softly.

He left without another word, closing the door behind him; Zoe sank into her chair and closed her eyes. God, why did it all have to be so complicated? Why couldn't Brandon see what a reptile Mark Burroughs was? And why were they mixed up together in the first place? She couldn't imagine a more unlikely combination. Did Mark have something on Brandon? It was the only thing she could think of – the only reason why Brandon would choose him as a business partner. Coercion of some kind. Maybe it was something to do with the farm, and Brandon was protecting his grandfather from some bad news – perhaps bad investments that would affect the farm if development didn't bail them out.

She was saved further thought by another rap on her door. 'Yes?'

'Miss Lynton?'

Apart from the fact that she'd established first-name terms with Betty and Sam early on, she didn't recognise the obviously female voice. 'Yes?'

'May I come in?'

'Who is it?'

'Helena Burroughs.'

Zoe thought swiftly. Helena Burroughs – Mark's daughter. A spoilt bitch, according to Sam, used to getting anything she wanted. Why would she want to talk to Zoe? Unless Mark had decided to mobilise the troops, see if feminist solidarity would work where he had failed. Zoe was aware that he thought her a hard feminist bitch. His mind worked in stereotypes; no doubt he thought her on a crusade of women against the world, and believed that Helena would be better able to persuade her to drop her opposition to the development.

He couldn't be more wrong.

'Come in,' she called.

The door opened to reveal a small, curvaceous woman

with pale blue eyes and a mass of curly blonde hair. The pocket Venus type: and even if Zoe hadn't already worked out who Helena was, she would have known within seconds. Her bone structure was finer than her father's, but she had exactly the same smile, confident and slightly predatory.

'I hope you don't mind me coming to see you,' Helena said, closing the door behind her.

Zoe was immediately on her guard. Those humble and almost apologetic words didn't match her reputation, her tone – or the look in her eyes. 'Not at all,' she said. 'What can I do for you?'

'I know you're probably tired of talking about it, but it's the development.'

She looked at Zoe through lowered lashes, and Zoe had to bite back a laugh. If she didn't know better, she'd say that Helena was trying exactly the same tactics as her father – seduction as an aid to getting her own way.

'Oh, that.' Zoe kept her tone light. 'Would you like to sit down?'

'Thank you.' Helena was wearing tight jeans that emphasised her curves, the soft swell of her hips and the tininess of her waist. She crossed the room, weaving her hips sinuously. Then she sat down on the bed, crossed her legs, and leant forward, resting her elbow on her knee and her chin on her hand. She looked up at Zoe, her huge eyes fringed with long mascaraed lashes, and pouted slightly.

Again, Zoe resisted the urge to grin. Helena was treating her as though she were a man, to be conquered by her coquettish smile. Well, she could remove that smile quickly enough. 'I met your father earlier today.'

'Did you?'

The look of surprise on Helena's face was genuine. Maybe Mark hadn't sent her, after all, Zoe thought. 'Didn't he tell you?'

'No – er – I haven't seen him today, to be honest. Daddy's so busy, you know. He works so hard.'

Leaving poor little you all on your poor little own. How my heart bleeds, Zoe thought. 'Indeed,' she said wryly. 'So what can I do for you?'

'It's about the development. I know you're against it – Brandon told me.'

Brandon. Aha. Now we're getting somewhere, Zoe thought, remembering what else Sam had said. That Helena wanted Brandon, and had her eye on the profits from the development. Except the profits wouldn't be quite as big as she was expecting; and Zoe also had the feeling that Helena Burroughs wasn't really Brandon's type. She couldn't see him with the fluffy bunny-wunny type; he'd prefer someone straight-talking.

She caught the direction of her thoughts and corrected herself. She and Brandon worked purely on a physical sense, and lust wasn't enough. Besides, what had happened between them was a one-off. He was in the opposing camp, which made him off limits – from now until forever. 'You know Brandon well, then?'

'You could say that.' Helena simpered slightly. 'We have . . . an understanding.'

'I see.'

'We know how each other's mind works. Almost to the point of being able to read it,' Helena confided. She licked her lower lip. 'We have . . . similar tastes.'

She inched forward slightly, sitting up straight and placing her hand on Zoe's knee. 'You're a woman of the world. You understand these things,' she said. 'Brandon likes to play games. So do I.'

Zoe's eyes widened. The woman really was making a play for her. And if she was telling the truth and she and Brandon really did have something going, did she know about what Brandon had done with Zoe in the churchyard? Had Brandon been there with her full blessing – and had he gone back to her to tell her every intimate detail? And had she been there when Brandon had called to arrange this evening's visit? Had she expected Brandon to make love with Zoe – and now intended to continue where he left off? Had she been expecting him to be there still, so that they could share Zoe's bed?

'Zoe – may I call you that?' Helena purred. 'I do so like to make new friends. I think that you and I could be . . . very good friends. Very good indeed.'

Zoe managed to bite back the retort that if Helena was anything like her father, she doubted that very much indeed. Instead, she said, 'Oh?'

'You have such nice hands.' Helena took her hand, stroking it. 'Such soft skin. So nice to touch.' She squeezed gently. 'Zoe.' Slowly, she brought Zoe's hand up to her lips. 'That's Greek for "life", did you know?' She answered her own question. 'Of course you do. You're a journalist, and you're bright. I've always liked bright women.' In a studied move, she began to suck Zoe's fingertips, holding her gaze.

Zoe was fascinated and appalled at the same time. Her sexual tastes didn't extend to making love with other women, but she could see what Sam meant about the men in the village wanting to get into Helena's knickers. Apart from the fact that Helena was a consummate actress and could probably switch between vamp and vulnerable at will, she knew all the right moves. Eye contact, touch, suggestion ... Everything to make her victim a willing one. Except Zoe.

She pulled her hand away. 'I'm very flattered, Helena, but I'm afraid I'm not what you think.'

'Not bright?'

'I'm strictly heterosexual,' Zoe said quietly.

'How disappointing.' Helena switched to little girl lost mode. 'And I was so hoping that we could be ...' She sighed deeply. 'Friends.'

That was the last thing on both their minds, Zoe knew. 'I'm sorry to disappoint you, Miss Burroughs. Now, what was it you wanted to tell me about the development?'

'That you're making a mistake in opposing it. There's a lot of money at stake – and God knows, the people round here could do with the jobs. There isn't a lot of employment, out in the sticks.'

'Obviously you care a great deal about the village.'

Zoe's irony was lost on Helena. 'Yes. That development has to be built.'

Zoe couldn't be bothered to argue with her. 'Maybe.'

Helena's lips thinned. 'Miss Lynton, you're wasting your time round here. That development's going ahead, whether you like it or not.'

Zoe could suddenly see why Sam had described her as a spoilt little Daddy's girl. All Helena needed was a lisp, lots of curls done up in bows, a frilly dress which showed even frillier knickers, and a stamping foot. Zoe had difficulty in hiding her smile. 'I see.'

'And, just for the record, there's no point in hanging around after Brandon, either. He's spoken for.'

If Helena had her way. Again. Sam's words flickered through Zoe's retentive memory. Miss Helena Burroughs would love to be Mrs Helena Mitchell – but Zoe had the feeling that it would be in dream only. Her brief time with Brandon had convinced her that he wouldn't be interested in the likes of Helena, even if she was his business partner's daughter and it would be very convenient for them to be together. All that nonsense about Helena and Brandon having shared tastes had been precisely that – nonsense. Helena might have kissed him, but Zoe would have bet large sums of money that he'd refused to take their relationship further. 'I see,' she said neutrally.

'He's going to marry me. We haven't announced it officially yet, of course, but everything's planned.'

Again, in Helena's dreams, Zoe thought. 'I hope you'll both be very happy.'

'So you'll stay away from him, won't you?'

Zoe shrugged. 'Bad-tempered country boys aren't to my taste, Miss Burroughs. You don't need to warn me off him. I'm more than happy to leave him to you.'

Helena's eyes narrowed. 'I beg your pardon?'

'I prefer sophistication. Though perhaps you could tell your father that I mean more than skin-deep sophistication. I prefer men who do at least know what they're talking about.'

Helena's nostrils flared. 'What are you talking about?'

'Next time you see your father, tell him to find himself a book on art history. Preferably one specialising in Victorian art – and to look up *Beata Beatrix*. Then *Proserpine* – he might learn something.'

'I don't have to listen to this.'

'No. But do pass on my message.' Zoe gave her a mocking smile. 'He'll understand perfectly. Goodbye, Miss Burroughs. I imagine you can see yourself out.'

'Oh!' Helena was obviously just seconds away from stamping her foot; she contented herself with stomping out of the room and slamming the door very hard behind her.

Zoe grinned to herself and picked up her mobile phone, calling Steve at the office. Again, the answerphone clicked in; she waited until after the long tone, then spoke. 'Marwick, if you're call-screening, pick up the phone.' She waited for a moment. 'Looks like you're not there. Ignore this message; I'll try you at home.'

She cut the connection and dialled Steve's flat. It rang six times, seven; then the receiver was snatched up. 'Hello?'

'Steve. It's Zoe.'

'Hello, sweetheart. How's it going?'

'Curiouser and curiouser,' she said with a grin. 'We got a good piece in the local paper. Did you see my fax?'

'Yup. Nice one. Any developments?'

'I've been warned off by both partners in the development – and the daughter.'

'Daughter?'

'Mm. Mark Burroughs took me out to lunch. I think he was expecting me to drop my knickers for him, then drop the opposition.'

'And did you?'

'No, to both.' She chuckled. 'He compared me to a Rossetti painting.'

'Shall I compare thee to a big-mouthed maid? No, thou art more lovely, more like a hamster.'

She burst out laughing. 'Thanks a lot!'

'Only teasing, sweetheart. Oh dear. Pretentious, *moi*, was he?'

'And a half. He decided that I was the culture-vulture type, so he played me *The Four Seasons* in the car – on CD – and then hammed it up in the restaurant. He talked about taking me to Paris or Rome.'

'He'd have done better offering you Florence or Seville,' Steve said drily. 'Or Venice, letting you wander to your heart's content round the old churches. So what happened?'

'He claims that he's already done a survey, and it showed nothing there. He reckons that the geophys results are a false lead – you know, like metal detectors and ring-pulls.'

Steve chuckled. 'I bet that went down well with you. Do you believe him?'

'I'm not sure. Brandon – Jack's grandson – believes that the survey's been done. But Mark Burroughs . . . I don't trust him, Steve. There's something about him that sets my teeth on edge. He's not sincere. He's obviously shown Brandon something to convince him; but I reckon he's not telling the truth about the results.'

'So it's full steam ahead.' Steve paused. 'You said both of them warned you off.'

'Yes. First of all, Mark – over an expensive lunch.' She chuckled. 'I think he was expecting payment in kind.'

'Were you tempted?'

'He's my type, physically,' Zoe admitted. 'But no. He doesn't have the same effect on me that certain scruffy journos do.'

Steve laughed. 'Flattery won't get you off the hook.'

'No, then. I wasn't tempted. I don't like fakes.'

'So he dropped you back at The Feathers in a temper, did he?'

'No. I walked out of the restaurant and found my own way home.'

'Second warning?'

'This evening. Brandon. He told me his reasons for building the development in the first place – it's all to do with keeping the village spirit alive.'

'As if.'

'I believe him,' Zoe said quietly. 'He might be on the other side, but he's got integrity, Steve.'

'And he's also your type.'

'Actually, he's dark-haired, well-built and doesn't wear glasses.'

'Zoe, your voice gives you away. You find him attractive, don't you?'

'That's beside the point.'

There wasn't a hint of jealousy in Steve's voice. 'Admit it.'

She sighed. 'All right. He's attractive. But he's off limits.' She wasn't ready to admit that she'd already done something about her attraction to Brandon.

'And the third warning – the daughter?'

'Mark's daughter. Apparently, she's a spoilt Daddy's girl, used to getting what she wants.'

'Oh dear. She's just met the brick wall called Zoe Lynton.'

'Yup.'

'So what was her argument?'

'She said it would provide jobs for the village, would you believe? Though I think the only reason she'd want builders around is so she could have a bit of rough,' Zoe said.

'Sounds like she rattled your cage.'

'How do you mean?'

Steve coughed. 'You're not usually bitchy about people.'

'Bitchy? Steve, she's one of these women who switch from vamp to vulnerable and back again – whatever it takes to get her own way.' Zoe snorted. 'She didn't just want to talk about the development. She warned me off Brandon, too.'

'Oh dearie, dearie me. How to thrust you into the guy's arms, in one easy move.'

'Not quite.' Zoe's voice was distinctly frosty. 'And she made a pass at me.'

Steve hooted. 'I wish I could have seen that! Tell me.'

'If you think I'm fuelling your sordid little fantasies—'

'Oh, there's nothing sordid about my fantasies, where you're concerned. Though I admit, you'd have to be with a blonde or a red-head, to contrast with your hair.'

'Helena's blonde and fluffy-wuffy. Even if I were tempted by the idea of another woman – which I'm not, Steve, it leaves me indifferent, so the lady doesn't protest too much – it certainly wouldn't be her.'

'You'd rather have the butch dominant type?'

Zoe sighed. 'No. I don't understand why men get so worked up about the idea of two women together, I really don't.'

'It's all that lovely soft warm female flesh, those curves – just waiting for you to join them,' Steve told her.

'A threesome, eh?' A sudden vision flashed into Zoe's mind: herself, Steve and Brandon. She shivered.

'Caught you there, Zoe-kins,' Steve said softly. 'You like that idea, don't you? Except it'd be two men and you, in your fantasy.'

'How come we always end up talking sex, when I intend to call you about work?'

'Because we can't help ourselves,' Steve said matter-of-factly. 'We share the same interests. Archaeology and sex. I'm half tempted to run a couple of articles about that – and I know just the person to write them.'

'And no doubt you'll help with the research,' Zoe teased.

'Indeedy. But that doesn't let you off the hook. What did Helena do to you?'

'Sat on my bed, pouted at me, gave me a come-hither smile – then took my hand and told me how soft my hands were. Then she kissed the tips of my fingers, sucking them. Routine stuff, really.'

'But a very nice thought.' Steve paused. 'I would have liked to see her take it further. See you respond to her.'

Zoe moved over to her bed, settling herself against the pillows and closing her eyes. 'Okay. Talk away.'

'Sure about this? I mean, you said it doesn't do anything for you.'

'It doesn't – but it obviously works for you. And I always enjoy having this kind of phone-call with you, knowing exactly what you're doing as you're talking to me; I can picture it, and *that* turns me on.'

She could almost see his smile. 'That's good.'

'Tell me, then. What do you see?'

'You, on a bed, in a white room. Bare polished floorboards, white walls, white muslin curtains at the window. At night: the room's lit by a dozen white candles. Vanilla-scented candles. And there's just you on the bed, lying naked on starched white sheets, just a couple of tones away from the alabaster of your skin. The bed-frame's wrought iron, and your wrists and ankles are tied to it by black silk scarves. You're blindfolded, too, with a black silk scarf. And you're lying there, just waiting.

'You don't know how long you've been there: there's no way of knowing the time. Your body's tingling with anticipation, and adrenalin's flowing through your fingertips. You're excited and scared at the same time. Your nipples are hard; the areolae have puckered and darkened to a rosy pink. You'd like to touch yourself, but you can't. It's frustrating and even more arousing.

'Your sex feels warm and puffy. To anyone who's watching you, it's obvious that you're aroused. Your legs are parted to reveal everything: the soft pink coral of your sex, the way it shades into vermilion in the centre, the hard little bud of your clitoris. All glistening with arousal, a pearly gold sheen on top, like the finest gossamer gold leaf. You look beautiful, desirable. Anyone who saw you like that would want to possess you, man or woman. They'd want to crawl between your thighs, touch you and taste you and drink in the musky aroma of your sex.

'Then, finally, you hear something. Music. You don't recognise the voice, but it's a pure, soaring tenor. He's singing an aria, an obscure Bizet serenade, from *La Jolie Fille de Perth*, melancholy and sweet – the kind of music that makes your stomach melt, it's so gorgeous. Haunting. You can also hear footsteps on the floorboards: very light, very soft. You have no idea who it is, because he – or is it she? – says nothing.

'You feel the mattress give slightly; and then, at long last, you feel a hand drifting along your abdomen. Just the fingertips: smooth, cool, such a light touch. That's when you know that it's a woman. You've never been attracted to other women – but you're so aroused, you can't help responding. Because the man who tied you up left you aroused: he talked to you before he left, painting a word-picture that had you wet within seconds, wet and wanting. He even touched you, licking your nipples and teasing your clitoris with his tongue, inserting a lazy finger into your quim, until you started to writhe and beg him to take it further. Then he stopped and left you, saying that good things happen to those who wait. And you've waited, Zoe. You've waited for so long.

'Now, you're on fire. You don't care who's touching you, as long as whoever it is doesn't tease you.' Steve's words grew husky, and Zoe smiled to herself. This was turning him on in a big way. His jeans would be down by his ankles, now, and he was stroking the long rigid shaft of his cock as he talked to her. She could tell every stroke by the timbre of his voice.

'What's she like?' Zoe asked softly.

'Beautiful. A blonde version of you. Her hair's exactly the same style as yours, but it's like spun gold. Natural, too: there are red and silver tones in it, caught by the candle-light. Her skin's like yours, pale and creamy – and delicate enough to flush like yours does, when she's aroused. Her body's the same as yours, too: lush and wanton. It's every man's dream, watching her sit on the bed next to you and stroke your skin.

'She wants you. Her lower lip's already full and red, and her nipples are hard: though she's actually wearing something. A black lacy teddy that reveals more than it hides: the curve of her breasts, the valley between them, the hardness of her nipples and the deep rosy colour. The contrast between the lace and her skin and yours is startling. Poetic, almost.'

He paused; Zoe knew that he'd just employed a delaying tactic, pressing hard just below his frenum to stop himself coming. 'She continues stroking you, in silence; because you're blindfolded, you have to concentrate on your other senses. And it's so good: that beautiful music, that voluptuous scent, the whisper of her skin against yours. It breaks down your last inhibitions, and you tilt your pelvis upwards, inviting her.

'She knows what you want, and smiles. She lays her cheek against your stomach; you can feel her hair, so soft and silky, drifting over your skin, and you're shocked at how aroused it makes you feel; your sex heats even more. You want to feel that silky softness against your thighs; you can't help a moan of pleasure, and you ask her to touch you. She doesn't speak: she simply shifts between your thighs, kneeling there, and dips her head so that the ends of her hair brush against your nipples.

'It drives you crazy; you writhe within your bonds and she laughs, pleased with the effect. She does it again and again, teasing you and inciting you; you plead with her, beg her to use her mouth on your breasts. And then she does; she places her hands either side of your body, and lowers hers to yours. You can feel the lace teddy skimming your body, and the friction excites you even more. And then, at last, her mouth closes round one nipple.

'You almost come at that moment; somehow, you hold back, and she begins to work on you. She sucks your nipple, drawing fiercely on it, then making her tongue flat and swirling across it. She pulls back, letting your skin chill slightly, and blows on you. It excites you even more: it's sensory overload. You want more, more. She does the same to the other breast, and you're tugging against your bonds, wanting to touch her, wanting to push a hand between your legs and rub yourself like a Maenad.

'She moves up to kiss you, and you open your mouth under hers, letting her kiss you properly; your tongue-tip duels with hers, and your pelvis tilts again. Your sex is so hot, so wet; you're almost coming from the thought of what she's going to do next. She breaks the kiss, and moves back down your body, kissing and licking and nipping. She caresses the soft undersides of your breasts, squeezing your nipples hard at the same time; the mixture of light and hard caresses excites you even further.

'And then, finally, you feel her hair brushing your lower abdomen, your thighs. You know that she's going to touch you, taste you. The moment that she places the flat of her palms against your inner thighs and widens your stance, you come; she watches you, the way your sex contracts so sharply, oozing soft silky nectar, then smiles and dips her head. She laps at you, drinking your wine, and pushes her tongue deep into you; you're already so keyed up that you come again, your internal muscles spasming against her mouth.

'She shifts up to kiss you, so you can taste yourself on her mouth; and she rubs her breasts against yours, the lace creating a beautiful friction against your nipples and hers. She asks if you want her; you nod. She tells you that you have to say it, tell her what you want. Then you tell her. You say that you want her to touch you, to taste you, to fill you.

'So she does. She crawls back between your legs; you feel her insert one finger, then another. The walls of your quim are soft and wet and velvety; you flex your internal muscles, teasing her back, and she grins. She withdraws her hand: you frown as you feel her climb off the bed. Surely she isn't going to leave you like this, half-satisfied, your sex drenched and desperate?

'Of course not. She's merely gone to snuff one of the candles and take it from its holder. A big, fat, warm wax candle – though you don't know that. She returns to her place between your thighs, and dips her head again; she plays with your clitoris, flicking her tongue against the hard peak again and again and again, until you're shuddering and trembling and begging her to do it harder, harder.

'Then you feel something pushing against your entrance. Something warm, but thicker than a finger or thumb. That's when you realise why she climbed off the bed; you can picture what she's doing to you. It's lewd and wanton, and it excites you even more, to think of yourself tied starfish-style to the bed, a candle protruding from your quim.

'She works you with it as though it were a cock, pushing it in so very slowly; you arch your back, and she changes rhythm, pumping it into you, back and forth, with short sharp thrusts. Then slow again, slow and deep; fast and short, almost out of you then pushing back in, driving you to a higher and higher pitch.

'When you come, you're almost screaming, it's so good; your sex clamps round the candle, the intensity of your climax making the wax cylinder shake. And then, finally, when the after-shocks die away, she removes the candle and brings it up to your mouth, making you lick it clean.'

Zoe was surprised to find just how aroused Steve's fantasy had made her; she realised that she'd unzipped her own jeans and her hand was working busily between her thighs. 'Wow,' she said.

'I haven't finished yet,' Steve said quietly. 'Because then, she unties the blindfold, so you can see her. She kisses you; and then she turns round on the bed, kneeling by your shoulders, and lowers her sex to your mouth. She's excited by what she's done to you, and you can smell the sweet musky tang of her arousal. As she lowers her face to your sex again, you stretch out your tongue and start to lick her – your first taste of another woman. You feel a little shy, a little insecure, worried that you're not doing it right, until you hear her whisper softly that you should just do what you like being done to you. A little hesitantly, you tongue her clitoris, and you're rewarded by a groan of pleasure. It gives you confidence, and you do it again and again; and then you work her properly, exploring the furls and hollows of her sex with your tongue, bringing her to a peak at the same time as she does the same to you . . .' He paused and gasped; Zoe realised that he'd come. 'And that's it,' he said softly. 'My ideal fantasy. Two beautiful women together, all softness and curves, their bodies moving sinuously as they bring each other the ultimate pleasure.'

'Hm,' Zoe said.

'It turned you on, too, didn't it?'

She coughed. 'Um – no comment.'

He chuckled softly. 'Next time I see you, I'm going to make you admit it.'

'Promises, promises.'

'I always keep my promises, Zoe. I'm a man of my word.'

'I know.'

'I'll talk to you tomorrow, sweetheart,' he said. 'Take care.'

'You, too.'

She cut the connection thoughtfully. Steve's fantasy had affected her more than she'd expected. So had she told Helena the truth – that she was a hundred per cent heterosexual? She smiled wryly. Maybe. Maybe not. Either way, Helena wasn't her type. All she'd done was convince Zoe that there was something more to the development than met the eye – and Zoe was going to get to the bottom of it.

Chapter Eight

'Tesserae.' Ed, the head of the dig, climbed out of the exploration trench, brushing the dirt off the tiny squares of pottery and handing them to Jack. 'It's a good start.'

Jack beamed. 'I knew there was something there. It's not just an old man's fantasy, you know.'

'I know,' Zoe said as he handed her the tesserae. 'I love this blue. It's such a gorgeous colour.' A deep, rich blue; she handled the squares lovingly, before reluctantly returning them to one of Ed's team. 'Is this the rough area where you found the coins, Jack?'

He nodded. 'Have any more been found?'

'Not yet.' Ed grinned at him. 'But you'll be the first to know when we hit treasure trove.'

'I'm not bothered about the financial side of it,' Jack said. 'I just want to find that grave.'

Ed nodded, brushing a muddy hand across his forehead; his grey eyes glittered. 'So do we. I haven't slept since Steve rang me and said we had the best lead ever on Boudicca.' He nodded at Zoe. 'I should have known that Zoe would be involved somewhere.'

'You two know each other, then?'

'Through *Archetypes*, yes,' Zoe told him. 'I know most of the leading archaeologists.'

'And Zoe's the only journo most of us will talk to. Apart from Steve, of course. She talks our language,' Ed said simply. 'Anyway – I'd better crack on.'

'And we'd better stop interrupting you,' Jack said wryly. 'Sorry.'

'No problem.' Ed gave him another cheery grin, and climbed back into the trench.

'Do you want to stay a bit longer?' Zoe asked.

Jack nodded. 'If you don't mind. It's fascinating, just

watching them. If I were younger . . .'

'You'd be in there with them, I know,' Zoe said, squeezing his hand. 'But you're the one who started this off. Without you, they wouldn't even be there. Remember that. You're as much a part of the dig as they are.'

Jack's blue eyes twinkled. 'Flattery, my dear, will get you anywhere.'

'Except with your grandson, hm?' Brandon had flatly refused to have anything to do with the dig – or to join them all for a meal in The Feathers, that evening. The exploratory dig was taking place over a weekend, and the team was staying at The Feathers; Betty had reserved a large table for them that evening, and Zoe had asked Jack to join them. On impulse, she'd asked Brandon if he'd like to eat with them, but he'd informed her coldly that he had a prior engagement. The male equivalent of washing his hair, she'd presumed.

'Don't worry about him. He'll finish sulking, one of these days.'

Zoe persuaded Jack to sit down on one of the collapsible chairs the team had brought with them; as the dig progressed, Jack asked her dozens of questions, and she answered them as best as she could.

More tesserae were found, and shards of cooking pots and oil lamps; what might have been the handle of a silver mirror was also logged. They hadn't found what they were really looking for, though: the burial place.

'It might not necessarily be a mound,' Zoe said. 'All we can go on is the geophys results – and they're not a hundred per cent definite. It might be just a settlement, without the burial chambers.' She paused. 'Jack . . . I hate to raise this, but have you considered that Brandon might be right?'

'He isn't,' Jack said, his jaw setting.

Zoe could see where Brandon had inherited his stubborn nature; she decided to let things be, and continued talking to Jack about the dig.

The evening at The Feathers was a lively affair, with the small team of archaeologists laughing and joking and swapping outrageous stories of digs they'd been on in the past. Jack enjoyed himself hugely; the only thing missing, for Zoe, was Brandon. She forced the thoughts out of her head. Yes, what their bodies had shared had been good. More than good. But it wasn't enough. And if he was too sulky to forget his differences and join them, that was his problem.

It was only later that evening, when she was alone in bed, that thoughts of him returned to haunt her. Why did he have to be so bloody difficult? Why couldn't he just swallow his pride and at least be there for his grandfather? Ed was staying overnight in a tent by the dig, to protect it from scavengers and bounty hunters – during the evening, the team had taken it in turns to do a shift on protection duty – and had taken Jack home on his way. If only Brandon could have unbent a little, and escorted his grandfather himself . . .

She sighed, shifting again in bed. Maybe if Steve had managed to get away for the weekend, he could have taken her mind off things: but he'd already been booked on a conference, and he couldn't get out of it. She couldn't even ring him like she had the other night, to fantasise down the phone to him.

She half-wished that she'd asked Dale to join them: but then again, he would have had to refuse, on the grounds of staying neutral where village politics were concerned. Restlessly, Zoe turned over, cupping her breasts and squeezing her nipples. There was only one way she was going to get to sleep, that night, she knew. She closed her eyes, pushing her head back against the pillows; it was only one step to think herself back in the churchyard, with the sky above her and Brandon kneeling between her thighs. To feel his breath warm against her thighs, the soft and insistent pressure of his hands as he widened her stance and lowered his mouth to her sex.

Zoe's hand slid down over her abdomen; she cupped her mons veneris, then slowly let one finger part her labia, smoothing a familiar path along her intimate flesh. She pushed her middle finger against her sex, scooping the honeyed moisture from her quim, then slicked her finger back over her clitoris. The hard bud of flesh pulsed under her touch as she began to rub softly, slowly, taking her time and teasing herself. As her clitoris grew harder, peeping out from its cowl, she rubbed harder, faster, jerking her hips to increase the friction.

She pushed her other hand between her thighs, inserting one finger into her sex and then adding a second and third; she set up a fast rhythm, bucking her hips as she pushed her fingers as deeply as she could into her sex, then rubbing her clitoris as her fingers withdrew again.

'Oh, yes. Yes,' she hissed softly as she felt her orgasm build, that sweet pressure in her lower abdomen that quickly became too much to bear and flooded through her, making her skin tingle and her nipples throb in time with her sex. 'Yes.'

She didn't bother showering; sticky and sated and languid, she curled up, breathing in the scent of her arousal and finally drifting off to sleep.

The next morning, she breakfasted with the team, then headed out to the dig with them. Jack was already there, sitting on the edge of the trench and talking to Ed; he smiled up at Zoe as she approached. 'Good morning.'

'Good morning.' She looked at him. 'Should you be sitting there?'

'You sound like Eileen. Don't nag,' he admonished her, lifting the edge of the material he was sitting on. 'There are such things as tarpaulins, you know. I'm not getting damp in my bones.'

Zoe grinned. 'Sorry.'

'That's all right.' He patted the tarpaulin next to him. 'Come and sit with me. There's a good view, from here.'

Zoe joined him; they spent the morning chatting idly, occasionally stopping to pass something from Ed to Jake, who was logging in all the finds. Ella, the only woman on the team, was in charge of the computer, and she showed Jack what they were plotting and how their finds compared with other burial sites.

'At the moment, it's too early to say, but I'd hazard a rough guess that there's some kind of settlement here. It might not be the burial area – but tesserae usually mean that there was some kind of flooring in the area, and the shards we've found definitely belong to a kitchen area. Samian redware – common enough stuff in these parts, I

105

know, but it's always good to see it. It means we're on the right track.'

After lunch – which Eileen brought out to them in a large wicker hamper – Jack and Zoe were peering over the computer with Ella again, when there was a whoop from the trench. 'That's it! We've got a wall!'

'A wall?' Ella saved the file and switched off her computer, jumping down into the trench. 'Show me.'

'Here.' Ed brushed aside some earth, revealing a flat upright stone. 'This is just the start. It's where the geophys said there would be a wall, too – I know I'm an old cynic, but half the time, geophys shows a wall and it turns out to be a water main.'

'You're an air-rec man, I know,' Ella teased, 'but technology does it better, sweetheart. And a lot quicker.'

'We'll agree to differ on that.' Ed cupped her face and kissed her lightly. 'This is great Jack, even if this isn't Boudicca's grave, there's a chance it's a villa.'

'Like the one they found in Holt?' Jake asked.

'Could be. It might just be a rich farmer, showing off; or it might be something more. It might be Prasutagus' palace. Or even something Suetonius decided to build, in memory of Boudicca. He respected her, even though they were on opposite sides,' Ed said.

A shiver ran down Zoe's spine. That could be said of another man and a woman, over a millennium later. On opposite sides, but still respecting each other. She respected Brandon's integrity, even though his stubbornness annoyed her; and he respected that she was a professional in her job, not a scandal-mongering hack.

She shook herself. That was the last thing she should be thinking about. 'Ed, if the rest of your exploratory dig reveals more evidence, can we have the field protected by English Heritage?'

'We certainly can,' Ed said. 'We've already lost God only knows how many sites, in the past, when farmers just ploughed them up without realising. No offence meant, of course,' he added hastily to Jack.

'None taken. I agree with you.' He beamed. 'But I'd like to be the one to give the news to my grandson.' He looked at Zoe. 'And I think you ought to be there too.'

106

'We don't have anything definite,' Ed warned. 'It still might be a dead-end.'

'But your gut feeling's the same as mine, isn't it?' Jack asked.

Ed nodded. 'I'd stick my neck out and say we have a settlement, here. Something worth excavating. We might be able to get a Lottery grant to fund more exploration – though they usually insist on publicity, and we need to keep this fairly quiet, to keep looters away.' He sighed. 'It's a sad fact that a lot of people dream about finding buried treasure, and they don't realise just how much they destroy in the search.'

'That's why I didn't go any further, when I found the coins,' Jack said, 'and the site's on private land. I've deliberately been vague about it to the press – except to Zoe and Steve, of course, and one or two people in the village. They won't say anything.' He shrugged. 'Norfolk people can be very reticent, if they don't like the person asking questions. And as people from London usually assume Norfolk born and Norfolk bred is thick in arm and thick in head . . . Well.'

Ed grinned. 'Go on. Sock it to him.'

Jack motioned for Zoe to take his arm; she walked back to the farm with him. To her surprise, Jack didn't head for the farmhouse, but for a low building on the other side of the yard. The farm office.

'Brandon's working? On a Saturday afternoon?'

Jack nodded. 'He loves this place. That's why he puts all the hours God sends into it.' He sighed. 'I just wish he wasn't mixed up with Mark Burroughs. I've never liked the man. He might be among the best when it comes to investment, but there's something about him that makes me . . .' He grimaced.

'I know what you mean. He's slimy,' Zoe said. 'I didn't like him when I met him, either.'

'You met him?' Jack was surprised.

'He tried to talk me out of interfering with his precious development. Needless to say, he didn't get very far.'

'Well.' Jack opened the office door and ushered her inside.

The room was nothing like Zoe had been expecting. It was a large open-plan space, with two desks and three four-drawer filing cabinets. On top of the cabinets were neat magazine boxes which held back copies of farming journals; there was a large pinboard on one wall, a whiteboard next to it, and a large map with various markings in different-coloured highlighter pens, which Zoe guessed to be a map of the farm and its crops.

Brandon was sitting at one of the desks, tapping into a computer; he looked up as Jack closed the door behind him.

'What are you doing here?' he asked Zoe.

'She's with me,' Jack answered.

Brandon saved his file and closed it. 'Gramps, I'm busy. On budgets – that's why I'm working this afternoon, to have some peace and quiet, away from the phones.' He looked pointedly at Zoe. 'I'm not in the mood to give quotes to the tabloids.'

'I'm not after any quotes,' Zoe said quietly, 'and I don't work for the tabloids.'

'What is it, then?'

'Just this.' Jack walked over to Brandon's desk and dropped a couple of tesserae on his desk. 'You know what these are?'

'I'm sure you're going to tell me, anyway.'

'Tesserae. Bits of mosaic flooring.' Jack beamed. 'Exactly where I said they'd be.'

'I'll bet.'

'I beg your pardon?' Zoe leapt immediately to Jack's defence.

'Finds like this, Ms Lynton, are ten a penny,' Brandon drawled. 'And I'm sure it's quite worthwhile for you to find them.'

'Meaning?'

'Meaning how easy it is to slip these into a pocket, then "find" them in a trench.'

'Are you saying I've planted the evidence?' Zoe demanded, outraged.

'I wouldn't put it past you. Journalists aren't exactly known for being scrupulous, are they?'

'She didn't find them. Ed did,' Jack said. 'And I was there to watch them being uncovered.'

'And who says they couldn't have been put there before you arrived?' Brandon asked.

'They've found other things,' Jack said. 'And a wall. You can't say that *that* was planted.'

'No, but it's not necessarily Roman, let alone Boudicca's gravesite. Gramps, we've been through all this. Mark did a survey. There's nothing there – and the development's still going ahead.'

Jack turned on his heel and walked out, slamming the office door behind him; Zoe caught a glimpse of his face before he left, and the moisture in his eyes. She snapped.

'You bastard! You patronising, chauvinist bastard!' She covered the remaining steps between her and Brandon, and raised her hand to slap his face. 'None of that was planted, least of all a wall. You just can't bear to be wrong, can you? Mr Brandon Perfect Mitchell, with your noble aims of patronising a village – you'd have been a squire in the old days, not a tenant farmer. I bet you're even going to name the bloody estate after you. Brandon Road, Mitchell Way, Brandon Meadows . . . I can see it now.' Her lip twisted. 'There's a settlement there, all right – and no one planted it. You might have outline permission for the development, but there's no way you'll get final permission. Not when the council hears about this. And as for what you've done to your grandfather—'

He caught her hand easily, before it connected with his face. 'It's none of your business. No one asked you to come here and stick your nose in. Everything was fine, before you arrived.'

'Like hell. Can't you see how miserable you're making him? And yes, it probably does stick in your throat that you were wrong about that field, but can't you be pleased for him?'

'As I said, it's none of your business.' Brandon stood up and began to walk towards the door, propelling Zoe backwards. 'As for upsetting Gramps, you're doing a pretty good job of that all by yourself, working him up to a frenzy about the dig. If he's ill over this, I'll hold you personally responsible.'

'Oh, and your attitude has nothing to do with it?' Zoe sneered. 'Brandon Know-all Mitchell was completely wrong about the site but isn't man enough to admit it.'

'I'm man enough, all right,' he said softly. 'And you should know. You were quick enough to fuck me in the churchyard, if I remember rightly.'

Her face whitened. 'You bastard! You started it!'

'And you didn't make any protest, did you?'

'You . . . you . . .' Zoe was, for once, at a loss for words. She struggled, trying to regain control of her hands so that she could slap him, but Brandon guessed her intention and held both hands above her head, making her arch upwards. He pinned her hands to his office door; she opened her mouth, about to lambast him again, and he lowered his head, effectively cutting off her protest with his own mouth.

Zoe struggled against him, refusing to respond. There was no way she was going to kiss him back. The self-centred, unprincipled bastard – and to think she'd admired his integrity! She couldn't have been more wrong about him.

She bit at his lower lip, hard, thinking that it would make him release her; far from it. If anything, it made him even more determined to make her bend to his will, and he changed tactic, biting at her lips, too. He pushed one hard thigh between hers, tilting his pelvis so that she could feel his erection; then, still holding her hands in one of his so that her struggles were ineffective, he eased his free hand between their bodies and unbuttoned her shirt.

Zoe was furious. Who the hell did he think he was, treating her like a slut? But she couldn't yell at him, because he'd already anticipated her move and was kissing her again, his tongue in her mouth deliberately arousing her. She flushed with shame as he pushed his fingers under the edge of her bra, pulling the cup down to bare one breast; her nipple tingled where he touched her.

He made a small sound of triumph in the back of his throat as her areola puckered under his fingertips, the nipple hardening almost painfully; Zoe felt a rush of moisture between her legs, and hated him even more. She tried forcing herself to think of things which turned her off. Her income tax return; the junk mail that was no doubt piling up at her flat; the over-smooth and falsely sophisticated Mark Burroughs . . . But as he did the same to her other breast, baring it and teasing the nipple with his fingertips, she couldn't help responding, her sex growing warm and wet and puffy.

As if he could sense it – or maybe even scent it – Brandon slid his hand over her bared abdomen, deftly undoing the button of her jeans. Zoe continued to struggle, but it was more for show than anything else, and both of them knew it. He lowered the zip and pushed his fingers under the edge of her knickers, cupping her delta for a moment before delving further, parting her labia and rubbing her clitoris.

Zoe couldn't help a groan, deep in her throat; Brandon released her mouth for a moment.

'Let me go, you bastard,' she said.

'Methinks the lady doth protest too much,' he said, his eyes glittering. 'Admit it, Zoe. You want me.'

'I don't.'

'No? Then why are you wet? Your sex feels like silk – warm, wet silk. Ripe. Like a peach.'

'You're mixing your similes.'

'Metaphors.'

'No. Go find yourself a grammar book and learn the difference.'

Brandon smiled and lowered his mouth to hers again, pulling her arms up a fraction and continuing to torment her sex with his fingers. When he broke the kiss again, she was breathing heavily, her face flushed and her eyes wide.

'Tell me.'

'No. You started this.'

'You did,' he corrected, 'because you knew that I'd stop you slapping me. And you knew how.'

'By hitting me back?'

He shook his head. 'I'd never hit a woman. Unless we're talking sophisticated sado-masochistic games – and I'm not interested in them. Neither are you, though I think you enjoy mind games. I don't get off on chastising women, and I don't think you get off on being chastised.' His pupils had expanded, she noted absently. He moved his hand so that he could remove her glasses, tucking them into the pocket of his shirt; then he tilted his hips again rubbing his erection against her. 'You knew this would happen.'

'Balls.'

'And you think I need a lesson in grammar . . . Hm. Sounds like I'm not the only one who needs lessons. I suggest yours is in anatomy.' He moved his hips from side to side.

'What you can feel isn't my balls.' There was a faint flush across his cheekbones, and his mouth was as swollen and as reddened as Zoe suspected her own to be. 'Just admit you're turned on, Zoe. You like fighting me. And you like it rough, when you're in this kind of mood.'

'No.'

'No?' He bent his head again, this time suckling one nipple. Zoe's knees buckled slightly as his teeth bit gently into her flesh, keeping the right side of the pain-pleasure barrier. She forced herself not to cry out in pleasure, holding her body as tensely as she could; Brandon guessed, and changed tactics, his mouth softening and coaxing, the tip of his tongue teasing her nipple. He released her for long enough to blow on her spit-slicked skin, and she couldn't suppress a shiver; she felt, rather than saw, him grin and take her nipple back into his mouth, sucking hard.

He gave her other breast the same treatment; then raised his head. 'Look me in the eye, Zoe, and tell me you don't want me.' She did, and he laughed. 'This time, with more conviction. You're a bad liar. Your eyes give you away.'

'So why do you believe I planted the tesserae?' she fenced.

'Okay, I'll say you didn't.'

'You patronising bastard.' She managed to kick him in the shins. 'Let me go.'

'Oh, no. Oh, no, no, no. Not until I've taught you a lesson in manners.'

'*What?*' Zoe was outraged. 'Considering that you haven't shown the slightest—'

Again, he silenced her by kissing her, and slid his hand back down her jeans. Her sex was even wetter and hotter: and she knew that he could tell. She wasn't sure whether she was angrier at him for the way he was treating her, or with herself for her response.

He broke the kiss. 'If you're going to kick, you need to be hobbled.' Before she could guess what he was going to do, he pulled her hands down, then wrenched her jeans and knickers down to her ankles, in one lithe movement, before pinning her hands above her head again. 'Now, what shall I do with you?' He put his head on one side, considering. 'There's a lot of things I'd like to do to you, Zoe Lynton.

112

And a lot of things I think you'd like me to do.'

'Don't even think about touching me.'

'I'm way past that stage,' he told her huskily. 'And it's the same for you, I know. I can see it in your eyes.' He used his free hand to unfasten his belt, then wrapped it round her wrists. He lowered her bound hands, then studied her again. 'Well, now. What a picture you make. If your colleagues could see you, now . . . I wonder what they'd make of it?'

Zoe suddenly realised that they were in the farm office, and anyone could walk in and see what was happening. The only thing preventing that happening was that she was leaning against the door. 'I . . .'

'It's not important.' Brandon, guessing what was disturbing her, locked the door. 'I don't think we'll be interrupted, somehow. And it would be unfair to leave you like this – don't you think?'

'You're a bully,' she muttered.

'So you want me to leave you?' He slid one hand between her thighs, stroking her sex. 'Leave you unsatisfied and aching, and unable to do anything about it yourself?'

'Don't play games with me,' she warned.

'All right.'

To her shock, he picked her up and carried her across the room. 'Put me down!'

'As you wish.' He set her on her feet again, in front of his desk. There was a hole cut towards the back of the desk to accommodate the wires for his PC; he pushed her forward so that her hands were next to it, then swiftly adjusted the belt round her wrists so that she was tethered to the desk. Then he put her glasses in the top drawer of his desk. 'Now, if you'll excuse me, I was working when you came in.' He sat down, turned the PC screen away from her view, and began to tap on the keyboard.

Zoe swallowed. Just what the hell was he playing at? He had her spread face-down on his desk, her jeans and knickers round her ankles, her shirt open and her bra pulled down to reveal her breasts. From his position behind her, he could see her sex clearly; she knew from the feel of his erection against her when they'd fought by the door that he was just as turned on as she was. And yet he was working calmly, as if nothing had happened . . .

If she asked him what he thought he was doing, he'd make a sarcastic comment about working – she knew that. Or he'd tease her, make her tell him what she wanted him to do to her. She flushed dully. They both knew that. And they both wanted it. She was uncomfortably aware of the flat hard surface against her nipples and the edge of the desk against her pubic bone; just how long was he going to keep her there, in suspense?

'This is unlawful imprisonment, you know,' she said finally.

'Really?' Brandon continued tapping away, sounding bored.

'I could sue you.'

'Because you're my unwilling prisoner?'

'Yes.'

He laughed. 'There's a small flaw there, Zoe.'

'What?'

'You're not unwilling.'

'You think I enjoy being held like this?'

'Possibly not,' he allowed, 'but anticipation is . . . one of life's sauces. And I think you're enjoying that, thinking about what I'm going to do to you when I stop working.'

'No way.'

'Need proof, do we?' He gave a heavy sigh, and the PC whirred, as if he were saving a file. Slowly, exaggeratedly, he moved behind her. 'Now. If you were unwilling, your nipples would be flat and unresponsive.' He slid a hand between her body and the desk, touching the hard peaks of flesh. 'But they're hard, erect.'

'Because I'm cold.'

He laughed. 'It's not cold, Zoe. But all right, let's say that it's a physical reaction to cold. Now, if you weren't enjoying yourself, your sex would be dry.' He smoothed the cheeks of her bottom, then dabbled one hand between her thighs. 'And it's not.' He leant over her, rubbing his erection against her buttocks, and brought his nectar-soaked fingers before her face. 'As you can see. And scent. And feel. And taste.' He rubbed the musky juices on her lower lip, so she could taste herself. 'So are you going to admit that you're turned on?'

She refused to answer.

'In legal terms, they used to say that silence indicated consent.'

'You bastard.'

'I assure you I'm completely legitimate. In all senses of the word.' She realised that he was kneeling behind her; he rubbed his face against her buttocks for a moment, then between her thighs. Then she felt his tongue parting her labia, teasing her. She closed her eyes. God. How had she thought that she could fight a man like Brandon? A man who could make her body sing with his slightest touch? It was sheer agony, forcing herself not to respond to the way his mouth worked on her sex: but she kept herself in check, remaining absolutely still.

He sucked her clitoris, varying the speed and pressure and arousing her until she almost cried out, but she managed to retain her composure. Just. Then he changed tactic, sliding one finger into her sex and working on her clitoris with his other hand. 'Did I tell you,' he asked huskily, 'how good you feel? I love the way your flesh clings to me, Zoe. You're so responsive. So warm and wet and willing – even if your mind won't admit it, your body will. And I love the way you taste, that sweet-salt tang of your arousal. And the scent, all honey and vanilla. Your skin's so soft, so creamy: you drive me to the limits of my control. You're forbidden territory – but I can't stop myself. Not when I'm touching you like this, and you're responding to me . . .'

Chapter Nine

Zoe couldn't suppress a shiver. She hated herself for it, but he didn't crow in triumph. If anything, there was a slight change in his voice, a lower and huskier timbre that made her even wetter. 'I want to do all sorts of things to you. We're on opposite sides, and I should be fighting you: and yet my insides melt every time I see you. All the time I'm with you, I'm torn between arguing with you and making you realise what I'm talking about, and wanting to touch you like this.' She felt something wet and hard pressing against the puckered rosebud of her anus, and realised that he'd moistened his finger to ease his passage.

She groaned sightly as he pushed against her, and her flesh yielded, admitting his finger. 'You've cost me sleepless nights, Zoe, since I first met you.'

'I'm sure Helena would be delighted to help you out.' The words were out before she could stop them.

He chuckled. 'Helena. Are you jealous, Zoe, my sweet?'

'Of her? No.'

'Good. Because I wouldn't touch Helena if she offered herself to me on a plate.'

'According to her, you're secretly engaged.'

He laughed. 'It's so secret that I don't know about it yet, then.'

Exactly as Zoe had thought. 'She wants you.'

'"I want" doesn't necessarily get,' he mocked.

'Take your hands off me.'

'I didn't mean where you're concerned. This is a case where I want, and I'm definitely going to get.'

'I'm off limits.'

'You just sent me over the limit,' he corrected huskily. 'And I think it's mutual. Hm, Zoe?'

He'd admitted it. She wouldn't lose face if she did the

same. She squeezed her eyes shut. It was so tempting. But it was tantamount to giving in – and she wasn't going to do that.

'Tell me, Zoe. Have you slept well, since you met me?'

'Give me one good reason why I shouldn't have.'

'I can give you several.' He pushed his fingers deep into her sex. 'Like this.' He rubbed her clitoris. 'Like this.' He moved his finger very slightly in her anus, sending a thrill through her body. 'And this. Tell me, Zoe.'

'No.'

'No, you won't tell me? Or no, you haven't slept well?'

'Who says that I don't already have a lover?' she parried. 'That I'm not involved with someone in London?'

'It isn't important. Not here, not now.' Brandon said softly. 'What's important, right now, is you and me.'

'So you'll stop the development?'

'No. It's going ahead, Zoe, whether you like it or not.'

She tensed. 'Brandon, leave me alone. Take your hands off me. Now.'

'Just forget about the bloody development, for now.' He continued stroking her.

'It isn't just the development. It's the way you treated your grandfather, a few minutes ago.'

He sighed. 'Zoe, how the hell you can think straight when I'm touching you like this . . . Either you're really not interested in me, or your mind's even more incredible than I already give you credit for.'

She shivered. 'Flattery's not going to work.'

'Zoe, I want you. And I'm going to apologise to Gramps, later. I hate working on budgets – it's a necessary evil, and it does nothing for my temper.' He dropped a trail of kisses down her spine. 'And I'm tired of you bugging me about the development. If I thought it really was what Gramps thinks it is, of course I wouldn't go ahead. But the site's already been surveyed. Whatever you've found isn't really of archaeological importance.'

'Let's leave the experts to decide that, shall we?'

'Agreed. Now – that leaves us. What now?' To her shock, he removed his hands from her body, stood up, and walked round the desk to face her. 'What now, Zoe?' he repeated softly.

'I . . .' Her body craved his touch. 'Oh, hell,' she muttered, her face flushing as she met his gaze.

He smiled ruefully at her. 'Looks like we both feel the same way. I want you, but you annoy the hell out of me at the same time. It makes me furious with myself for being so weak, where you're concerned.'

'Why didn't you come to the meal, last night?'

'Because I would have started remembering the last time I saw you at The Feathers. In your room, with that beautiful big bed right beside you. I was even sitting on your bed, and I could smell your perfume. It drove me crazy. How I stopped myself ripping your clothes off and taking you, right there and then, I'll never know.' His eyes had darkened almost to black, Zoe registered: and his zip was straining to bursting point. Brandon was turned on by her, in a big way. 'I wanted to strip you naked and look at you, touch you.'

Part of her thought that she could use it in the fight over the development: but she knew that she was kidding herself. She was in exactly the same state. She could barely think straight, when he was around; it had taken a supreme effort to argue with him, rather than give in and let her body go into free-fall. 'Like you've just done.'

'You pushed me over the limits, Zoe.' He licked his lower lip. 'Like you're doing, now. I want to touch you. But I won't do it unless you want it, too.'

She swallowed hard. 'I . . .' This is as hard for me, she wanted to tell him. I don't know how to cope, either. It's against my professional code to get involved with you, but I want you so badly. 'Do what you like.'

He shook his head. 'That's not good enough. You have to want it, too, not just submit.'

She smiled wryly. 'You're a bully.'

'Tough negotiator, yes; bully, no. It's not my style. I believe in win-win situations.'

'It can't be one. Not with the development.'

'Fuck the development.' There was a brief flash of anger in his slate blue eyes. 'I'm talking about you and me, right now. You're over my desk, bare-arsed and beautiful, your hair mussed and your lips red and swollen with passion. It's driving me insane, just looking at you. I want you. But only if you want me, too.'

118

'You've touched me. Judge for yourself.'

He smiled. 'Your body wants me, yes. But I want to hear you say it.'

'And if I don't?'

He shrugged, and unfastened her wrists. 'Then you're free to go.' She stood up again, rubbing her wrists, and his face registered concern. 'Zoe. Did I hurt you?'

'No,' she admitted. She made no attempt to pull her jeans up or restore any order to her clothing; the bulge at his crotch grew even larger.

He followed the direction of her gaze, and grinned ruefully. 'Yeah, well. If you had the view I have, you'd be in the same state.'

'But you're fully clothed,' she pointed out.

'And you want me to do something about it?'

Their surroundings were forgotten. Neither of them cared whether someone came to the office, heard them talking, tried the door and found it locked, then looked through the window and saw them. Nothing else mattered other than the energy surge between them.

Zoe looked at him, remembering how good his body had felt against hers in the churchyard. Remembering how he'd just touched her; how, even when they'd been fighting, their bodies had responded to each other. The rational side of her knew that it wouldn't solve the problem, but she was barely capable of rational thought. 'Yes.'

'Right, then.' He kept his gaze locked on hers, and slowly stripped, undoing his white cotton shirt. He was muscular without being over-developed; Zoe itched to touch those beautiful pectorals but stopped herself. For now, she was just going to look. He discarded the shirt, and undid the button of his jeans. He paused for a moment, then unzipped the fly and slowly pushed the soft faded denims over his hips. His rigid cock was clearly outlined by the thin cotton of his underpants, and Zoe couldn't help a sharp intake of breath.

He noticed, but his smile held no triumph. If anything, it held a tinge of humility, she thought. He removed his jeans, kicking off his shoes and removing his socks at the same time; then he stood with his arms folded.

'What?' she demanded.

'If you want to see any more, you'll have to do it yourself,' he told her.

Zoe moved, then caught the edge of the desk before she fell. She'd forgotten that Brandon had hobbled her with her jeans. She steadied herself, then rubbed her heels against each other to remove her trainers, before shedding her jeans and knickers. She left her shirt and bra as they were, knowing that the disorder in her remaining clothing was as much of a turn-on for him as for her, then walked round the desk to him.

If he saw the purpose in her face, he made no sign; he stood passively while she hooked her thumbs into the waistband of his underpants and drew them down. He shivered slightly as she dropped to her knees in front of him, but made no sound. He let her pull his underpants down to his ankles; he was about to lift one foot to step out of them, but she stopped him softly. He smiled in understanding – she wanted to hobble him, as he had hobbled her earlier.

Slowly, she brushed her hair back from her face, and looked up at him, holding his gaze. Then she ringed his shaft with one hand, cupped his balls with the other, and lowered her head, swirling her tongue round his glans and lapping at the small bead of clear moisture in the eye of his cock. He made a small noise of pleasure in the back of his throat, and Zoe began to suck him in earnest, taking him as deeply as she could and caressing his balls, setting up a swift counterpoint between her mouth and the hand still ringing his cock.

He bucked his hips slightly, just once, and held still; she could tell how much effort it was costing him, and redoubled her attempts to make him lose control. Finally, he wound his hands in her hair, tugging it gently. 'Zoe. Stop. I can't take much more.'

She lifted her head for an instant. 'That's the idea,' she told him with a wicked grin. 'I want you to let go, give it all to me.' Then she resumed sucking him, teasing the sensitive ridge with her lips, increasing the pressure until she felt his balls lifting and tightening. She was ready for the jet of creamy fluid, and swallowed deeply, holding him in her mouth until his cock had stopped throbbing. Then she stood up, and looked him in the eye. 'Well?'

'Words fail me,' he told her, equally softly. 'The way you make me feel . . .' He wrapped his arms round her, pulling her close and kissing her deeply, tasting himself on her mouth. Then he kicked his underpants away and lifted her, carrying her over to his desk; he was tidy to anal retentive standards, in her opinion, so there were no papers to sweep to one side before he spread her on the table.

To her surprise, he picked up his shirt, folding it up and tucking it under her head in a makeshift pillow; he smiled, smoothing the backs of his fingers against her cheeks. 'I'm not the callous bastard you think I am, Zoe.'

She winced. 'Don't talk, Brandon. I don't want to think about Boudicca and that bloody site. Not right now.'

'Neither do I.'

'Then we're agreed on one thing.'

'More than one thing, I think.' he said unsteadily, parting her legs. 'God, Zoe, you're so beautiful. You've driven me out of my mind, this week. I've picked up the phone to ring you more times than I care to think – including one night, at three a.m.'

'Now, that, I would most definitely not have appreciated,' she told him. 'Anyway, my mobile would have been switched off.'

'I know. I wanted to tell you exactly what I wanted to do to you,' he said. 'In explicit detail.'

'But you held yourself back.'

I held myself, all right,' he said huskily. 'Even when I was a teenager, at my randiest, I've never had to relieve myself so much.'

Zoe thrilled. 'You masturbated – over me?'

'Not literally, no.' He gave her a lazy grin. 'Though maybe I will. But yes, thoughts of you drove me to touch myself.'

'Show me,' she whispered. 'Show me.'

'Like this.' He curled his fingers round the thickening shaft, much as Zoe had been doing, a few minutes before, and began to stroke it. He worked himself gently, until he was fully hard, then changed the rhythm of his strokes, alternating between bouts of quick short strokes and slow deep ones.

Zoe felt her sex pool. 'Brandon.'

121

'Hm?' his eyes were barely focused.

'I can't handle this. Seeing you . . . seeing you do that, it makes me so hot, so wet.'

'Then touch yourself,' he told her. 'Touch yourself as you'd like me to touch you.'

'I'd rather you did it.'

'Please? I want to watch you, Zoe. I want to watch you touch yourself for me.'

She paused for a long moment, then nodded. 'All right.' She leaned back against his desk, supporting herself, and widened her stance. She slid one hand between her thighs, parting her labia with her index and ring fingers, then curled her middle finger, placing it just above her clitoris before straightening it, letting it traverse the length of her sex. She curled her finger again, then straightened it, each time brushing her sex delicately, lightly, teasingly.

Her control lasted for only a short while: she began to rub herself harder, forgetting the finesse, wanting to feel that inner sparkling. She pushed her finger deep into her vulva, scooping out the moisture and slicking it along the furrow, then closed her eyes and tipped her head back, rubbing herself with abandon.

Then she felt another hand join hers, resting lightly against her skin for a moment to gauge her rhythm and pressure; she opened her eyes, surprised, to find Brandon next to her. 'I want you,' he repeated. 'I want you.'

'Then do it.'

'Do what?'

She knew what he wanted to hear. 'Fuck me, Brandon. Touch me. Taste me. Fill me with your cock. Make me come.'

He smiled. 'Oh, I'll do that, all right.' He pushed her hand to one side, and masturbated her deftly, keeping to the same rhythm and pressure that she'd used. Zoe cried out as her orgasm snaked through her, turning her legs to water and her belly to fire; then he hoisted her onto the edge of his desk, spreading her legs wide and fitting the tip of his cock to her still-flexing quim. Zoe gasped and opened her eyes as he pushed into her, sliding easily into her silky wet flesh, filling her to the hilt. Her own excitement was mirrored on his face, and he began to thrust hard, cupping her buttocks and pulling her against him to maximise his penetration.

She wrapped her legs round him, tilting her pelvis and pushing back against him. It felt so good, so very good; it couldn't be wrong, she thought. Not when the sex was as good as this. She no longer cared about their differences; all that mattered was the way his body possessed hers.

'I've been dreaming about this,' he said softly. 'Even this afternoon, when I was supposed to be doing those bloody budgets – I kept thinking of you, wondering what it would be like to have you sprawled naked on my desk.'

She grinned. 'Now you know, don't you?'

'And it's incredible,' he breathed. 'Even better than my dreams. I love the way your body feels, wrapped round mine. I love your softness, the way you fit me perfectly.' He reached up to cup her breasts. 'I love the way your body curves, all woman.'

'And I love the way you fill me,' she admitted. 'I kept remembering the way you felt inside me, that night in the churchyard.'

'Did you touch yourself, Zoe?' he asked her huskily. 'Did you touch yourself, thinking of me?'

She nodded.

'More than once?'

'More than once,' she confirmed.

He groaned as he reached his climax; at the same time, Zoe felt her quim rippling round him, her muscles contracting sharply. He didn't stop, though: he continued touching her, caressing her, refusing to pull out of her. She felt him softening; and then he bent his head to kiss her, still playing with her nipples, and she felt him growing hard again inside her.

'I can't get enough of you, Zoe,' he told her hoarsely, breaking the kiss. 'It's driving me insane.'

'Me, too.'

'There are so many things I want to do with you, in so many places. I want to carry you to a big sunken bath, fill it with bubbles, and wash you all over, arousing you until you come. And then I'd take you, leaning you against the side of the bath and taking you from behind, the bubbles sliding between our bodies.'

'Oh, yes,' Zoe murmured as he slowed his pace, pushing deeply into her.

'I want to lie you on a bed of deep red roses, the same crimson as your beautiful cunt. And then I want to take you on them, smell the scent of the roses as our bodies crush them, mingled with the scent of your arousal.' His eyes glittered. 'I'd like you dressed up as an *houri*, in silks and silver bangles, with your beautiful eyes outlined in kohl and your nipples reddened with henna and an emerald in your navel – and then I'd like to rip the clothes from you and take you fiercely, like a warrior.'

Zoe thrilled as he spoke to her. Brandon Mitchell was a man with the kind of imagination she responded to: the kind of imagination that matched her own. Men like him were few and far between. Why the hell did they have to be on opposite sides? She forced the thought from her mind. Now wasn't the time for arguments. Her body craved him too much – and it was mutual. Very much so.

'Then do it, Brandon. Take me hard.' She unwrapped her legs from his waist, pushing gently at him; he frowned, withdrawing, and she turned over, thrusting her buttocks into the air. 'Take me,' she repeated.

His body shuddered and he pulled her against him so that she could feel the hard length of his cock against her buttocks. He held her there for a moment, just long enough to make her wonder quite what was in his mind; then he altered their positions slightly, widening her stance, and fitting the tip of his cock back against her sex. As he pushed hard into her, his balls slammed against her quim. He caressed her buttocks, then slid his arms around her waist, moving one hand up to caress her breasts and the other down between her legs to seek her clitoris with his fingertips. She moaned as he rubbed her, driving her closer and closer to the edge.

He changed tactic, moving his hand from her breasts to her buttocks, squeezing the soft globes gently and then pushing the tip of his finger against her anus; she let her head drop as he penetrated her, pushing her buttocks back at him to urge him deeper. The combination of his thrusting cock and questing fingers was enough to tip her over the edge into a mind-bending orgasm; she cried out his name

124

as she came and he held her close, resting his cheek against her shoulder and breathing in the scent of her hair. They remained there for a long time until finally he slipped from her; he kissed her shoulder, then moved away.

They both dressed in silence; as they restored order to their clothing, tension grew again between them.

'What now?' Brandon asked softly.

'I don't know,' Zoe admitted. 'Why can't you believe that there's something there, Brandon?'

'Because there's already been a survey. There's nothing important there, believe me.' He raked a hand through his hair. 'Why can't you drop it?'

'Gut feeling,' Zoe said.

'And you want me to trust that, deprive the people around here of jobs and homes and hope?'

'It doesn't matter what I want, does it? Because you won't do it.'

'I can't, Zoe.'

'You mean, you won't.' She sighed. 'I don't know, Brandon. I need time to think. We need some space between us.'

'Maybe.'

He made no attempt to touch her, merely taking her glasses from his drawer and handing them to her. Zoe felt oddly disappointed. She finished dressing, hoping that he didn't notice the way her fingers fumbled with the fastenings of her clothing, and walked over to the door. He didn't say a word; holding her head high, Zoe made a dignified exit, unlocking the door and closing it quietly behind her, ignoring her body's clamour to make love with him again.

Several days later, work was still continuing at the site. More finds had been uncovered, convincing both Zoe and Jack that they were right about the field. Since their last encounter in the office, Brandon had given Zoe a wide berth; she, in turn, refused to admit just how much her body craved him, and continued as she was, spending her days at the dig and her evenings working on her column and the outline of her article about the church. She worked every night until she could hardly see, in the hope that it would make her too tired to think about Brandon, but it didn't work. Every time she crawled into bed and closed her eyes, she remembered the feel of his skin against hers and the way his cock had filled her to the hilt. And every time, she couldn't help touching herself, bringing her body to a sharp climax and crying out his name as she came.

On the Wednesday morning, she went out to the excavation as usual, to see a grim-faced Ed.

'What's up?' she asked.

He gestured at the ruined equipment in front of him. 'This. God, I'd just gone into the main tent to check something. When I came back, I found this.'

She looked at the broken tools. Not only would it cost money to replace them – money they didn't really have – it would also take time. They were working against the clock, as it was; the last thing they needed was for this to happen. 'Did you see anyone?'

He shook his head. 'Not a soul. I didn't hear anyone, either. Whoever it was, they knew exactly what they were going to do. They'd probably been hiding for ages, watching for their chance.'

Zoe had a sick feeling in the pit of her stomach. Surely Brandon wouldn't . . . But he felt as passionately about his development as she and Jack felt about the site. If she were in his position, and felt that desperate to stop the dig, what would she do?

'Zoe?' Ed asked, noticing the look on her face.

'I'll be back in a bit. There's something I've got to do,' she said, refusing to be drawn any further. The only way she could be sure was to confront Brandon, and she didn't want to accuse him until she was certain that her facts were straight. She walked quickly to the farm, opening the office door without knocking and ignoring the rush of desire that filled her at the memory of her last visit to his office. Brandon was sitting at his desk, talking to someone on the phone, tapping a pencil on a pad; he didn't look up as she closed the door behind her.

She cleared the line on the phone, cutting him off; he stared up at her. 'What the hell do you think you're playing at? That was an important call!'

'This is more important,' she said quietly.

His eyes narrowed. 'My grandfather?'

'Jack's fine.' She rolled her eyes. As if he really cared. 'I think you know what I'm talking about.'

He scowled at her. 'I don't have the faintest idea.'

'Let me refresh your memory. We'll start with you breaking equipment at the site, shall we?'

He frowned. 'Before you start making slanderous accusations, I suggest you check your facts.'

'You're denying it, then.' It was more of a statement than a question.

'I just did – if you'd bothered listening.'

'You're telling me you had nothing to do with the damage at the dig this morning?'

He rubbed a hand across his face. 'Zoe, I'm busy. I don't have time for hysterical questioning. I haven't been near your bloody dig, let alone done any damage.'

'Then who did it?'

'How the hell should I know?' Brandon sighed, exasperated. 'If you're going to blame me every time something goes wrong with—'

'Not just something,' she interrupted. 'Whoever did it waited until Ed left the trench for a moment. He didn't see or hear anyone. There's only one person besides Jack who knows the farm well enough to be able to move around without being seen or heard.'

Brandon rolled his eyes. 'God, give me strength! Zoe, I've told you, I had nothing to do with whatever happened at the dig. I'm not a criminal, and I'll use the proper channels to stop the excavation.'

'So you admit that you want the dig stopped.'

He drummed his fingers on the table. 'That's a stupid question. You know I do. But I'll do it legally.'

Zoe wanted to believe him. Desperately. But she couldn't think who else it could be. 'Legally?' she prevaricated.

'By court injunction. That's what you just interrupted, actually – a discussion between me and my solicitor.'

'Oh.'

He regarded her coldly. 'I told you, we've already had the site surveyed. You can see the report any time you like.'

'In that case, right now.'

'It's with Mark,' he told her quietly. 'I'll ring him and ask him to give you a copy.'

'Do that,' she answered, her voice equally cold and quiet. 'Tell him to drop it in at The Feathers. By lunchtime.' She turned on her heel and walked out.

The team couldn't do much more with their equipment ruined; a furious Zoe spent the morning on the phone, helping Ed secure replacements. Then, just before lunchtime, Sam came up to Zoe's room. 'Delivery for you,' she said. 'By courier.'

'Courier?' Zoe was surprised. 'Thanks.' She took the parcel and opened it; her mouth thinned. 'Ah, yes. The famous survey.' Brandon had at least kept to one thing. He'd asked Mark to get a copy of the survey to her before lunchtime, as she'd wanted.

She spent the next hour studying it; according to Mark's survey, even the wall didn't exist. So either the survey was wrong, or it was of a different field. Frowning, Zoe went to Ed's room, knocking on the door.

'Come in. It's open,' he called.

She put her head round the door. 'Hi, Ed. Got a moment?'

'Yeah, sure.' The burly archaeologist smiled at her. 'Bringing me some good news, are you?'

'I don't know.' She sighed, and handed him the survey. 'What does this mean to you?'

Ed examined it. 'It's a field survey.'

She grinned. 'I know that.' She sobered again. 'But what's your professional opinion?'

'From studying this? That it's just an ordinary field that's been cultivated for years and then allowed to lie fallow for a while. Why?'

'It's meant to be our field.'

Ed shook his head. 'Jack's shown me the map. Our field's a different shape.'

'Could someone pass it off as our field?'

Ed caught on quickly. 'To someone who didn't know it was our field, you mean?'

'Yes.'

He nodded. 'What is this, Zoe?'

'Mark's survey. The one that says there's nothing of

any archaeological significance.'

'There isn't – in this field. But it's not the same as the one we're working on.'

'That's what I thought.' Zoe's heart sank. 'It's a false survey, then.' And Brandon, who'd grown up with the farm, must have known that it was a different field. So much for integrity. Her respect for him died instantly. Had he and Mark really been so desperate to make money that they'd filed false particulars with the planning office? And yet he'd seemed so sincere when he'd explained his reasons for the development. Could it be that Mark had pulled the wool over Brandon's eyes? But then again, Brandon must have known about the survey . . .

'Are you okay, Zoe?' Ed looked at her white face, concerned.

'I'm fine.' She took a deep breath. 'I just need to check a few things.'

'Don't do anything stupid, will you?'

She smiled wryly. 'No heroics, Ed. I promise.'

She returned to her room and rang London. She had a couple of friends who owed her favours – the kind of friends who could find out what she wanted without it being traced back to her. By the end of the afternoon, Zoe had all the facts marshalled. Mark Burroughs was heavily in debt, his investment business mortgaged to the hilt, thanks to a habit of card games and casinos. Without the profits from the housing estate, his business would go under: no wonder he was so desperate for it to go ahead.

She took a deep breath. Well, now was the time to confront Brandon. She wouldn't drag Jack into it – not yet – but eventually he'd have to know what a devious bastard his grandson was. Swallowing, she left her room and headed for Whiteacres.

Chapter Ten

Jack had mentioned before that his grandson was a workaholic; there was a good chance that Brandon would still be in the office, even this late in the day. She tried the door, and it opened instantly.

Brandon looked up from his desk, and scowled when he saw her. 'What do you want?'

'To talk to you.'

He folded his arms, looking at her. 'To apologise for your outburst this morning, hm?'

She shook her head. 'Far from it. Look at this.' She marched over to his desk and dumped the survey on his desk.

He picked it up. 'Oh, Mark's report. Showing that there's nothing there. I'm glad you've finally realised that I was telling you the truth.'

'Come on, Brandon. I'm not that naive. Look at it properly and tell me what you see.'

'A report from an archaeological surveyor.'

'Look at the bloody pictures, will you?

He did, and frowned. 'What am I supposed to be looking at?'

'Are you telling me you don't know which fields are which on your farm? After you've grown up on the place, and with that bloody great map of the farm on your wall pinpointing the crops?'

'What are you implying, Ms Lynton?'

'I'm not implying, I'm telling you. It's not the same field.'

Brandon looked closely; his eyes widened. 'My God.'

She smiled thinly. 'Don't tell me – you haven't seen this before?'

'I've seen the survey. Not the pictures, though. Not the map.'

'And you're supposed to be a businessman? Come on. I don't believe that for a second. No way would you do a deal without knowing exactly what was going on. So you're as bent as your bloody business partner. Well, we're on to you, now. You might as well drop the pretence.'

Brandon stood up. 'Firstly, Ms Lynton, I am not "bent", as you put it. Any more comments like that, and I'll sue you for defamation. Secondly, Mark's been my financial adviser for five years. He has impeccable references, and he's on the level.'

'He's a liar, Brandon. A smooth talker.'

'Whatever he is in his personal life, he's as straight as a die professionally. He has to be. He's registered with all the financial bodies,' Brandon pointed out.

'And why should that stop him being a crook?' Zoe shook her head. 'You just can't admit to being wrong, can you?'

'Zoe, I'm too busy to give you the pleasure of a fight.' He gave her a contemptuous stare. 'Or was it something else you wanted from me?'

Stung, Zoe gathered up the papers she'd dumped on his desk. 'I don't want anything from you. But it's over, Brandon. You might as well face facts. Your little money-spinner just bit the dust.'

Brandon watched the door close behind her, as he tried to focus his thoughts. What she'd just told him . . . He could hardly believe it. He wouldn't have believed it, had he not seen the pictures for himself. Mark had deliberately lied to him about the survey. He'd shown Brandon the report, let him read it through – but he hadn't shown him the pictures or the map. The survey was above board, in that the surveyor concerned had reached the right conclusion. There was nothing of any archaeological importance in the field. The only thing was, it was the wrong field.

Brandon's eyes narrowed. So had Mark done it deliberately? And, if so, why? Frowning, he picked up the phone and dialled Mark's number. It rang three times, four: then the answerphone clicked in. He waited for the brief message to end, then spoke curtly into the receiver. 'Mark, it's Brandon. It's Wednesday evening, seven p.m., and I need to talk to you. I'll try your mobile – but if I haven't spoken to you before you get this message, ring me urgently.'

He cut the connection and dialled Mark's mobile number; he drummed his fingers impatiently, then scowled as he heard the polite female voice on the line. 'The cellphone you are calling is unavailable or may have been switched off. Please try calling later.'

He tried a third option – Mark's home number – and again was confronted with an answerphone. He left a curt message and hung up. Where the hell was Mark? Probably chatting up some potential client somewhere . . . Hell. As soon as Zoe took that report to the planning authorities, that would be the end of the development. The end of his dreams.

'I'm sorry, love, I haven't seen him all afternoon. He left the dogs here, so I assumed he was with you, at the dig.' Candy and Belle had been banned from the excavation, after trying to join in the dig and nearly damaging one of the finds.

Zoe shook her head. 'The excavation's on hold, at the moment. Someone did a bit of damage to the equipment – enough to stop us continuing work.'

Eileen winced. 'Ouch.'

Zoe couldn't quite bring herself to tell Eileen the truth about Brandon. 'My guess is it's something to do with Mark. Either he did it himself, or he paid someone to do it; but we're still going ahead.' She sighed. 'Well, when Jack turns up, would you tell him I was asking after him, please?'

'Of course I will, love.' Eileen looked at her. 'Are you all right?'

'Yeah. Just a bit angry about something.' Someone. How she could have been taken in so easily by Brandon Mitchell . . . it made her temper rage way, way out of control. 'I'm going to take a walk and calm down. If you could ask Jack to ring me either on my mobile or at The Feathers, I'd really appreciate it.'

'I will. Are you sure it's nothing I can help with?'

Zoe smiled at the older woman. 'Thanks, but it's something I need to sort out for myself. I'll see you later.'

When she left the farmhouse, Zoe headed for the dig. She knew she'd be alone there, and she wanted to think. How could she possibly tell Jack that his beloved grandson was a dishonest, cheating crook? That he'd lied from the start about the development? The shock and upset would be too much for the old man. On the other hand, there was no way Brandon was going to get away with it. She couldn't just pretend that he'd nothing to do with it. Either way, Jack was going to get hurt.

Bloody, bloody hell. She kicked at a stray flint. There had to be some way she could limit the damage. But how?

She reached the excavation, still in an introspective mood, and was just about to sit on the side of the trench when she noticed that an area slightly further down had caved in. Frowning, she went over to inspect it – and noticed the body in the bottom of the trench.

Jack.

'Oh, my God!' she exclaimed, leaping into the trench. 'Jack?' If he didn't answer . . . if he was dead . . .

The old man groaned. 'Help me.'

Zoe only realised then that she'd been holding her breath. 'Jack, it's Zoe. Are you all right?' No, that was a stupid question. If he was all right, he wouldn't be lying on the bottom of a trench. 'What happened?'

'Don't know. Slipped. Leg hurts.' He was obviously finding it difficult to talk.

Zoe remembered Brandon talking about his grandfather's illness, but she couldn't remember whether it was heart or lungs. Either way, she wasn't taking any risks. 'Jack, I'm calling an ambulance.' Thank God for mobile phones, she thought, dialling the emergency services.

The next couple of minutes saw Zoe at her most efficient, telling the operator exactly where they were and giving directions for the ambulance. In the meantime, although she knew better than to try to move Jack – there might be more damage than just to his leg – she stripped off her light jacket and covered him with it. Then she rang the farm, to tell Eileen what had happened and ask her to pass on a message to Brandon. Crooked bastard he might be, but she didn't doubt his love for his grandfather.

She continued talking to Jack, keeping him going until the ambulance arrived; then she accompanied him to the hospital.

* * *

133

An hour later, it was established that the only damage was a broken leg, although Jack would be kept in overnight for observation. Relieved, she was about to call a taxi and head back to Lower Yareham, when Brandon stormed in. 'I hold you personally responsible for this,' he informed Zoe, through gritted teeth. 'And when I've seen Gramps for myself and know he's all right, I'll deal with you.'

'Go to hell,' Zoe told him, her lip curling. 'I don't want anything to do with you.'

He gave her a withering look, then walked into the ward; she could hear him charming the nurses on duty. With disgust, she left the area and called a taxi.

Later that evening, there was a knock on her door at The Feathers.

'Yes?' she called.

'I think you'd better let me in, Ms Lynton. We have unfinished business.'

Brandon. Her sex throbbed treacherously, and her temper flared even more. How the hell could she still find him attractive, after all that had happened . . . 'Yes, we do,' she snapped, opening the door. 'Like the damage you've done.'

'The damage *I've* done? My grandfather's in hospital with a broken leg – and it could have been a hell of a lot worse. I told you, he has a heart condition. He could have died out there.'

'Pity you didn't think of that earlier, then.'

'*What*? Hold on. You're the one who started all this. Interfering, when I asked you to let things be.'

'So you could get your crooked scheme underway and destroy yet more of England's heritage?'

'So he wouldn't be upset by all this and made ill. And now he's in hospital – well, I hope you're satisfied. Because I won't be, until I've dragged you through every court in the system. You'd better just hope that Gramps doesn't get any worse, hadn't you?'

'*I'd* better hope? My God. If you hadn't weakened the trench, in the first place, he wouldn't have fallen.'

'If you hadn't got your friends to dig – hang on, what do you mean, I weakened the trench?'

'You know exactly what I mean. I don't suppose it

134

occurred to you that your grandfather might go there – you probably meant it to cave in under Ed or Ella. But it backfired – and now Jack's in hospital.'

'Zoe, I don't know what you're talking about.' Brandon frowned. 'What do you mean, weakened the trench?'

'The side of it. Come on, Brandon, don't try and pretend. We both know it was you.'

'I haven't touched the bloody trench. If anything, I've been trying to put it out of my mind. Are you telling me that someone deliberately weakened the side of the trench?'

Zoe curled her lip scornfully at him. 'That's exactly what you did. Maybe you didn't intend to hurt anyone – maybe it was just like the last time, when you damaged the equipment, so the dig would be put on hold again.'

'I didn't damage any equipment, and I haven't been near the trench.'

'Like hell. Who else would have done it? Me? Jack? Ed?' she spat. 'Come on. It's time you faced the consequences of what you did.'

'What *I* did?'

Her eyes blazed. 'For God's sake, stop repeating me.'

'You're not making a lot of sense.'

'No? Right. Come with me.'

'I'm not going anywhere until you promise to stay away from my grandfather and stop interfering.'

'If I hadn't been interfering, as you put it,' she pointed out, 'Jack could still be lying in the trench, now.'

'If you hadn't interfered, there wouldn't have been a trench for him to fall into.'

'Or for you to weaken.' She gave him a contemptuous glance. 'You say I'm not making any sense. Let's prove it, shall we? And I'll drive.'

Without another word, Brandon followed her down the stairs. They drove in silence to the lane by the excavation, then Brandon followed Zoe across the fields. Although her legs were shorter than his, he had to quicken his pace to suit hers: anger gave her strength and speed she didn't know she had.

When they reached the dig, she pointed at the wall of the trench. 'There. Now do you "remember" what I'm talking about?'

Brandon bent down and inspected the trench; the anger on his face increased, but it was no longer directed at Zoe. 'Who the hell did this?'

'Don't play-act with me, Brandon.'

'Zoe, it wasn't me. Believe me. My God. What happened to Gramps could have happened to any one of your team – to you, too.' He looked at her. 'I want to stop the excavation, yes, but no way would I hurt anyone in the process. I told you, I was going through legal channels.' His voice was very quiet, very sober. 'If you hadn't come along, Gramps could have been here for days. Or anyone else, for that matter – maybe one of the village children, or one of your colleagues.' He paused. 'As a matter of interest, just why did you come out here, when work wasn't scheduled to start again until the weekend?'

'Because I wanted to think, and I knew I'd be alone, here,' Zoe told him. 'I guess Jack did the same. Came here to think and dream – and the side of the trench gave way under him.'

Brandon closed his eyes. 'I can't bear to think of what could have happened to him. If he'd been out here, for hours . . .'

Zoe looked at him. The pain on his face was genuine. He really didn't know anything about what had happened to the trench. Which left Mark and Helena as the most likely suspects. 'Do you know where Mark is?' she asked.

He opened his eyes again. 'No. I've been trying to get hold of him, ever since you came to see me about the survey.' His face darkened. 'If he's got anything to do with this, I'll—'

'You'll take it through the courts. Beating him to a pulp might make you feel better, but it won't change what happened to Jack, and it'll land you in a heap of trouble. Jack's going to need you, when he comes out of hospital,' Zoe reminded him.

'Which is where I ought to be, now. At his bedside.'

'He needs his rest. Besides, if there's any change, the hospital have my mobile number.'

'Your mobile?' Brandon was incredulous.

'I told them I was his granddaughter,' Zoe admitted, wincing. 'I wanted to make sure he was all right, and it was the only way I could think of to make sure they'd let me know.'

'His granddaughter,' Brandon repeated. 'And you've accused me of lying?'

'This was a white lie. Justifiable.'

'Yeah. I suppose.' A rueful smile crossed his face. 'His granddaughter. I'll tell him that, tomorrow.'

'I'll tell him that, myself.' Zoe looked at him. His face was ashen; he looked tired, hungry and nearly out of his mind with worry. 'Have you eaten?'

'No. I was busy at the farm office – then I got the message about Gramps, and went straight to the hospital.' He shrugged. 'Eileen is off duty, now. I'll make myself a sandwich or something.'

For some obscure reason, Zoe suddenly wanted to make amends for doubting him. There was one way . . . She shook herself. Her head had to rule her heart, for once. And her libido. 'Come on. I'll drive you back to the house and make you an omelette.'

'Complete with arsenic?'

She grinned. 'Don't tempt me. No, I believe you – I don't think you did damage the equipment, or the trench.'

'But you think Mark did?'

She nodded. 'He's got the motive. And I think you need to know a little more about your business partner – he's not quite what you think he is.'

'Meaning?'

'Meaning you'll eat, first; then, when your blood-sugar's back to normal levels, your brain will be in a state to take in what I have to tell you. And then, we can decide what to do next.'

They walked back to Zoe's car in silence, but the anger and tension between them had dissolved. Zoe drove them to the farm, and Brandon let them both into the house. The dogs came rushing up to greet them; Zoe made a fuss of them, bending down and ruffling their fur.

'Hey, it's all right. Your master's going to be fine.' She looked at Brandon. 'Do you want to feed these two, while I cook you something?'

He grinned wryly. 'Make yourself at home, Zoe. You're in charge.'

She winced. 'Sorry. I'm just used—'

'To doing things your way. I noticed.' He bent down to fuss the dogs. 'Come on, hounds. Dinner time. Though at one point, I reckon she had me on the menu – for you.'

Zoe's mouth went dry. If it hadn't been for those last two softly added words, she could have sworn that Brandon was inviting her to . . .

She shook herself. Now was most definitely not the time to let her imagination go into overdrive. She busied herself in the kitchen, fixing a salad and preparing a fluffy cheese omelette while Brandon fed the dogs and laid the scrubbed pine table.

'I take it you're eating with me?'

'I . . .' Her voice tailed off, and she shook her head.

'Have you eaten?' He echoed her earlier question.

She shook her head again. 'At first, I was too angry; then, I was more concerned about Jack. I didn't feel like facing a meal in The Feathers.'

'Then you're eating with me. You've made enough there for two.' He took a loaf of crusty bread from the cupboard, and a bottle of white wine from the fridge.

Zoe felt suddenly shy when she came to sit at the table, bearing two plates; this was oddly intimate, and she had a nasty feeling that she could get used to it where Brandon was concerned. Though that was impossible. It would never work, and they both knew it.

'It's good,' Brandon said, after the first mouthful.

'Don't sound so surprised. Not all hack journos are smart-talking wise-crackers who can't do anything else.'

He chuckled. 'Ouch. I wouldn't describe you like that.'

Zoe didn't ask him how he would describe her. She wasn't sure that she wanted to know.

They ate in near-silence; finally, Brandon pushed his plate away, sated, and topped up their glasses.

Zoe looked at him. 'I'm driving.'

'A glass and a half is within limits. Unless you were drinking earlier?'

She shook her head. 'I was otherwise occupied.' She sighed. 'Brandon – I'm still not sure about any of this. I mean, in the village, they think you're some kind of god. The women do, anyway.'

He coughed. 'Listen, I'm not the squire who's decided to bed every maiden in the village, as of right, you know.'

'I don't mean that.' She rolled her eyes. 'But everyone speaks pretty highly of you. I don't understand why you're mixed up with that slimy bastard Burroughs.'

'He's been my financial adviser for about five years. He's been good, too – he's given me some excellent advice.' Brandon shrugged. 'We were talking, one day, about the village, and I suppose I was running on about my pet project, building back the community spirit in the village. Anyway, he suggested that we develop some of the land on the farm.'

'And what did you get out of it?'

'Part-share in the development.'

'He's out for profit, but your motives are different.' Zoe frowned. 'I can't see how they go together.'

'You can make money ethically, you know.'

'Yeah, right.' She scowled. 'That's why he did that bent survey.'

'Without the maps, it was perfectly legitimate.'

'Exactly. Without the maps. No shrewd businessman would accept a survey like that, without maps.'

Brandon winced. 'It's called trusting your partner. Like I said, Mark had played fair with me for the past five years. I didn't have any reason not to trust him.'

'The fact that no one else could stand the man didn't affect your judgement at all?'

'I've known a few people who've fallen foul of the village, had a reputation as a thug, and no one would give them a second chance,' Brandon said softly. 'I did. And they've all turned out okay.'

Zoe nodded. That was more or less what Dale had told her. 'Mark's not in the same league, though.' She bit her lip, remembering what she'd found out, that afternoon. 'I don't know how to tell you this.'

'Tell me what?'

'Did you know that Mark gambles?'

Brandon shrugged. 'It isn't a crime.'

'I'm talking about big-time gambling. Cards and casinos.'

'It's the circle he mixes in, I suppose. Finance.' Brandon didn't seem fazed.

How could she make him understand? 'I called in a couple

of favours, asked some friends to find out a few things for me about him. He's up to his neck in debt, Brandon. If your development doesn't go ahead, his business will go under. He's mortgaged to the hilt, and it wouldn't surprise me if he'd borrowed clients' money, too.'

'You're making some very serious accusations, Zoe. I hope you have the proof to back it up.'

'I do.' She sighed heavily. 'But it all makes sense, now. I suppose I knew you weren't the type to damage equipment and weaken that trench.'

'You accused me, anyway,' he reminded her.

'You were the obvious suspect. You had the motive, and you had the means – whereas Mark's a city boy who'd never get his shoes dirty.' She bit her lip. 'It's my guess that he paid someone to do it. Someone who knows the area; maybe someone with a grudge against you, who could fix it so that everyone thought you were to blame.'

'But I'm his business partner. If I went down, so would he,' Brandon pointed out. 'Without me, the development couldn't go ahead.'

'Couldn't it? He's a devious bastard, Brandon.'

'I vetted the contracts myself. So did my solicitor.'

'But who's to say that he didn't pull a fast one, like he did with the survey?' Zoe asked softly.

Brandon digested what she'd just said. 'If he had . . .'

'Then he had everything to gain by getting you out of the way. Not to mention Jack. For all we know, he could have had Jack in mind when he weakened the side of the trench.'

'I feel like beating the hell out of him for what he's done.'

'Join the queue,' Zoe said. 'But that won't solve anything.'

'We'll talk to the police, in the morning,' Brandon said grimly. 'Though you'd better have proof of what you're saying, or we'll end up with a libel action.'

'Settlement being one field, hm?' Zoe followed his train of thought. 'Don't worry, I've got all the proof you need.'

'I'm his business partner, and you thought I had something to do with it. What changed your mind?'

'The look on your face when you saw the trench,' Zoe admitted. 'Though I suppose I've always wanted to think you were . . . well, innocent.'

'Innocent in some ways,' Brandon said.

And completely knowledgeable in others. Zoe felt a shiver of desire ripple down her spine at the thought, and coughed to cover her confusion. 'We can't leave this mess for Eileen. I'll clear up,' she said.

Brandon helped her in silence; the uneasiness between them had changed back to awkwardness. Zoe couldn't help remembering the way he'd stripped her in his office, belting her hands to the desk and touching her in the most intimate way; she was aware that her nipples had hardened, and she was sure that Brandon could tell. The back of her neck grew hot; she was on tenterhooks, waiting for him to act. What was he thinking? Was he remembering, too?

She turned to put another plate on the draining board, and Brandon's hand brushed hers; the momentary contact was enough to push her pulse rate up another notch or two. She shivered, trying to concentrate on the washing up.

When it happened a second time, she realised that it was deliberate, on his part. She looked up at him, her green eyes widening; Brandon gave a muffled curse. 'I don't know what it is about, you, Zoe, but . . . Oh, hell.' He dropped the tea-towel and pulled her to him, moulding her body against his. 'I can't think straight when you're in the same room,' he told her, sliding one hand under her hair to stroke the nape of her neck. 'All I keep doing is seeing you, in my office, that time. The way you touched me. The way I touched you.'

'Don't,' Zoe said.

'Don't what? Don't tell you how I feel? Don't touch you? I can't help myself, Zoe. I don't care if you're off limits. I don't care if we're on opposite sides. I just . . .' He groaned, and bent his head, touching his mouth lightly to hers.

It was enough to break down the last of her defences. She slid her hands round his back, pulling him closer, and opened her mouth to allow him the access he wanted. He kissed her deeply, hungrily, his tongue pushing against hers; then he pulled back slightly, taking tiny nibbles at her lower lip, arousing her.

Zoe felt her breasts swelling and her nipples peaking to the point of pain; she longed to feel his hands there, his mouth, relieving her urgent need. As if he sensed it, he tilted his pelvis, rubbing his erect cock against her body and leaving her in no doubt that he felt the same way.

'Zoe, I want you, so badly,' he breathed. 'I want you in my bed, your hair spread over my pillows, your body scenting my sheets. I want to feel your body fusing with mine, see your eyes as you climax. I want you.'

'Yes,' was all she said.

Chapter Eleven

He kissed her again, hard, then took her hand and led her out of the kitchen. Part of her was faintly disappointed that he hadn't turned macho on her and carried her up to his bed, but the practical side of her knew that she'd be too heavy to carry up the stairs. Besides, she wanted him to conserve his strength for something else.

It took a long, long while to reach his bedroom. He stopped, every few steps, to kiss her and to undo a button or zip, caressing the skin he revealed with his fingertips and his mouth. Zoe did likewise, revelling in the feel of his skin under her fingertips. By the time they reached the top of the stairs, Zoe was wearing only her undone shirt and her bra with the cups pulled down to expose her breasts, just as she'd been that day in his office, and he was wearing only his underpants. There was a trail of their clothing all the way back down the stairs and the hall.

'More domesticated by the day,' Brandon murmured as he pushed his bedroom door open.

'What?' Zoe's mind wasn't working clearly.

'The first time . . . we were in the churchyard. Then my office. And now, you're where I really want you.' His eyes had darkened almost to black. 'One of the places, anyway.'

'One of the places.' She was aware that there was a stupid smile on her face, but it didn't matter. It was reflected on his own.

'Mm. As well as the bath, the shower and the kitchen table. Oh, and on the chamomile lawn, at the back of the house. The scent's amazing, particularly in summer.'

'You know that from experience, do you?'

'I haven't been a monk, Zoe.'

'No. I was warned that half the women in the village would drop their knickers for you if you clicked your fingers.'

He grinned. 'I haven't gone that far. Just one or two – and strictly on a no-strings basis.'

She took the hint. 'No strings. Haven't we said that before?'

'I don't know. I don't care,' he said simply. 'All I know is that my body craves you.' He slid one hand between her thighs, cupping her delta. 'And I think it's mutual. Your quim's warm and wet and beautiful, Zoe.'

'Silk and peaches,' she murmured.

'Hm?' He licked the hollow of her collarbone, tasting her skin.

'That's what you said before. That I remind you of silk and peaches.'

'And all sorts of things. Even doing the farm accounts makes me think of you.'

'That dull, am I?'

'Stop fishing.' He pushed his finger into her sex, and she shuddered with delight.

'Who's fishing?' She was aware that her voice was slurred slightly. Not through the wine – she'd barely touched her topped-up glass. Simply through the way he was touching her. It was like a drug, and she wanted more and more. 'Brandon.'

'Uh-huh.' He was lost in a dream of his own, she noticed. A dream about her.

She cupped his face, drawing his mouth down to hers and nibbling gently at his lower lip. He opened his mouth, giving her the access she wanted, and she kissed him deeply, exploring him with her tongue. He swivelled his thumb over her clitoris, making her gasp with pleasure; then he withdrew his hand from her sex, picking her up and carrying her over to the bed.

'Macho man,' she said.

He grinned, rubbing his nose against hers and removing her glasses, putting them on his bedside table. 'Complaining, are you, woman?'

As his hand cupped one breast, Zoe shivered. 'Yes.'

He flicked his fingertip against the hard peak of her nipple. 'Liar.'

'Mm.' She almost purred at his touch.

He bit her earlobe, making her arch against him, and

took advantage of her position to finish removing her shirt, dropping it on the floor next to the bed. Her bra went the same way, as did his underpants. 'That's better,' he said. 'Skin to skin.'

'Skin to skin,' she echoed, stroking his shoulders. He was muscular, but she knew that the muscles were due to hard work, not to pumping iron. His skin felt like velvet against her fingertips; she explored further, working down his spine and brushing the dimples at its base, then cupping his buttocks. 'You feel good, Brandon.'

'Indeed.' He rolled onto his back, giving her a lazy look through half-lowered lashes which gave her permission – no, incited her – to explore further. She settled on her side, next to him, letting her hand drift over his chest. His pectorals felt as good as his shoulders and buttocks, firm and hard; she drifted lower, over his abdomen, following the arrow of dark hair. There wasn't an ounce of fat on him: his body was perfectly toned, she thought.

She deliberately avoided the hard stem of his cock, moving down to caress his thighs instead.

'Tease,' he complained, moving so that he could kiss the top of her head.

'What did you want me to do, then?'

He grinned. 'I feel like a kid in sweetshop who's just been told he can have whatever he wants.'

'I didn't say that I'd actually do it,' she pointed out. 'I was just interested.'

'Oh, yeah?' He flipped her over onto her back, nudging a thigh between hers. 'If teasing's the game, I can play better than you.'

'Oh, yeah?' she mimicked.

'Yeah.' He pulled a face at her, making her laugh, then gently stroked her jawline. 'Zoe. You're lovely. Such soft, creamy skin.' His fingers cupped her throat for a moment, then drifted down to caress the hollows of her collar-bones. 'Beautiful. And here, you're like some incredible sculpture.' He bent his head to kiss her throat. 'You taste as good as you feel, too.' He cupped one breast, weighing it. 'The perfect voluptuary. All you need is the red hair, really, and I can imagine you as Boudicca. The woman with the cold and distant face befitting a queen – but her body's all fire, like

145

her eyes and her hair. Green fire, red fire – every colour, fusing into one.'

Boudicca. Her eyes narrowed. 'Brandon—'

'Sh. I don't want to fight you. Not right now. Later.' He dipped his head, taking one nipple into his mouth, playing the tip of his tongue against it. Zoe shifted slightly on the bed, making herself more comfortable, and he took advantage of her position to move to her other breast, teasing her nipple with his mouth.

Zoe pushed against him, arching her back, and he slowly trailed his mouth downwards, nuzzling the soft undersides of her breasts and then moving over her ribcage. She found it the most exquisite torture, knowing exactly what he was going to do next – just not how long it was going to take him to get there. She wriggled as he traced the outline of her navel with the tip of his nose, and tilted her pelvis impatiently; he grinned against her abdomen.

'More haste, less speed.'

'Tease.'

'I told you I could do it better. Believe me now?'

She was caught. If she said yes, she'd be submitting; if she said no, he'd dawdle even more before he finally used his mouth on her aching sex. Mind over matter, she told herself fiercely.

There was a brief argument between her mind and her body. Her body won. 'Yes,' she breathed. 'Now, will you stop teasing me? Please?'

'Nope.' He continued to take his time, moving down to her hip-bones and exploring every millimetre of her skin; then he purposely avoided her delta, moving down to her thighs and caressing them with his hands and mouth. Zoe whimpered in frustration. 'I told you once that anticipation's the best sauce,' he said softly. 'And it's only going to get better.'

She didn't quite believe him, but she had little choice in the matter; he was already licking the backs of her knees, and lifting her left leg, working very slowly down it. By the time he'd worked his way back up to her right knee, Zoe's sex was wet, puffy and throbbing with urgency. Still, he didn't hurry, taking a leisurely route back across her thighs; finally, she felt him breathing against her sex.

146

'Yes. Please. Please,' she begged.

He paused, as if he'd intended to make her ask him properly, explicitly; unable to bear the torture any more, Zoe pushed her hands into his hair, pulling him closer to her sex and thrust downwards.

'I can take a hint, you know,' she heard his muffled voice say. And then he stretched out his tongue, making it into a sharp point which travelled the full length of her quim, and she stopped thinking, merely revelling in the sensations his mouth was creating.

He explored her folds and hollows thoroughly, savouring her nectar and nipping gently at her labia with his lips; when he took her clitoris into his mouth and began to suck, she almost came, it felt so good. She urged him on, massaging his scalp in the same rhythm as his mouth moved over her sex; he began to lap at her clitoris, making his tongue swirl softly over it and flattening it against her pubic bone, then making his tongue into a hard point and moving it rapidly over the sensitive knot of nerves.

Zoe's climax took her by surprise, pulsing through her with a force that made her cry out. Brandon lifted his face, then, and she could see how his mouth was smeared and glistening with her juices. He smiled at her – a long, slow, sexy smile – and shifted up to kiss her mouth, so she could taste herself on him.

'Good?' he asked softly.

She couldn't speak; she merely nodded.

He stroked her face with the backs of his fingers. 'I haven't finished with you, yet. And that's a promise, not a threat.' He bent his head to kiss her again, then rolled her onto his back, pulling her on top of him so that she straddled him in a kneeling position. Her quim was still throbbing when he lifted her slightly, curling his fist round his cock and fitting its tip to the entrance of her sex; finally, he let her slide down very gently onto him.

'I'm all yours, Zoe,' he invited her softly. 'You set the pace.'

Slowly, she began to raise and lower herself over him. She could still remember the last time this had happened, under the stars. That time, too, he'd made sure that the first time was for her.

'Stop thinking,' he told her softly, pulling up into a sitting position so that he could kiss her. 'No thinking, no analysing. Just you and me, doing what we both want. What we both need.'

'I know,' she said wryly. 'I was just remembering.'

'The first time?' He rubbed the tip of his nose against hers. 'Yeah. Me too. Except I didn't realise then how addictive you are.'

'Addictive?'

'I can't get enough of you,' he told her, his voice husky. 'This is how I'd want to spend eternity. Making love with you. Feeling your sex ripple as you come, your internal muscles contracting round my cock and pushing me over the limit.'

'We don't have—' Zoe began, but he silenced her with a kiss.

'No analysing,' he said again. 'This is just for you and me. Right now.'

'Right now,' she agreed. Tomorrow, maybe she'd hate herself; maybe she'd hate both of them. But right now, the feel of his cock stretching her, filling her to the hilt, was so very good. She abandoned herself to pleasure, tipping herself back slightly to alter the angle of his penetration and then cupping her breasts.

He spread her hair over her shoulders, then slid one hand between their bodies to massage her clitoris, his other hand fondling the soft curves of her buttocks. 'Oh, yes. You feel so good,' he told her. 'And you look just as good as you feel. Wanton. Warm and sexy. I love the contrast of your skin, the way your hair's so dark and your skin's so creamy. And the way your nipples grow dark when you touch them.'

Zoe gave him a smile of pure wickedness, spreading her fingers and letting her nipples peep through them. 'Like this, you mean?'

'Exactly like that,' he agreed. 'And I love the look on your face when I touch you here.' He continued rubbing her clitoris. 'Your eyes go all dark, like emeralds melting into night. And your lower lip's all red and swollen. You look like every man's wet dream. Snow White just discovering her sexuality.'

'I think Snow White had blue eyes.'

He groaned. 'Zoe, shut up. I'm trying to pay you a compliment.'

She grinned. 'You don't have to use your mouth to pay me a compliment.'

His gaze held hers. 'Not good enough, was it?'

'I meant, in words.'

He laughed. 'Tell me, Zoe. Tell me you liked what I did to you.'

'I liked what you did to me.'

He licked his lower lip. 'Tell me properly.'

'All right. I liked the way you used your mouth on my sex.'

'Properly,' he insisted.

Zoe gave him a lascivious look. 'Okay, honey. I liked it the way you licked my cunt,' she drawled, in her best impersonation of Mae West. 'That what you wanted to know?'

'Yes.' He smiled, and reached up to touch her lips; his fingers still smelt of her arousal. 'I don't know whether I like it more when that beautiful mouth talks dirty to me – or when it's being used on my body.'

'Any part in particular?'

'This part.' He pushed up into her.

'Don't say you're going shy on me,' she teased.

'Oh, no. Not in the least.' He stroked her back. 'I can't get enough of you, Zoe Lynton. What did you put in that omelette?'

'Eggs, cheese and milk,' she responded, dead-pan.

He grinned. 'And I like your sense of humour. I like a lot of things about you, Zoe. It's not just physical between us.' He shivered as she continued to ride him. 'Though, right now, I'm fast losing control.'

Me, too, Zoe thought. Me, too. She began working her internal muscles round him, tightening them as she pulled up, then relaxing her body as she slammed down again, hard, grinding her pubis against his. She rocked her body against his, moving faster and faster; he twisted his head against the pillow, baring his teeth.

'Zoe – I can't hold back much longer,' he muttered, the words almost ripped from him.

'Then don't,' she said huskily. 'I want to see your face as

you come. I want to see your eyes.' She reached over to cup his face; he looked up at her, and she saw his pupils dilate at the instant his cock began to throb inside her. His mouth opened in a cry of pleasure; as she felt her own climax begin to shimmer through her, she lowered her head, kissing him deeply.

When the aftershocks of their climax had died away and his cock had slipped from her, she allowed Brandon to roll her onto her side and hold her close. She settled with her head on his shoulder and her arm thrown loosely over his waist.

He moved his head to kiss her ear. 'I could stay like this all night,' he said.

She suddenly realised how late it was. 'God. I have to be—'

'You don't have to be anywhere,' he told her softly. 'Betty won't mind if you stay out all night. She won't quiz you – she's the soul of discretion.'

'I know, but . . .' Zoe flushed.

'Stay with me,' Brandon said huskily. 'I've had a hell of a day. So have you. Let's comfort each other.'

'But—'

'Don't argue with me, Zoe. Please. Not now.' He stroked her face. 'I need you, tonight. And I think you need me, too.'

'Yes,' she admitted, eventually.

They lay in companionable silence for a while; then Brandon shifted again so that he was lying on his side, facing her. He rubbed the tip of his nose against hers. 'I don't know what you do to me,' he said quietly, 'but I should be almost comatose. Instead, I feel alive and awake . . . and I want a shower. With you.'

Zoe remembered the fantasy she'd had about him in the shower, and desire rippled down her spine. 'With me,' she repeated.

'Mm. I'd like a jacuzzi with you, actually, but I'm afraid Whiteacres just has a functional bathroom. Not even a sunken marble thing.'

Her lips twitched. 'Farmers are always complaining about how poor they are – the weather's always either too dry or too wet for crops. No wonder you can't afford any luxuries.'

'No wonder,' he agreed, his eyes sparkling with amusement. 'So . . . will you wash my back for me? Please? I'll wash yours, too.'

She grinned. 'As you put it so nicely, how can I refuse?'

'Good.' He kissed her lightly, then climbed out of the bed, taking her hand as she followed suit.

She eyed the trail of clothing as they left the room. 'Oh, God.'

He smiled ruefully. 'Looks like we both got carried away.'

'We'd better—'

'I'll do it later,' he cut in. 'Before Eileen comes in, in the morning.'

'Eileen. God, I'd better not be here when—'

'Zoe. I thought journalists weren't supposed to mind what people think?'

She flushed. 'I . . .'

He kissed her. 'You're deliciously teasable. Delicious, full stop.'

He led her into the bathroom: as he'd told Zoe, it was plain and functional, but she could imagine what it would look like, given a designer's free hand. Black and white tiled flooring, an original roll-top claw-footed Victorian bath, colour-washed walls and—'

She stopped herself. What was happening between them was – well, far from permanent. No strings. It was pointless redecorating his house in her mind. It wouldn't happen in real life.

'Hey. Don't look so serious. It isn't *that* bad,' he said, spinning her round to face him.

'No.'

He switched the shower on, letting the water heat up before lifting her into the bath and joining her. 'I can imagine you in a Roman bath,' he said. 'Reclining while a slave tended to your every need, cleaning your skin and pouring clean warm water over you.'

'Oh, yes?'

'Mm.' He squeezed shower gel into his cupped palm, rubbed his hands together to make it lather, then smoothed it over her skin. 'Like this.' He washed her slowly, tenderly, everywhere from the curve of her neck down to the hollows of her ankles. Zoe arched her back as he smoothed down

151

her spine, gently kneading her buttocks; he spun her round to face him, then worked on her breasts, teasing her nipples into hardness as he washed her. When he washed between her legs, Zoe felt her sex grow warm and puffy again.

He smiled knowingly at her, then unhooked the shower head, directing the jet between her legs. He held her labia apart, playing the water over her clitoris; Zoe moaned his name, and his smile broadened. He continued to tease her with the water, arousing her still further; finally, her knees buckled slightly, and she climaxed sharply.

'That was unfair,' she said.

'I didn't touch you.'

'You knew exactly what you were doing,' she accused.

'Mm.' He leant forward to kiss the tip of her nose. 'Wash my back for me, sweetheart?'

It was a request rather than a command; Zoe complied, revelling in the touch of his skin as she soaped him and then sluiced the lather away. He shivered as she stroked his back and buttocks, copying his earlier actions, then turned him round to face her.

His cock reared from the cloud of hair at his groin; she gave him a wicked look, then lathered her hands again and began to wash the hard rod thoroughly. He closed his eyes as her hand slid back and forth over the shaft, and moaned aloud when she cupped his balls, massaging them to the same rhythm. He clenched his fists as she continued to masturbate him; finally, his balls lifted and tightened, and he opened his eyes again as he came, pearly white fluid covering her body.

Lasciviously, she massaged it into her breasts and belly. 'It's the best moisturiser there is,' she said. 'Full of protein.'

'You're incredible, Zoe,' he told her, his voice hoarse as he washed her clean. 'The way you make me feel . . .' He pulled her to him, kissing her hard and lifting her, balancing her weight against the wall. She wrapped her legs round his waist, kissing him back and pushing her hands into his hair.

When he was hard again, he guided his cock into her sex, slamming in fast and taking her roughly against the tiles; Zoe matched him thrust for thrust, urging him on with her heels against his buttocks. He took her to another shattering climax and another, then finally withdrew and cleaned her up again. Then he switched off the shower, climbed out of the bath and wrapped a large fluffy bath towel round her before lifting her out of the bath. He dried her thoroughly, finally towelling her hair into a cloud, then kissed the tip of her nose. 'This is what I'm going to be thinking about, all day tomorrow. My accountant's going to wonder what the hell's put such a smile on my face.'

'Indeed.'

He towelled himself dry, then led her back into his bedroom. 'But, right now, all I want to do is sleep, with you in my arms.'

She kissed him lightly. 'Sweet dreams.'

'Oh, they will be,' he said, as he turned out the bedside light. 'They will be.'

Chapter Twelve

The next morning Zoe woke, stretched luxuriously, and opened her eyes. She frowned, not recognising her surroundings: then sat bolt upright as she remembered. She was in Brandon's bed, at Whiteacres. Naked. And she was alone.

She looked round the room. Her clothes were neatly folded on a chair, and her glasses were on the bedside table. Of Brandon, there was no sign. Only the dent in the pillow next to her gave her any indication that he'd slept there. That, and the pleasurable ache of her body, testifying how many times they'd made love the previous night.

Even thinking about it made her wet. She smiled wryly. Brandon had said something to her about addiction. She was just as much of a junkie as he was, craving the release his body could give her. But where the hell was he?

She glanced at her watch. It was nearly seven. He was probably in the farm office, sorting out something or other, but had decided to let her sleep in. He could have left her a note, she thought ruefully. Or maybe he just thought that she'd be able to work out where he was.

She dressed quickly, not wanting to be at the farm when Eileen arrived. It wasn't that she was ashamed of what she'd done with Brandon: more that she didn't want to answer any awkward questions or embarrass Eileen. She had just enough time to make them both some coffee and toast, she thought, and then she could be on her way, back to The Feathers, with no one any the wiser about where she'd spent the night.

On her way down the stairs, she heard the phone ring in the hall. Then the answerphone clicked in.

'Brandon, it's Mark. Sorry I didn't get back to you, last night. I was with a client. You know how it is.' He chuckled.

'I suppose it's about that Lynton woman – well, you know how to deal with her, like we discussed. You've got most of the women in the village panting for you; she'll be just the same. Have your way with her. Then maybe she'll get off our case. Ring me back when you get a moment.'

Her eyes widened. Discussed? What the hell did he mean, *discussed*? Had what had happened between her and Brandon been a set-up, orchestrated by Mark Burroughs? Did they both think that she'd be so overcome by lust for Brandon that if he took her to his bed, she'd forget all about the site?

As the answerphone clicked off again, she scowled. The dogs were nowhere to be seen; she assumed that they were with Brandon. Well, if he was expecting her to take him a cup of coffee and breakfast, he'd have another think coming. Now she knew what his game was, and it left a nasty taste in her mouth. A very nasty taste. He'd lied to her consistently, and she'd believed him. How the hell could she have let herself be duped like that?

She drove back to The Feathers without bothering to go to the farm office to confront him. She really didn't trust herself to face him; all she wanted to do was reassure herself that Jack would be all right, talk to the police, and then head back to London.

The police. Brandon had talked about going to the police, the previous evening. He really was a consummate actor, she thought savagely. He'd made her believe that he was innocent, when he'd been in on the deal all the time. And as for that nonsense about wanting to sleep with her in his arms – well, if he'd cared that much, if he'd been genuine, he would have left her a note.

Angrily, she drove past The Feathers and headed for the city, instead. An hour later, she'd given a statement at Norwich police station that would have Mark Burroughs convicted for fraud, criminal damage and actual bodily harm. It would certainly put paid to the development. What it would mean for Brandon . . . she just didn't care any more.

She called in to a couple of shops on her way to the hospital; Jack was delighted to see her, and appreciative of both the flowers and the book on Boudicca she brought him.

'Zoe! Thank you for coming. How are you?'

'Fine, thanks,' she lied. 'More to the point, how are you?'

'I'll live.' He rolled his eyes. 'It's just a broken leg.'

'Just?'

'It could have been worse,' he said wryly. 'I suppose it's my own fault for being a silly old fool and tottering around the fields.'

'It's far from being your fault.'

He picked up on her grim tone. 'How do you mean?'

She explained about the weakened trench side. She couldn't quite bring herself to tell him about Brandon's betrayal, so she concentrated on Mark, instead. 'The survey was completely false – he'd had the wrong field done, deliberately. I've spoken to the police, and the development won't be able to go ahead until the case comes to court; so in the meantime, we can finish the excavations. As for what'll happen to Mark – I don't know and I don't care. He'll certainly pay for trying to act like a mobster and dealing underhand. I think his licence to trade will be revoked – there's no way you can be in financial services, with a record of fraud – and I know he's in debt up to his eyeballs.'

'Does Brandon know any of this?'

'I expect so,' Zoe said lightly. 'Anyway, I really called in to say goodbye. I need to head back to London.'

'But you'll be back, won't you?'

'I . . . I don't know,' she admitted. Part of her wanted to – she'd taken a liking to Jack and Eileen, as well as several other people in Lower Yareham – but she couldn't face Brandon again. Not after the way he'd lied to her. 'I'll keep in touch, though.'

'Just make sure that you do,' he said.

She kissed him on the cheek. 'Take care.'

'I don't think I'll have any choice. Eileen will see to that,' Jack said ruefully.

'Good.' She smiled at him, and left the ward.

Her final call in Norwich was to Shannon; over a coffee and a pastry that she barely touched, she outlined events to the local journalist, who made swift notes and said that she'd keep Zoe informed about developments on the site.

Then she drove back to The Feathers in silence, not even bothering with the radio. Her throat hurt with unshed tears, and she was torn between wanting to cry and wanting to

156

punch Brandon, hard. She packed her bags swiftly, then went downstairs to settle her bill with Betty.

'Going already?' Betty was surprised. 'I thought you were staying until the dig was finished.'

'No. I need to be back in London. Work calls,' Zoe said. 'But thanks for your hospitality.'

'Brandon called. He left a message for you, asking if you'd ring him.' Betty gave her a perceptive look. 'It's none of my business and I'm not going to interfere, but if the reason you're going so quickly has anything to do with him—'

'It hasn't,' Zoe lied, interrupting her. 'I really do have to get back to London. Thanks for everything, Betty.'

'It's been a pleasure, love.' Betty looked concerned. 'Are you all right, Zoe?'

'I'm fine, thanks,' Zoe lied again, She was very far from fine. She was furious and hurt and miserable, all at the same time. 'Well – thanks again.' She said goodbye to Sam; she was half tempted to call in at the doctor's surgery, but decided that it wouldn't be a good idea. It would only fuel village gossip and, although she wouldn't have to live with it, Dale would. She decided to send him a postcard instead – in a sealed envelope – when she got back to London.

Roadworks and contraflow systems on the A12 meant that she had to concentrate on the drive home; she was grateful for them rather than annoyed, because it meant that she didn't have time to think about Brandon and his betrayal.

By the time she parked in her road, she was tired and aching; she had just about enough energy to drop her bag in the hall and run herself a bath. She hadn't told Steve that she was on her way back, so she was unsurprised to find no milk in the fridge; she made herself a black coffee, which revived her slightly, then stripped off for a bath.

That was her first mistake. It brought the memories flooding back: the way she and Brandon had made love in the large functional bathroom at Whiteacres, with him using the shower to arouse her still further. She closed her eyes, grimacing. So much for being a hard-headed, intelligent woman. She'd just let her libido run loose, carrying her on its rush of energy, and ignored every warning sign about Brandon.

'Hell,' she growled. She scrubbed herself clean and climbed out of the bath, not wanting to wallow in the bubbles. That would be fatal: she knew that she'd only start thinking of Brandon, and she didn't want her body to take over from her mind again. What she needed was action. Anything to stop her thinking. She dressed swiftly, then grabbed her notebook and went into the sitting room.

There were a number of messages on the answerphone – as well as a list of messages, in Steve's half-legible writing. She smiled to herself. Good old Steve. At least he was one man she could rely on. He'd obviously checked her answerphone when he'd kept an eye on the house, knowing that her tape would fill quickly and not wanting her to miss anything. They were nearly all work-related – her friends all knew that she'd taken a brief sabbatical and would be in touch when she got back from Norfolk – and she put them in priority order.

Next, she checked her email, doing the same thing. Then she sorted through a pile of post next to the kettle, throwing away all the circulars and putting the rest into priority order, separating personal mail from business mail.

And finally, she decided to clean the flat. Housework was far from being her favourite activity, but she wanted to make sure that she was really tired, that night. Tired enough not to think about Brandon – or dream about him.

It worked: she slept well, that night. But in the morning, all the memories surfaced again. How she'd woken, the previous day, realised that she was still in his bed – and realised that she was alone. How she'd worked out that he was probably already in the farm office and hadn't wanted to disturb her sleep, and how she'd planned to make them both breakfast. Until she'd heard that message from Mark Burroughs. The message that proved to her, beyond all doubt, that Brandon was as untrustworthy as his business partner, and the whole thing had been a set-up.

An hour later, she was in the *Archetypes* office, sitting in Steve's chair and amusing herself by changing the screen-saver on his PC.

'Zoe!' he said, shocked, when he came out of his meeting and saw her at his desk. 'I didn't know you were planning to

158

head back yet. I thought you'd still be in the wilds of Norfolk, poking round little churches.'

'Nice to see you too, Steve,' she said.

He smiled at her. 'Someone got out of bed the wrong side this morning. Coffee?'

'Please.' She winced. 'Sorry. I shouldn't take it out on you. Thanks for looking after the house for me – and for taking all those messages.'

'Pleasure. You could read them, I assume?'

She grinned wryly. 'I'm one of the half-dozen people in the world who can decipher your messy scrawl.'

'Yeah.' He put the kettle on, then sat on the edge of his desk, looking at her. 'So what brings you back so early?'

'A few developments.' Quickly, Zoe outlined what had happened with the trench and the survey; she skated over what had happened between her and Brandon. 'It looks like the excavation can go ahead without having to be rushed now,' she said. 'So there really wasn't much point in my hanging around. Anyway, it was about time I came back.'

'You haven't been away that long. Not even long enough for the average summer holiday,' Steve pointed out.

'Yeah, well.' He looked at her. 'Are you sure you're all right, Zoe?'

She nodded. 'I'm fine.' It was a lie, and they both knew it. Zoe had to distract him – and quickly. There was one sure-fire way, but not in the middle of the *Archetypes* office. She smiled at him, choosing the other fail-safe method. 'I've nearly finished that article on the wall paintings.'

As she'd hoped, Steve took the bait and spent the next ten minutes talking to her about which issue it could appear in, how long it needed to be, and what he thought of the pictures she'd taken earlier in the week. Then she took her leave, pleading that she had a lot of people to see and a lot to catch up on. It was true, to some extent: but she knew that Steve wouldn't give up until he had the full story from her. The full story, which she really didn't feel like repeating. Having someone make a fool of her was one thing: but to fall so heavily for him, as well . . . She was hurt, embarrassed and angry, and didn't want to talk about it.

She half-expected there to be a message on her answerphone,

when she returned, but the light on the little machine wasn't flashing. She scowled. She was being ridiculous. Of course Brandon wouldn't ring her. Even if he knew her home phone number – which he couldn't possibly, because she hadn't given it to Jack, and no one in the *Archetypes* office would give out her phone number without checking with her first – there was no way he'd call. Not after she'd shopped his business partner to the police and ruined the development. And not when he knew that she knew that he'd duped her.

She moped around the flat feeling listless and angry with herself for being miserable over someone like Brandon. Yes, the sex had been good, but she could get that just as well elsewhere. Steve, for a start: he was a good lover, and her friend, to boot.

And yet the chemistry between them wasn't as explosive as it had been between her and Brandon.

She swore loudly; it didn't make her feel any better. Neither did going into central London and doing serious damage to her credit card bill in half a dozen small and exclusive shops. The designer silk lingerie, half a pound of expensive seventy per cent cocoa chocolate, six CDs, three pairs of shoes and a pair of black leather trousers didn't make her feel any better at all.

'Get a grip, Lynton,' she told herself savagely when she returned home and dropped her bags in the hall. She put her favourite Del Amitri CD on at high volume, thinking that it would cheer her up to bop around the sitting room to it – but it was a mistake. Justin Currie's voice was like melted chocolate, and so sexy that it reminded her of Brandon. Brandon in the churchyard, his voice urgent and insistent. Brandon in his office, when he was kissing her and holding her against the door and stripping her: then when he was fantasising about what he wanted to do to her. Brandon in his bed. In his shower, making love with her – arousing her body to fever pitch, and then some.

Grinding her teeth, she ejected the CD from the player and took it upstairs. She had to get that man out of her system – and there was a quick way to abate him for a little while. She slammed the CD into the player in her bedroom, whacked up the volume, closed the curtains and stripped swiftly. She pulled the duvet from her bed, took her vibrator from her bedside cupboard, and switched it on.

The little machine failed to hum. She turned it off, shook it, and tried again. Still it refused to buzz. 'Well, who needs batteries, anyway?' she snarled. She flung herself on her bed, closed her eyes, and spread her legs. She pushed the tip of the plastic against her sex: the music was enough to arouse her, and she was already wet. 'And who needs *you*, Brandon Mitchell?' she sneered as the vibrator slid in all the way to the hilt.

Deftly, she worked the little machine, thrusting it in and out in time to the wailing guitar and the sexy voice on her stereo. She placed the soles of her feet flat on the mattress, arching her back on the bed and tilting her pelvis as she plunged the geloid vibrator in as deeply as she could.

The next track was slower, with the backing of a harmonica and a soft bluesy piano; in response, she slowed the furious pace of her thrusting, tipping her head back hard against the pillow and squeezing her eyes tightly shut. She rubbed her clitoris with the thumb of her other hand, as she continued to push the vibrator into her, trying hard not to think about Brandon and fantasise about some other man. One of the actors or rock stars that she and her friend Lissy had fancied, in their student days; Steve, Curtis, one of her past lovers. Anyone but him.

At last, her movements and the music had the desired effect; she gave a small groan as her internal muscles flexed against the plastic. As the aftershocks of her climax died away, she relaxed against the bed, still keeping her eyes shut and listening to the music. When the CD finished, she removed the vibrator, then picked up the phone, dialling a number rapidly.

It was answered on the third ring; she grinned to herself. Alicia was definitely in efficient librarian mode today. 'Hello, UCL Library, Alicia Field speaking.'

'Lissy, it's Zoe.'

'Hi! I thought you were off chasing a story, completely inaccessible to the modern world? At least, that's what your email said.'

'I was. I'm back now. Are you busy tonight?'

'I've got nothing more exciting planned than a pile of ironing. Why?'

'What time can you finish work?'

'About half six.'

'Good. See you in Leicester Square, outside the Häagen-Dazs café, at seven. We're going for large quantities of pasta, even larger quantities of wine, and ice-cream. My shout.'

'Okay.' Alicia paused. 'Zoe, you sound a bit . . . well, flat. Are you all right?'

'Yup. See you tonight.' Zoe put the phone down before her friend could quiz her any further.

Seven o'clock saw Zoe waiting at the appointed spot. When Alicia arrived a couple of minutes later she hugged her friend, then stood back and scrutinised her.

'Crisis level nine and a half out of ten – right?'

Zoe decided to play it cool. 'How do you mean?'

'Don't lie to me, Zoe. I've known you for too long.' Alicia had shared a room with Zoe during their undergraduate days, and they'd remained good friends ever since. She was definitely Zoe's best female friend, and ranked as highly as Steve in Zoe's life, with the exception that Zoe had never slept with Alicia. 'From the look of you, you've given your credit card one hell of a hammering.' Zoe was wearing her new black leather trousers, high-heeled black leather lace-up ankle boots and a black chiffon shirt which showed off rather than concealed her black lacy push-up bra. She was also wearing more make-up than usual and had left her glasses at home. 'What's his name?'

Zoe smiled wryly. 'What makes you think that it's a bloke?'

'Unless your sexual orientation's changed in the past fortnight, which I can't see, why else would you be dressed to kill? And your invitation out, tonight – that's a classic Lynton cheering-up idea.' She eyed Zoe's trousers. 'They're gorgeous. They also look new – and bloody expensive.'

'They were,' Zoe admitted. 'Though you know I've wanted a pair for ages.'

'Ever since we saw Del Amitri, and we could only get right at the back, and you didn't have your glasses on, so you reckoned that Justin Currie looked like Fox Mulder in black leather trousers, and spent the next month fantasising about him and that incredibly sexy voice,' Alicia teased. 'I wonder what your neighbours had to put up with, when you got back from the shops?'

'They were out, actually, so they didn't have to put up with anything,' Zoe said. 'But yeah, I was playing the last three Del Amitri albums.'

Alicia knew the shorthand of old. Zoe was seriously unhappy about something, if she was playing CDs that she could sing to and bop around the house to and cry to, depending on which tracks she'd chosen. 'You definitely need that wine, then.' She brushed her chestnut hair from her eyes. 'And I've had a crap day, with students being lippy and my boss changing his mind half a dozen times about what he wanted . . . so I do, too.'

'Come on. Dinner,' Zoe said, linking her arm through her friend's.

Once installed in one of the pasta cafés in Leicester Square, and half a bottle of wine later, Alicia looked at her friend, her grey-green eyes perceptive. 'Time to talk. Tell Aunty Lissy.' It went without saying that their conversation would be in complete confidence. They were old enough friends not to need to ask.

Zoe sighed. 'I've really screwed up this time.'

'Work?' Alicia was surprised.

'Not exactly. You know I went off to Norfolk on one of Steve's hare-brained ideas . . . well, there's a pretty good chance he was right.'

'Is Steve the problem?'

Zoe shook her head. 'We've got it about right between us. No strings.'

'Who is he, then?'

Zoe gave her a potted explanation about Whiteacres, Brandon, Jack and Mark Burroughs. Alicia burst out laughing when Zoe told her about Helena's seduction bid, but sobered again when Zoe finished her tale, ending with Mark's incriminating answerphone message and her walking out of Whiteacres.

'You were serious about him, then.' It was a statement rather than a question.

Zoe sighed. 'I was a bloody fool, Lissy. I don't know what's upset me more: that Brandon took me in like that, or . . .' She didn't finish her sentence, and Alicia was too tactful to do it for her. What was upsetting Zoe was that she'd fallen for Brandon, hard.

'I'm not standing up for the guy – he's behaved like a shit – but is there any chance that it might be some kind of misunderstanding?' Alicia asked.

'I doubt it.' Zoe pulled a face, and took a deep draught of wine. 'I thought I was a good judge of character.'

'You are.'

'So how did I get it so wrong?' She scowled and answered her own question. 'Pheromones.'

Alicia reached over the table and squeezed her hand. 'Hey. We all do it.'

'Yeah.' Zoe gave her a rueful smile. 'I didn't intend to spend all night whinging.'

'Yes, you did, or you would have called Steve and seduced him,' Alicia informed her with a grin. 'You wanted a girly night: wine and talk and sympathy.'

'I thought it was supposed to be "tea and sympathy"?'

'Not in our case,' Alicia said, laughing.

'No.'

Zoe spent the rest of the evening flirting outrageously with their attractive waiter – who was a good ten years younger than them, she reckoned: probably a second-year student topping up his grant – and drinking far too much wine. Alicia encouraged her, knowing that it would do her friend good to talk rather than bottle it up and pretend to bury herself in work.

'Large quantities of pasta, even larger quantities of wine.' Zoe beamed, when they'd finished. 'And now, ice-cream.'

'I don't know if I can. I haven't got my professional eating trousers on,' Alicia groaned.

'Neither have I – but it's not going to stop me. You can either join me, or watch me,' Zoe said, 'and I prefer it to be the former.'

'You,' Alicia said, 'are bloody bad for my diet. I'm glad I don't go out with you like this more than once a month.'

'Life's too short for dieting. And for giving up things you enjoy.' Zoe spread her hands. 'And for being sensible all the time.' A trace of hurt flickered across her face, and she balled her fists for a moment, until her feelings were back under control. Bloody Brandon. She wasn't going to let him spoil a night out with her best female buddy. 'If I'd been sensible, I would have ignored Steve. And I'd have missed the story of the century.'

'So you reckon this grave really is there?'

'The dig isn't finished yet – but, yes, I'm pretty sure.'

'It's the stuff of dreams. Like me going through the archives at work and finding some long-forgotten Brontë letters,' Alicia said. 'I'm really envious.'

'It isn't a hundred per cent certain,' Zoe said.

'But your gut feel's almost never wrong.'

Except where Brandon Mitchell was concerned, Zoe thought, suppressing a sigh. 'Yeah, well. Ice-cream,' she said firmly. She called for the bill, signed the credit card slip with a flourish, then left the waiter an outrageously large tip. In return, the waiter gave her a small booklet.

'Special offers,' he said. 'And my phone number's on the back.'

Zoe grinned. 'I'll remember that,' she said.

'*Ciao*, baby.' He blew her a kiss.

'I'm beginning to feel green, round and hairy,' Alicia said as they left the pasta café.

Zoe shook her head. 'He's not my type.'

'It might make you feel better,' Alicia suggested.

'Mindless sex with a gorgeous man?' Zoe took a deep breath. 'I think I've done that enough, these past few days. As far as I'm concerned, men can be replaced by six inches of plastic, a good imagination and a decent selection of CDs.'

Alicia winced. 'Not all men are complete bastards.'

'No. There's Steve. And I'm sure our waiter is a sweetie, in his way. Or maybe he flirts like that with all his female customers in the hope of large tips to supplement his grant, the poor sod.'

'I think he was more bowled over by what you're wearing,' Alicia remarked. 'I might as well be wearing a tweed skirt and brogues, with my hair in a bun.'

Zoe grinned. 'If you ever turned up at work like that, even for a bet, you'd never live it down.'

'I know.'

Two ice-cream sundaes later, Zoe was more cheerful. 'Thanks, Lissy.'

'What for?'

'Putting up with me in this mood.'

Alicia grinned. 'I've known you in worse. And you've done the same for me.'

'Yeah.' Zoe glanced at her watch. 'How early do you have to be at work tomorrow?'

'Early shift. Eight on the dot,' Alicia said. 'Why?'

'I was going to suggest going clubbing,' Zoe said, 'but it wouldn't be fair to make you face the rush hour *and* an early start with a hangover.'

'You hate clubbing, anyway.'

'Looks like I'll be winding up the neighbours, then. Or putting a long lead on my headphones,' Zoe said. As Alicia was about to protest, Zoe held up her hand. 'I'm fine, Lissy. Really. It helped a lot, just talking about it. The man's out of my system now.'

They both knew that she was lying; but eventually, Zoe persuaded Alicia that she'd be fine, and would call her tomorrow. They caught the tube in opposite directions; although Zoe attracted more than her share of admiring glances, the look on her face was enough to warn the men concerned that it was strictly look and not touch – in fact, not even approach.

When Zoe arrived home the answerphone was flashing. Her heart leapt – then sank again when it turned out to be a business message.

'Get a grip, Lynton,' she told herself sternly. Her attention was caught by the special offer booklet from the pasta café, which had fallen from her handbag; she was half-tempted to ring the telephone number on the back, but decided not to. There was no point in complicating her life still further, and she'd probably despise herself even more in the morning.

Ruefully, she went upstairs, stripped and cleaned off her make-up. No. Mindless sex, fun though it might be at the time, wasn't going to help. She'd just use her work to keep herself from thinking. Luckily she'd remembered to buy some batteries, while she'd been waiting to meet Alicia . . .

166

Chapter Thirteen

Two days later, Zoe changed her mind. She was looking through her handbag for some stamps when she came across the pasta café's special offer booklet with the telephone number and a name scrawled hastily on the back. Whatever she'd said to Alicia, she didn't really believe men could be replaced by six inches of plastic. She missed the warmth of another body holding hers in the afterglow of orgasm.

She knew that she could always ring Steve, but it wasn't fair to make love with him. Not when she was constantly thinking of another man. She didn't want to ruin their friendship. But the young waiter was another proposition entirely: it could be a mutual, no-strings arrangement . . . She glanced at her watch. It was half past ten. If she was right, and he was a student, there was a chance he'd be at home, before going to a lecture. On impulse, she dialled the number.

The phone rang nine times, ten; she was about to hang up when the receiver was picked up and a male voice mumbled, "Lo?'

'Hello. Is Gareth there, please?'

'Dunno. Hang on.' There was a lengthy pause; finally, he returned. 'No. He's gone to lectures. Do you want to leave a message?'

'I . . . No. What time's he likely to be back?'

'God knows. Try him about six,' the voice suggested. 'Sure you don't want to leave a message?'

'It's all right. Thanks for your help.' Zoe put the phone down. Maybe she'd had a lucky escape. She wasn't thinking straight or acting sensibly. If Gareth had been there to take her call, what then?

'Ah, forget it,' she said, and headed for her PC.

* * *

Six o'clock that evening, she grinned ruefully at herself. She knew that she was going to ring that number again. She'd been thinking about Gareth all day, wondering and fantasising. Quickly, she dialled it; again, there was a long pause before it was answered. She could hear music in the background, some kind of Britpop; and it was the same voice answering, although this time he sounded much less hung-over.

'Can I speak to Gareth, please?'

'Yeah, hang on. I'll get him for you.' There was a pause. 'You rang this morning, didn't you?'

'Er – yes.'

'Right.' There was a trace of amusement in the voice. 'Just a minute, then.'

A long minute later, she heard another voice. 'Hello?'

'Gareth?'

'Yes?'

'It's Zoe. You gave me your number the other night, in the pasta café.'

There was a pause, then a surprised. 'Oh! The woman in black, right?'

'Yes. I – er – was wondering what the special offers might be.'

There was a pause. 'This isn't a wind-up, is it?' His voice was filled with suspicion.

'No, it's not a wind-up. I wondered if you fancied having a drink, that's all.'

'Yes. Yes, I'd love to.'

'Are you free tonight?'

'Sorry – I'm working. I might be able to swap shifts, though.'

'How about tomorrow night?'

'Tomorrow's fine. Where do you want to meet?'

'Wherever. Do you know any good places?'

'There's the Kirtle and Kettle, just round the corner from me – oh, I'm in Ealing. Where are you?'

'Doesn't matter. I'll meet you at the Kirtle and Kettle at seven o'clock tomorrow night.' She paused. 'I'll need directions, though.'

'Sure.' He began to rattle off a string of directions, then stopped. 'Sorry. I should take it slower.'

'That's okay. Carry on. I can do shorthand.'

'You're a secretary?' He sounded shocked. 'You – well, I'd never have taken you for one.'

'I'm a journalist,' she told him, laughing. 'Don't be so sexist.'

'Sorry. Secretaries are the only people I know who do shorthand.'

'Well, you learn something new every day,' she quipped lightly.

'Right.' He gave her the rest of the directions. 'See you tomorrow night in the bar, then?'

At ten past seven the next evening, Zoe strolled in to the Kirtle and Kettle. Gareth was sitting at the bar, nursing a pint and glancing towards the door every so often. He was as nice-looking as she remembered, with floppy light brown hair, green eyes and a very winning smile; he was dressed in the typical student garb of jeans and T-shirt. Something very similar to her own, she thought with a smile.

'Hello, Gareth,' she said, coming to stand beside him.

'I . . . Zoe?' He looked surprised.

She grinned, guessing at the reason for the look on his face. 'You weren't expecting me to wear *that* outfit to go out for a pint, were you?'

He flushed. 'I suppose not.'

She chuckled. 'I don't normally dress like that, actually. I'd just had a shit day and wanted to indulge myself a bit.'

'Right.' He smiled at her. 'What can I get you, then?'

'A bottle of Bud, please.'

He ordered her drink. 'I didn't think you'd call me.'

'No?'

'What would a sophisticated woman in leather trousers want with a waiter in a pasta café?'

Her grin broadened. 'That'd be telling. Why did you give me your number, then?'

'Hope?'

She chuckled. She was going to like Gareth, she knew. 'Lissy – that's my friend – and I reckoned you were a second-year student supplementing your grant.'

He nodded. 'That obvious, was it?'

'An educated guess. I did part-time barmaiding during my degree.'

'In leather trousers?'

She laughed. 'I didn't buy them to impress men.'

He gave her a searching gaze. 'You don't look like a dyke.'

'I'm not,' she said simply. 'I bought them to please myself.'

'Fair enough.'

Over the next hour or so, she learnt that Gareth was reading history, loved his course, wanted to be a researcher for historical TV documentaries, and shared a house in Ealing with four other male students and a cat. She took a liking to his easy-going, talkative manner; when her stomach rumbled, she looked at her watch. 'Have you eaten tonight?'

'Sort of. Beans on toast – I didn't want to be late for you,' he admitted, slightly shame-faced.

'This is a stupid question to ask a student, I know, but do you fancy going for a meal? My shout,' she said.

'I'll pay my own way.'

She shook her head. 'I can afford it, Gareth. No strings.'

'Pity,' he murmured. 'I wouldn't mind being a gigolo.'

Her lips twitched. 'If that's the best offer I'm going to get all night . . . Look, I'm hungry. It's up to you if you join me. But it's definitely my bill.'

'Thanks. As long as we don't go for pasta. I mean, I used to love the stuff, but when you work with it, it's kind of overkill.'

'How about Chinese?' she suggested.

'There's a good one round the corner from here,' he told her. 'It's more reasonable than the West End, too.'

'You're on.' They finished their drinks, then headed for the small Chinese restaurant.

'I can't believe you're half my age again,' Gareth told her, after they'd ordered.

'Thanks. How to make me feel like an ageing crone, in five seconds flat,' she said drily.

'No, seriously. You don't look your age. And in those trousers . . . you know, the minute you and your friend walked into the place, we were all drooling. We tossed for who was going to serve you.'

'And you won?'

'Actually, I lost.'

'Oh, thanks.' She pulled a face at him. 'You really know how to make a woman feel good, Gareth.'

He grinned. 'I bribed the guy who won by offering to swap shifts with him I'm doing his Saturday night for the next couple of weeks, and he's doing my Thursdays instead.'

'I see.'

He tipped his head on one side. 'You were going to tell me just what a sophisticated woman would want with a waiter.'

'Perhaps I liked your face.'

He grinned. 'Well, it certainly wouldn't have been the uniform!'

'Aren't women supposed to fancy men in uniform?'

'Not that kind of uniform. It's meant to be brass buttons.'

'Oh, yes? And why's that?'

He laughed. 'Don't ask me. I'm reading history, not psychology!'

Zoe found herself relaxing in his company and enjoying herself immensely. The food was good, and so was the bottle of Chardonnay they'd ordered with it. When they'd finished their meal, Gareth looked at her. 'Would you like to come back to my place for a coffee? I mean, the house is a bit of a tip, but I'll make sure the mug's clean.'

'Sounds like an offer no woman could possibly refuse,' she said, her lips curving in amusement.

'As a sort of thank you for dinner. No strings. I won't ask you to come and see my etchings, or anything.' His green eyes sparkled with mischief. 'Now, if you'd been wearing those leather trousers . . .'

'Yeah, I know. It would have been a different offer.'

'Special of the day,' he quipped.

She chuckled, and paid the bill; they walked back to Gareth's house in companionable silence. It was as untidy as Gareth had said, but not quite as bad as she remembered student houses being in her own undergraduate days. He ushered her through to the kitchen, directing her to sit at the kitchen table while he made them both coffee.

'What I don't understand,' he said, bringing two steaming mugs over to the table and sitting next to her, 'is why you're on your own. I mean, you're attractive, you're intelligent, you're good company . . .' He frowned. 'I don't get it.'

171

'I've been busy with my career,' Zoe said simply. She'd told him that she was a journalist, but she hadn't mentioned her surname; he obviously hadn't twigged that she was Zoe Lynton of *Dry Bones* fame, and she didn't feel like enlightening him.

'Even so.' He tipped his head on one side. 'Divorced?'

She shook her head. 'Never married.'

'Hurt badly, then,' Gareth said.

'I thought you said you weren't reading psychology?'

'I'm not. I'm just . . . intrigued, I suppose. I'm nothing special to look at; yeah, I suppose I do turn on the charm a bit at work, but it's more or less expected of me, there. I still can't quite believe that you're here with me – that it's not a wind up of some sort. A bet.'

'Suspicious, for a twenty-year-old, aren't you?' she said lightly. 'Maybe I just wanted a change of scene, a good night out with someone different. Don't analyse it. I'm not.'

'No.' He took her hand, raising it to his lips. 'Sorry.' He kissed the tips of her fingers in turn, then drew her middle finger into his mouth, sucking hard.

Zoe felt herself grow wet instantly – particularly as he kept his gaze very firmly trained on hers, and she could see the desire burning there. 'Gareth . . .'

He released her hand. 'Sorry. I did say coffee, no strings.'

She leant over to stroke his face. 'You also said something about special offers.' Slowly, she cupped his chin, then pressed her lips against his. He gave a soft groan and opened his mouth, letting Zoe explore him.

She wasn't quite sure how it happened but, a few moments later, she found herself sitting on his lap, kissing him, with her arms round his neck and his hands up her T-shirt. He'd unclasped her bra and was cupping one breast, squeezing it gently and teasing the nipple into hardness, while his other hand stroked the length of her spine.

When she broke the kiss, he rubbed the tip of his nose against hers. 'Zoe. I'd like to make love with you – very much – but I don't think the kitchen's a very good place. Not if you'd like some privacy. I'm not sure who else is in – but they'll be down for a coffee, if they're working. And whoever's out will be back, pretty soon.'

'Then let's go to your room,' she suggested.

'Sure?'

'Sure,' she nodded.

He kissed her lightly; she climbed off his lap, and he stood up, leading her up the stairs. His room turned out to be like all the other student rooms she remembered – huge posters of rock bands and postcards hiding patchy wallpaper, a desk piled high with books and papers, and a shelf full of CDs and tapes.

'Takes me back to old times,' she said.

He grinned. 'You're not *that* old,' he said. 'And I'll prove it to you.' He walked over to his stereo and put a CD on.

Privately, Zoe felt even older. In her student days, Dire Straits and ballads by David Bowie, U2 and Chris de Burgh had been standard seduction music. She half-recognised the singer, but didn't dare ask who the group was. Some young Indie band, she presumed. The singer had a good voice, slightly plaintive; it had much the same effect on her as early Bono and Justin Currie, turning her on.

He closed the curtains, then took her in his arms, kissing her hard. Zoe found herself responding to his ardour, pressing her body against his and rubbing her pubis against the hardness of his cock.

'Oh, yes,' he breathed as he pulled her T-shirt over her head, discarding her bra at the same time. 'You're just as beautiful as I imagined, the other night. That shirt you were wearing drove me insane, I hope you realise that. I added up your bill completely wrong.'

'Yeah?'

'Yeah. I was too distracted by thoughts of what you really looked like, under that black chiffon confection.' He stroked her breasts. 'Beautiful. Such beautiful creamy skin . . .' He dropped to his knees and cupped her breasts, lifting them slightly and pushing them together. He rested his face against the shadowy vee for a moment, breathing in her scent, then moved his head slightly so that he could take one hardened nipple into his mouth.

Zoe closed her eyes as he began to suck. It felt so good; she could forget everything and just drown her thoughts in the way her body reacted with his. He made his tongue into a sharp point, flicking it from side to side and teasing her nipple until she gasped; then he sucked again, grazing the

173

sensitive tissues with his teeth but keeping the right side of the pleasure-pain borderline.

He shifted to pay attention to her other breast; as he did so, she felt him undo the button and zip of her jeans. She made no movement to stop him when he started to ease the soft denims over her hips; she stayed still, just revelling in the way his mouth was working on her breasts. When her jeans reached her ankles, she allowed him to help her step out of them; then she widened her stance slightly, in response to the gentle pressure of the flat of his palms against her inner thigh.

His lips travelled down, paying homage to the soft undersides of her breasts, then continuing southwards, over her ribcage and her abdomen. He stopped as he reached the edge of her knickers, then urged her to widen her stance again. Zoe waited, eagerly anticipating his next move; he teased her, cupping her delta and making her wait. She gave a small moan of frustration, and then at last she felt him pull the lacy crotch of her knickers to one side.

He breathed on her quim, making her wriggle impatiently; then, at last, she felt the long slow sweep of his tongue, in one movement from the top to the bottom of her musky furrow.

'Oh, yes,' she murmured, her voice husky with pleasure. She slid her hands into his hair, urging him on, and he continued to lap at her. When he took her clitoris between his lips, nipping on the sensitive nub of flesh, she almost howled with delight; she tilted her pelvis towards him, wanting more.

He teased her, the movements of his tongue becoming slow and languorous; when she bucked against him, he quickened his pace for a moment, then slowed down again. Finally, Zoe could take no more. 'Please, Gareth,' she said. 'Please.'

'Please what?' he murmured against her skin.

'You know what I want.'

'Sorry. I don't read minds.'

'Make me come. Lick me. Make me come,' she pleaded.

He continued to tease her, licking slowly and bringing her nearer and nearer the edge, pulling back whenever he felt she was too close to climax; she writhed against his mouth. 'Gareth. Don't torment me. I want you.'

'Whatever you say, madam,' he teased, and resumed his task, lapping at her until the waves of pleasure reached a crescendo. She climaxed with a yell, and he sat back on his haunches, pleased with himself. 'Okay?' he asked.

Zoe's pupils had expanded with lust. 'More than okay,' she said.

'Good.' He stood up again, and pulled her to him, kissing her hard. She could taste herself on his mouth, the sweet-salt musky juices, and it turned her on even more. She slid her hands under his T-shirt, kneading the muscles in his back and delighting in the firmness of his body. His cock would be just as good, she knew. Suddenly, she wanted to feel him inside her, unable to hold back any longer, she undid his jeans, feathering her hands over the bulge at his groin.

'Mm,' he moaned, tilting his pelvis towards hers.

He allowed her to remove his T-shirt, then helped her to remove his jeans and boxer shorts in one movement. Then he walked her back towards his bed, kissing her. He pushed the duvet aside, then sat down, drawing her down with him. 'Sure about this?' he asked. 'Because now's the time to stop, if you're not.'

In answer, she cupped his face and kissed him hard. He pushed her back against the bed, kneeling between her thighs. She was still wet from her earlier orgasm and the way he'd licked her; when he rolled a condom onto his cock and fitted the tip against her sex, he slid in easily.

'Oh, Christ, Zoe,' he moaned as he was sheathed inside her. 'You feel so good.'

She flexed her internal muscles, delighted by his response. 'Yeah?'

'Yeah.' He half-closed his eyes in pleasure. 'Oh, yeah.'

She wrapped her legs round his waist, tilting her pelvis so that he could penetrate her more deeply; he began to thrust, timing his movements to the music. Zoe reached up to hold the headboard, pushing her head back into the pillow and luxuriating in his movements. Gareth might be young, she thought, but he had a good cock, and he knew exactly what to do with it. He moved his lower body in small semi-circles, almost stirring his cock in her; in answer, she pushed against him, pressing against his buttocks with her heels.

'Mm, Zoe.' He stroked her legs, gently disentangling them from his waist, and rocked back on his haunches, still sheathed inside her, so that her body was arched up from the bed and her buttocks were resting on his thighs. Her feet were flat on the mattress; the position meant that he could stimulate her clitoris with his fingers, as well as pressing against it when he thrust in deeply.

Zoe began to pant as he continued to push in and out, taking it slowly and working on her clitoris. The sensitive bundle of nerves thrilled under his ministrations, and she felt the beginnings of her inner sparkling, radiating out from her clitoris and spreading through her whole body. As it gathered momentum, she pushed against his body and cried out, her knuckles white as she gripped the headboard even more tightly.

He didn't stop as she climaxed; he quickened his thrusts, continuing to rub her clitoris and taking her to a higher peak, and still higher. By the time he came, Zoe's whole body was quivering, and every muscle was drained.

He buried his face in her shoulder for a moment; she felt his cock pulse deep inside her. Then he moved so that he was lying on his back, and she was resting with her shoulder on his chest; neither of them said a word. There was no need. In companionable silence, they listened to the rest of the CD; finally, Gareth dealt with his condom and turned to Zoe. 'I'll make us both a coffee,' he offered. 'If you want to freshen up, the bathroom's the third door on the left, from here.'

'Thanks.' Her lips twitched as she glanced down at her lack of clothing. 'Though I'm not sure if your house-mates would appreciate me wandering around naked.'

He grinned. 'I think they would, actually, but if you want to spare your blushes . . .' He opened his wardrobe door and pulled out a shirt. 'Will this do?'

'Thanks.' Zoe took the soft cotton garment gratefully and slipped into it. It reached to just below her buttocks, making her decent.

'See you in a minute, then.' He pulled on his jeans. 'Oh, the towel on the rail's clean.'

'Thanks.' She suppressed a grin at his afterthought, and

176

followed him out of the room. She locked the bathroom door before removing his shirt, then took a quick shower, half regretful that Gareth hadn't suggested joining her; then she remembered the last time she'd made love in the shower, and her face hardened. Bloody Brandon. Even tonight, she couldn't keep him completely out of her mind.

'I don't need you, Brandon Mitchell,' she hissed quietly. 'I'm doing fine by myself.' Crossly, she scrubbed herself dry on the slightly rough towel, then slipped on Gareth's shirt and headed back down the corridor to his bedroom.

Just as she was within reach of his door, the door next to his opened and a tall, dark-haired man walked out, colliding with her. His hands instinctively shot out to steady her; he winced. 'Sorry. I didn't mean to nearly knock you over. I was miles away.'

'That's okay.' Zoe was aware as he took a step backwards that the only thing between his gaze and her naked body was a thin cotton shirt. A shirt that stuck to her semi-damp skin and left nothing to the imagination.

'I'm Nico,' he said, stretching out a hand.

She took it, shaking it warmly. 'Zoe.'

He glanced meaningfully at the door. 'And you're with Gareth, are you?'

She flushed, suddenly aware that it had been a far from quiet coupling. 'Sorry. Did we interrupt your studies?'

He grinned. 'No. I work with headphones on. But . . . Gareth? He's a nice bloke, don't get me wrong, but you don't look his type.'

'Oh?'

'Too sophisticated,' Nico enlightened her.

'If that's meant to be a compliment, thank you.'

'Oh, it is.'

Zoe's flush deepened as his dark eyes studied her body – partly from embarrassment and partly from arousal. Nico was just as attractive as Gareth, but in a complementary way: his hair was slightly curly, its darkness in sharp contrast to Gareth's light brown floppy hair, his eyes were dark, and his skin had an olive tone which looked as if it owed more to the Mediterranean than Gareth's fair English complexion.

'Mitts off, Nico,' Gareth said, joining them and obviously recognising the look on his housemate's face. 'Zoe, just ignore him. He tries to charm the knickers off every woman he meets.'

Her lips twitched. 'Not in my case.'

'Then he's just working up to it,' Gareth said, his affectionate tone belying his words. 'Dominic here plays on the fact that he's half Italian. Any minute now, he'll start telling you that Italian is the language of love and start quoting poetry at you.'

'Not just any poetry. Boccaccio,' Nico said.

Zoe grinned. 'Could be worse. Catullus.'

'Mm, intelligent and well-read as well as beautiful,' Nico said admiringly. 'I told you that you weren't Gareth's type. Way, way too sophisticated.'

'Don't start charming her knickers off,' Gareth groaned. 'Please.'

'Not possible, in my case,' Zoe said. She stood on tiptoe to whisper in his ear. 'I'm not wearing any.' The look on Gareth's face made her grin, knowing that she'd given him an instant erection.

'I heard what you just said,' Nico said, echoing her grin. 'Now, this could be very interesting.'

'Yes, it could.' A wicked idea was forming in Zoe's brain. One man might not be enough to make her forget Brandon – but two might well be. It was an age-old fantasy of hers, one which Steve had almost latched on to, in one of their long-distance late-night phone calls. Now was her chance to make it real. She smiled, and undid the top three buttons of the shirt, letting the material gape to show the upper swell of her bare breasts. 'Very interesting,' she said breathily.

Gareth and Nico looked at each other. There was a very long pause; finally, Nico reached out to trail his forefinger from the cleft in her chin, down her throat and between her breasts. 'Just how interesting do you have in mind?'

In answer, Zoe undid the next button of the shirt, revealing more of her breasts. Her nipples were erect, and she knew that the thin material did nothing to hide the fact.

'I think,' Gareth said softly, 'that we'd better go back to my room.'

'Who's "we"?' Nico asked.

They both turned to Zoe, who smiled. 'Two's company. Three's even more pleasure,' she said.

'My room, then,' Nico said. 'A double bed's more comfortable than a single.' He walked back into his room; Gareth and Zoe looked at each other, and followed him in. Gareth put the coffee mugs on Nico's desk, then he walked over to Zoe and kissed her, hard. He undid the buttons of her shirt; Nico stood behind her, and slid the garment from her shoulders.

Zoe felt Nico trailing his mouth down her spine, pushing her hair to one side so that he could start at the sensitive spot at the back of her neck, then slowly moving downwards along her spine. She shivered in delight, particularly when, a few moments later, Gareth started doing the same thing at her front, licking the hollows of her collarbones and then working on her breasts.

Gently, Nico parted her thighs; she realised that he was kneeling when she felt him take tiny erotic bites at the soft globes of her buttocks. Her sex pooled: what she was about to do was way beyond the kind of things she usually did, but she needed this. Some kind of sexual healing, to help take away the pain of Brandon's betrayal.

She stopped thinking altogether as Gareth, too, knelt before her. Nico was holding one ankle; Gareth followed suit with her other ankle, so that she was fully supported. And then, with near perfect timing, Gareth set his mouth to her quim, flicking his tongue-tip over her clitoris, while Nico eased a finger into her warm wet sex.

She gave a moan of pleasure as they began to work her, touching her and teasing her with their fingers and their mouths all the time. Nico was whispering how beautiful she was, how her skin was like cream and honey, and how he wanted to take her to the limits of pleasure.

She gave herself up to them completely; after they'd made her come, twice, she was in no state to deny them anything. Nico lay on the bed, and she climbed on top of him, directed by Gareth. She was vaguely aware that he was wearing a latex sheath, though she had no idea when he'd put it on; she was merely glad of his thoughtfulness. Gareth held her labia apart, guiding her onto the hard rod of flesh; then, as she sank down onto Nico's hard cock, Gareth knelt by Nico's shoulders, presenting his own erect cock to her lips.

Zoe smiled and opened her mouth, allowing him access;

he moaned with pleasure as she tongued his frenum, teasing him, before taking him as deeply as she could. The two men worked in perfect rhythm, one thrusting into her quim and the other into her mouth; Nico was stroking her breasts and rubbing her clitoris, murmuring endearments in Italian, while Gareth was stroking the nape of her neck and her hair, urging her on.

She rocked back and forth on Nico's cock, enjoying the sensations coursing through her body; then, finally, she felt his cock throbbing deep inside her. Almost at the same moment, she felt Gareth's cock twitch, and her mouth was filled with his warm tangy fluid. She swallowed every drop; then, as he withdrew his cock, she licked her lips and smiled up at him.

'God, Zoe, you're incredible,' he said. He looked at Nico. 'Now do you believe what I told you about the gorgeous woman dressed in black?' he asked teasingly.

'Mm.' Nico's voice was husky. 'I can just see you in black leather trousers, Zoe. And I'd love to peel them off you.'

'Some other time, hm?'

He eased her off him, then rolled her onto her back, pulling her into his arms. 'I'll hold you to that. But you don't have to go just yet, do you?'

Chapter Fourteen

She was enjoying herself far too much to leave. 'No. Though if you've got early lectures tomorrow—'

'I haven't, but it'd be worth cutting them,' Nico said softly. 'To have you spending the night with us.'

Gareth moved to lie beside her, sandwiching her between the two men. 'Agreed,' he said, equally softly. He turned Zoe to face him; she could feel two hard cocks against her thighs, and shivered inside with delight. That was the thing about younger men: they had a faster recovery rate. One of her ex-colleagues, a notorious man-eater, had once said that to her, and she'd scoffed. Now she realised that Cherry had had a point.

'Zoe.' Nico kissed the hollow behind her ear. 'I like to play things dark. Just stop me any time I go too far for you, hm?'

Another shiver rippled down her spine. 'Dark?'

'Sophisticated, you might say.' He nipped her earlobe. 'Give me a second.' She felt the mattress give as he climbed out of the bed, but didn't have time to register what he was doing, as Gareth began kissing her again, taking one of her hands and curling her fingers around his erection. She frotted him gently, making no protest when he stroked her buttocks and thighs and lifted one of her legs over his to give him access to her sex. He pushed one finger into her still-wet quim, then added a second and a third.

Zoe was in the throes of another climax when Nico climbed back into the bed; as she floated down through the aftermath of orgasm, she realised that he'd put a CD on. Not the same kind of music Gareth had played: this was opera. A tenor, singing *a capella*. Something obscure, something she didn't recognise, but something that sent a thrill through her.

'Like I said. Sophisticated,' he murmured. She made as if to turn towards him, but he stilled her. 'Stay just where you are,' he said softly. 'That's just how I want you.'

He kissed his way down her spine again; but this time, instead of nipping at her buttocks, he pushed his tongue-tip against the puckered rosy hole of her anus. Zoe gasped, and he stopped instantly. 'Okay?' he asked, his voice tender and solicitous.

'I . . . Yes.'

'Want me to stop?'

Zoe had an inkling of what he'd meant by 'dark', and it both scared and excited her. 'No.' The denial was firm.

'*Bellissima*,' Nico said, and resumed his attentions.

Zoe was slightly shocked at how arousing she found it. She'd only met him a few minutes before, and here he was, doing something more intimate than any of her lovers had done at this point in their relationship. Except Brandon . . . She shivered again as she felt Nico's finger pressing against the tight ring.

'Easy, sweetheart. Easy,' he soothed; she relaxed her muscles, allowing him the access he wanted, and squeezed her eyes tightly shut, trying not to think of Brandon.

Gareth began kissing her again, exploring her mouth gently but insistently; the dual onslaught was enough to make her switch off her thoughts and let her body enjoy what was happening.

Nico kissed his way back up her skin; then she heard paper ripping, followed by a snapping sound. When it happened again, she realised that Nico had sheathed Gareth's cock as well as his own; a ripple of excitement ran through her, both at the vision of Nico's hands on Gareth's cock, and at what she now knew they were going to do with her.

Slowly, very gently, Nico pushed the tip of his cock against her anus.

'I . . .' Zoe's stomach clenched with mingled excitement and fear. 'I don't think I can do this. You're too big.'

'Trust me. It'll be pure pleasure. Though I can stop any time you tell me, Zoe,' he assured her, kissing her shoulder. 'Any time it's not comfortable, not good for you, just tell me.'

Her mouth went dry as the tip of his cock nudged past the tight ring. 'Nico . . .'

'Easy, babe, easy,' he murmured, increasing his penetration millimetre by millimetre. 'When your body gets used to this, you're going to love it.'

Zoe was shocked at the sensations running riot in her body. She'd never done this before, ever: she'd fantasised about it more than once, but had always held back from living it out. And now . . .

Before she could register exactly what she was feeling, she realised that Gareth was lifting her leg slightly higher, and the tip of his cock was pressing against her sex. 'I . . . I'm not sure I can take both of you,' she said.

'You can,' Nico assured her. 'Believe me, you can. And this is going to be good for you, Zoe. I promise, you're going to enjoy this.'

He remained still, letting her body grow used to the unfamiliar invasion; all the while, Gareth's cock was sliding deep into her vagina. He, too, remained still when he was in her up to the hilt; both of them stroked her and kissed her and nuzzled her, cherishing her. Their combined ministrations, together with the sensual music Nico was playing, was enough to relax her; when they felt the tension in her body ease, they began to move in synchronisation. As Nico pulled out, Gareth pushed in; as Gareth withdrew, Nico entered her again.

Zoe began to moan as her excitement increased. The sensations were indescribable; she simply stopped thinking about it, revelling in the way they took her. As if they sensed the change in her, they quickened their movements, tipping her into such a convulsive orgasm that she yelled out her delight. Her flexing muscles were enough to push them into their own climaxes; she could feel their cocks throbbing almost in tandem, an erotic counterpoint to her own involuntary convulsions.

Finally, they withdrew, turning her onto her back and lying on their sides, both of them sliding an arm round her waist.

'Beautiful, beautiful Zoe,' Nico said, kissing the tip of her nose. 'That was incredible.'

'Seconded,' Gareth said huskily.

Zoe smiled at them; her whole body ached pleasurably. 'I don't know what to say.'

'Don't say anything,' Nico said softly. 'Just relax here, with us.'

Relax. Yes, at last, she felt that she could. She closed her eyes, concentrating only on the movements and the lazy caresses of her lovers, and eventually drifted off to sleep.

The next morning, Zoe was woken by her two lovers covering every inch of skin with kisses; she feigned sleep for a little longer, wondering just how far they'd go. She soon discovered, when they lay either side of her, one pushing his fingers into her sex and the other playing with her clitoris. At the same time, they each took one of her hands, curling her fingers round their cocks.

She couldn't resist grinning and doing what they wanted, masturbating them both at the same time.

'I knew you were faking it,' Nico teased, leaning over to kiss her mouth.

She opened her eyes. 'I thought you had to go to lectures?'

'And you have to go to work,' he countered swiftly. 'That makes us quits.'

'I'm freelance. I decide my own work-pattern.'

'And we're Arts students. We do the same,' Gareth told her. 'Within a few limits.'

'Mm.' She concentrated on the two erect penises she was massaging. It felt delightfully lewd and wicked, to be starting the day like this. Making love with not one, but two young studs . . . She could feel their balls lifting and tightening as she continued to rub their cocks, and smiled to herself. Yes, they might be in the dominant position, right now, intending to let their semen jet over her breasts – but she'd make them clean her with their mouths, afterwards.

And so it proved. Twin pearly jets spattered onto her skin, and she rubbed them harder, almost as if she were milking them; when they groaned their pleasure, she smiled. 'And now, you'd better clean me up.'

Nico reached down for a shirt to wipe the sticky mess from her breasts, but she stopped him. 'I meant with your mouths.' Deliberately, she massaged the semen into her skin, mixing it together, and laughed as his eyes widened. 'You told me last night that you like it dark.' Her smile was pure wickedness. 'So do it.' She glanced at Gareth. 'That goes for you, too.'

'Bossy-boots,' he said, but did as she demanded, cleaning her left breast with his tongue while Nico licked her right.

Afterwards, they made love again, settling Zoe on her hands and knees with Nico kneeling in front of her and Gareth kneeling between her thighs, pushing his cock into her sex and rubbing her nipples while Nico slid his hands into her hair and urged her to take him as deeply as she could into her mouth.

'What a breakfast,' Zoe said afterwards, curled into them and feeling relaxed and lazy.

'Makes a change from toast and marmalade,' Nico added with a grin, kissing her lightly.

'Yeah. And how.' Zoe sat up. 'But I really do have to be going, now.'

'At least stay for a cup of coffee,' Gareth said. 'We're bound to be out of bread, but I think there's some cornflakes or something, if you want some cereal.'

She shook her head. 'It's been great – thanks – but I really ought to be getting home.'

'Thank you for last night. And this morning,' Gareth said.

Nico echoed his sentiments. 'Any time you want company, just let me – us – know.'

'Thanks.' Zoe smiled at them. 'I might just take you up on that.'

Three weeks later, she came back from a morning at the British Museum's reading room to discover a message from Steve to call into the *Archetypes* office when she got a chance. She rang him. 'Steve? What's up?'

'Ed's just called me. They've finished the preliminary excavations.'

'And?'

'Put it this way, we're all drinking champagne here. I think you should come and join us.'

'Now?'

'Flat champagne's repulsive – anyway, I don't think there will be any of this left, by tomorrow.'

'Okay. I'll be there,' she said. 'Give me an hour.'

Exactly an hour later, she was at the office. 'Congratulations,' Steve said, putting an arm round her shoulder and hugging her. 'How does it feel to be in on one of the finds of the millennium?'

'Good,' Zoe said as he gave her a glass of champagne.

'Good? My God. The woman has just been part of the discovery of the grave of her hero, the most prominent woman in Roman Britain. It's like Napoleon's lot discovering the Rosetta Stone – and she's blasé about it.' He rolled his eyes. 'Zoe, you're impossible. Do I take it this means you won't go down and have your photograph taken with the team, by the grave?'

'Correct.' The thought of going back to Norfolk made her voice sharp. 'I don't have a window in my schedule.'

He whistled. 'Wow. You sound more like a hot-shot marketeer than a journo.'

Zoe gave him an old-fashioned look. 'Drop it, Steve. I was there at the start, and that's more important to me than messing about with photo-calls and the like.'

'Okay, okay. I'll drop it.' Steve coughed.

He told her what they were planning next: a full-scale excavation of the site, and possibly opening it to the public, or at least the local schools. He didn't ask her if she would cover the story for *Archetypes*, and Zoe felt slightly guilty; it was clear to her that he wanted to ask her, but he also knew that she'd bite his head off at the suggestion.

She finished her champagne, and kissed him on the cheek. 'I'd better be off, Steve. I've got a few things to do.'

'Do you have a window in your schedule for lunch with me?'

Zoe glanced at her watch. 'As a matter of fact, no. Sorry. I have deadlines to meet.'

He looked hurt. 'Call me when you can fit me in, then.'

She knew that she was behaving badly, but she couldn't help herself. The idea of having to go back to Lower Yareham and maybe facing Brandon . . . Being sharp was the only way she could deal with it. Because otherwise, she knew she'd start crying. 'Yeah, I will. See you later.'

The next week was difficult. Ed and Ella kept her up to date with what was happening with the site. Jack, of course, was delighted, and was the toast of the village. Zoe spoke to him a couple of times, and he tried to persuade her to come back for a celebratory party that he and Eileen were organising at The Feathers, at the weekend. But the minute he mentioned his grandson's name, Zoe changed the subject, and made some excuse or other not to be at the party. She was aware that Jack didn't really believe her excuse, but there was no way she was going to risk facing Brandon again.

Shannon also rang her a couple of times and told her that the housing development was still going ahead – but on a different site, and not with Mark Burroughs, who was currently facing charges of fraud and the wrath of the county council.

Zoe couldn't resist reading the articles in various newspapers and magazines about the site, but Brandon's name was never mentioned. She wasn't sure whether she was relieved to hear nothing about him, or miserable and desperately craving to glean some tiny snippet of news. Instead, she threw herself into work, refusing all social invitations – even from Lissy and Steve. She didn't ring Nico or Gareth, either, and as she hadn't given them her number, there was no way either of them could get in touch with her.

A couple of weeks later, Steve rang her mobile number. 'Zoe?'

'Yes?' she said cautiously.

'Are you busy tonight?'

'Well, actually—'

'If you're working,' he cut in quietly, 'then you know as well as I do that freelances can plan when they want to work. We're old friends, aren't we?'

'Yes.'

'So can I ask you this without pussy-footing around the subject. Are you trying to avoid me?'

'No, I'm not,' she told him honestly. 'I'm just busy.'

'All right, we'll try another tack. Have I done something to upset you?'

'No.'

'Then come over to dinner. Tonight, at seven.'

'Steve, I—'

'No excuses.' His voice softened. 'I miss you, sweetheart. I miss my good pal Zoe Lynton. I haven't seen her for a while, and it worries me that she's working too hard.'

'I'm fine, Steve. Really.'

'Then come over to dinner. No excuses acceptable.'

Zoe paused suspiciously. If Steve had talked to Jack, who had talked to Brandon . . . 'Just the two of us?'

'Just the two of us,' he confirmed.

Steve wouldn't lie to her. He wouldn't set her up with Brandon. This was a genuine invitation to dinner. She made an effort. 'All right. I'll be there. Do you want me to bring red or white wine?'

'Either. Just be there, okay?'

At seven o'clock precisely, Zoe rang the doorbell to his flat. Steve buzzed her back immediately. 'Hi, Zoe. Come on up.'

She sniffed as she walked into his flat. 'Something smells good. Italian, I'd guess.'

'Pasta, walnut bread, salad and ice-cream.'

She tipped her head on one side. 'Are you trying to tell me something?'

'Only that I've missed seeing you,' he said simply. 'You've sent your copy in on disk, and I was beginning to wonder if I'd done something to upset you. I know you said I haven't but, for all I know, you might have just been polite. If I have done something, then I'm sorry, and I'll make amends.'

'It's not you,' she said. 'It's me.'

'Want to talk about it?'

She shook her head. 'It's something I'm trying to forget.'

'Fair enough. Just warn me if I put my foot in it, okay?'

She hugged him appreciatively. 'I don't deserve a friend like you.'

'Of course you do.' He ruffled her hair. 'So how are things with you? Apart from busy, of course.'

'Fine.' She smiled wryly. 'I had a bit of a shopping bender. I've just needed to earn enough to pay my credit card bill.'

Steve's look was disbelieving, but he said nothing. 'I'll just go check on the pasta sauce.'

'Anything I can do to help?'

'Light the candles,' he said.

She grinned. 'Vanilla ones?'

'Would I dare put anything else out for you?'

She followed him into the kitchen, putting the bottle of red wine on the worktop and retrieving a box of matches from a drawer.

'One thing, Zoe.'

'Hm?' She turned, frowning. He wasn't going to mention Brandon, was he?

'Just what did you buy to put such a huge dent in your credit card?'

'Chocolate.'

He gave her a knowing look. 'And?'

'A pair of leather trousers.'

'And you're not wearing them, to show me?'

'Nope. But they exist – ask Lissy.'

'Right. And?'

She sighed. 'Three pairs of shoes, six CDs and some underwear.'

Steve looked hopeful. 'Do I get a view?'

'No. I want feeding.'

He pounced. 'So you're wearing the underwear tonight?'

'Might be.' Zoe stuck her tongue out. 'Just feed me, Marwick. I've been working hard, and I'm starving.'

'Okay, okay.' He stirred the sauce. 'Three minutes for the pasta – it's fresh vermicelli – and we're all yours.'

Zoe went back into the sitting room and lit the candles on the table. Steve had already opened a bottle of red wine, letting it breathe: vintage Barolo, she noticed with pleasure. The green salad looked good; she dipped her forefinger into the bowl of dressing. Home-made, she recognised instantly. This was going to be good.

'I saw that,' Steve teased as he walked in, carrying two plates.

'Yeah, well.' Zoe look slightly embarrassed, then shrugged. 'What's a finger, between friends?'

He grinned. 'That's a leading question, and one I might answer when we've had a couple of glasses of wine.'

'Indeedy.' She sat down. 'Shall I pour?'

'Sure.' He put a plate in front of her. 'The sauce is home-made, too. Sun-dried tomatoes, mozzarella, bacon and black olives.'

'If it tastes as good as it sounds and smells, there'd better be seconds,' she warned.

'Nope.'

'Come on. You said it was ice-cream for pudding. That doesn't take up a lot of room.'

'Not just ice-cream. White chocolate semifredo: also home-made.'

She gave him a sidelong look. 'You're up to something.'

'Nothing, I assure you. Like I said, I thought I'd done something to upset you, so I'm making amends.'

She smiled wryly. 'And like I said, it isn't you.' She took a mouthful of pasta. 'This is seriously good, Steve. Have you ever thought about give up *Archetypes* and becoming the next Gary Rhodes?'

He shook his head. 'I can do the attitude, yes; I could even do the weird haircut. But he's got the edge on me when it comes to talent.'

'Ooh, now if I've ever heard someone fishing for com—' Zoe's voice faded. The last time she'd bantered with someone about fishing for compliments was just before she and Brandon had made love. God, was she ever going to get that man out of her system?

'You okay, Zoe?'

She nodded. 'I'm fine.'

Steve, who had had an interesting phone conversation with Alicia, that morning, thought otherwise. He also thought that if he pushed the subject before Zoe was ready to talk about it, she'd simply walk out on him. 'Must be the sun-dried tomatoes,' he said lightly. He turned the conversation to something neutral, steering well clear of Norfolk and Boudicca; he didn't even mention Zoe's big passion, the *mementi mori*.

She found herself relaxing and even laughing again; by the time she and Steve had finished both bottles of red wine and the majority of the semifredo, she was leaning back against her chair, groaning. 'Why do I always over-indulge in your company?'

'Because we're a bad influence on each other,' Steve said

with a grin. 'Hey, Zoe . . . dance with me?'

'Dance with you?'

'Yes. I'm in that kind of mood, tonight,' he said. 'I'll even let you choose the music, if you like.'

'I'm too lazy to make decisions. I'll leave it to your discretion.'

Steve picked a jazz compilation, then turned out the overhead light, leaving the room lit only by the scented candles on the table. He turned to Zoe, holding out his arms, and she walked over to him, letting her cheek rest against his chest and sliding her arms round his waist. Steve held her close, resting his own cheek against her hair and breathing in her scent.

They danced in silence for a while; Zoe closed her eyes, and Brandon's face inevitably floated into her mind. They'd never actually danced together; she couldn't help wondering what it would be like to dance with him. On his chamomile lawn; he'd be wearing a dress shirt, an undone bow tie and dark trousers, having discarded his dinner jacket earlier, and she'd be wearing something floaty. Something white and floaty, she decided. They'd be dancing to a solo piano, or maybe Sarah Vaughan's husky tones, and they'd have been drinking champagne all evening. It would be late, the stars would be out, and it would be just the two of them . . .

The thoughts were so strong that, for a moment, she thought she actually was dancing with Brandon; as her arms tightened round the man dancing with her, he moved slightly so that he could kiss the top of her head. Her eyes still closed and her mind still filled with Brandon, she lifted her head, tipping her face up for a kiss.

His lips touched hers, very gently; she reached up to slide her hands into his hair, opening her mouth under his, and the kiss turned explosive. He slid his tongue into her mouth, teasing the tip of her tongue with his own; they continued swaying in time to the music, and Steve deftly freed Zoe's dark shirt from her jeans. He slid his hands under the material, stroking her back, his fingertips moving in slow circles down her spine. She arched against him, making a sound of pleasure in the back of her throat; his hands slipped down to caress her buttocks through her soft faded denims, and she felt his erection pressing against her.

Gently, he eased one hand between their bodies, undoing her shirt; Zoe made no protest as he pushed the material from her shoulders.

'You're so beautiful,' he murmured.

His voice didn't break the spell: Zoe still had her eyes closed, still saw Brandon, still felt his skin against hers. She simply smiled, lifting her ribcage in offering; he undid the clasp of her bra, removing the lace confection and dropping it on the floor, before cupping her breasts in his hands, lifting them up and together.

He dropped to his knees before her, making his tongue into a hard point and tracing her areolae with it, teasing her nipples into hardness. She pushed her fingers into his hair again, urging him on; he blew against her spit-slicked skin, making her shiver and arch her back, then took one nipple into his mouth and sucked hard.

Meanwhile, he undid the button of her jeans and then the zip; as the faded denims were eased down over her hips, Zoe gave a soft moan of pleasure. She felt his smile against her abdomen, rather than saw it, and allowed him to remove her jeans properly, leaning against him as he guided the material down to her ankles and lifted her feet in turn, helping her step out of the jeans.

When she stood before him, wearing only a pair of hold-up lace-topped stockings and a tiny pair of black lacy knickers, Steve rocked back on his haunches, watching her; she still had her eyes closed, and he smiled wryly before getting to his feet and picking her up. He'd never actually met Brandon Mitchell, but he must have been one hell of a guy to get Zoe in this kind of state, he thought. It was obvious that she was fantasising about him, rather than making love with Steve; part of him felt a flicker of jealously but, then again, Steve knew that he and Zoe had a no-strings arrangement. He couldn't complain about it now. All he could do was try to make her feel better, in the best way that he knew how.

He carried her through the flat to his bedroom, pushing his duvet aside and laying her gently on the bed. He knelt between her thighs, and bent his head to kiss her lightly on the mouth. Then he continued his trail of kisses downwards, over her throat, lingering on the sensitive spots he knew so well. He nuzzled the hollows of her collarbones, moving downwards to cover her breasts with kisses, sucking hard on each nipple in turn and then caressing the soft undersides, making her shiver with longing.

Slowly, he moved down over her ribcage, then the soft swell of her abdomen. She arched up widening the gap between her thighs; smiling, he moved down, rubbing his face against the soft skin of her inner thighs, then pulling the lacy crotch of her knickers to one side. He breathed on her quim, teasing her; when she tilted her pelvis, he bent his head, lapping delicately at her sex. He traversed all her intimate furls and hollows with his tongue, exploring her thoroughly, before teasing her clitoris from its hood and taking it into his mouth, sucking gently.

She gave a sharp intake of breath, pushing her hands into his hair again and using the pressure of her fingertips against his scalp to urge him on. He continued licking patiently; although the scent of her arousal enticed him to slide his cock deep inside her, he wanted to take this slowly, give her what she needed. She began to whimper, moving her head from side to side on the pillow, and the pressure on his scalp grew more intense; he quickened his pace, alternately pushing his tongue as deeply in her vagina as possible and sucking on her clitoris.

At last, he felt her quim rippling against his mouth, and tasted the sweetness of her nectar as she came, making small incoherent noises of pleasure. He waited until her breathing had slowed again before shifting up the bed to kiss her, letting her taste herself on his mouth.

'Better?' he asked softly.

'Steve . . .' She opened her eyes and promptly burst into tears.

'Hey, hey.' He sat up, pulling her into his arms and letting her cry on his shoulder. When the racking sobs had abated, he gently held her at arm's length. 'Zoe. Come on, sweetheart. Talk to me.'

She gulped. 'Steve, I . . . I'm sorry. I – we shouldn't be here. Not like this.'

'That's what friends are for, remember.'

'I mean, I shouldn't be here in your bed. It's not fair to you.'

He stroked her face. 'I know you were thinking of someone else. And we've been no-strings for years, haven't we?'

'I know, but it's still not fair to you.' She swallowed. 'I . . . I can't.'

'Finish what we started? Hey, that's no problem. Look, I'll make us a coffee while you get dressed, and then you can sit down and talk to me. That's an order, not a request,' he added.

He kissed the tip of her nose, then climbed off the bed and grabbed a towelling robe from the back of the door. 'You know where the shower is, if you want it. I'll get your clothes,' he said.

Zoe felt even worse at the way he was being so understanding: she wasn't sure if guilt or self-pity had the upper hand, but she felt bad. Steve had known that she was thinking of someone else. He probably knew exactly who, too.

She showered quickly; the heat of the water made her feel better. She forced herself not to think of Brandon, and what he'd done with her when they showered together, though it took a hell of an effort, and her face was white with strain when she dried herself.

Finally, she went back into Steve's bedroom. As he'd promised, all her clothes were waiting for her on the bed. She dressed, put her wet towel in his laundry basket, and went to join him in the kitchen.

'Steve, I really am sorry. I had no intention of leading you on. Tonight, it was just going to be a meal between friends – what you suggested originally.'

He gave her a swift hug, then resumed making the coffee. 'It's okay, Zoe. I was the one who started it, trying to make it something else.' He handed her a steaming mug. 'Come and sit down. I promise I'm not going to leap on you.'

She chuckled ruefully. 'I know. You're too much of a gentleman.'

'Far from it – but I value your friendship. There's no way I'm going to stuff that up by pushing you too hard.' He smiled at her, ushering her into the sitting room. 'Isn't it about time you talked about things, Zoe?'

'I don't know what you mean.' She concentrated on her coffee.

'Yes, you do.' He sat beside her on the sofa. 'Would I be right in saying that Zoe the free spirit has finally fallen in love?'

'No.'

The denial was too quick and too vehement, and they both knew it. 'Zoe.' He took her hand, squeezing it. 'We've been friends for a long, long time, right?'

She nodded.

'Well, then. You're not your normal self at the moment. You're working too hard, you hardly ever smile, you're acting like a ruthless businesswoman, driven by time – and it's obvious to me that there's something wrong. To Lissy, too.'

'Lissy? What does she have to do with this?'

Steve winced. 'Okay, if you must know, Lissy and I were talking about you the other day. We're both worried about you. You wouldn't talk to her, so I thought I'd give it a try. Except I stuffed up, trying to comfort you in other ways.'

Zoe's eyes narrowed. 'What did Lissy say?'

'It doesn't matter.'

'Yes, it does.'

'She didn't tell me everything you told her when you went out for pasta. Just that she thought you'd fallen for someone who was on the opposite side from us on the dig. I don't think it could have been that Burroughs character, so I reckon it must be Jack's grandson – right?'

Zoe sighed heavily. 'I made a complete and utter fool of myself, Steve. I thought . . . well, it doesn't matter what I thought. I was wrong. And no, I'm not in love with the guy.'

Steve made no comment, but she could see on his face that he didn't believe her.

'I'm *not*, Steve. And I'm fine, really. I just need a bit of time to get my head together.'

'If you say so. But if you do want to talk about it, I'm here for you. So's Lissy.'

She nodded. 'Thanks. I appreciate that.'

He lifted his mug in a toast. 'To friends. Good friends.'

'Good friends,' she echoed.

Chapter Fifteen

Zoe walked down the road to her house, tired and rolling her aching shoulders to ease the strain in her muscles. She'd spent the day researching in the university library; Alicia was already doing something that night, but Zoe felt too tired to go out for a meal or to the cinema, anyway.

Since that scene with Steve, she'd thrown herself even more deeply into her work. She was at the point, now, where she was tired nearly all the time, but she continued to drive herself on. If she slackened off now, she'd end up thinking of Brandon and feeling even worse. Although she'd been tempted to call Gareth and Nico again, she decided to leave it as a one-off; a memory of a very pleasurable night. Acting like a bitch on heat wasn't going to make her feel better, except in the very short term.

She stopped, frowning, when she saw the light on in her sitting-room window. Apart from the fact that she'd turned all the lights off before she'd left the house that morning, her curtains were drawn. Someone was there. Her frown deepened. She couldn't remember asking Steve over, but he was the only one she could think of who had a key.

Maybe he'd decided to surprise her, cook her something nice. Or maybe he'd lent it to Lissy, who was planning a sybaritic girlie night as a surprise. Pizza, lots of chocolate, and a good soppy video . . . She wrinkled her nose. No. Lissy would have phoned her, rather than trying to make it a surprise. On balance, it was more likely to be Steve. She tried the front door: it was locked. He was playing safe, then. Shrugging, she unlocked the door. 'Hello?'

There was no answer, and she couldn't smell the enticing aroma of cooking that she'd been expecting. She frowned. 'Steve?' When there was still no answer, a cold shiver ran down her spine. Maybe she'd assumed wrongly, and it wasn't

Steve at all – maybe she'd walked into the house in the middle of a burglary.

She grabbed her mobile phone from her handbag, about to dial 999; then a figure appeared in the door of the sitting room. Her mouth opened in shock as she recognised him. He was the last person she'd expected to see in her house. 'How the hell did you get in?'

'Since you've already pigeon-holed me as a criminal, you can assume that I broke in, can't you?' His voice was cold.

She recovered her composure fast. 'In that case you can leave the same way you got in. Through the window or whatever.'

He dangled her front door key before her. 'Actually I used this.'

She frowned. 'Where did you get that?'

'Does it matter?'

'No. Just give it to me, and get out.'

'Or else what? You'll call the police?'

She realised that she was still holding her phone. 'Maybe.'

'Don't you think the police have got more important things to do than sort out arguments between people who are grown-up and sensible enough to do it themselves?'

She flushed. 'Just get out, Brandon.'

'You're not very magnanimous in victory, are you?'

'I don't know what you're talking about.'

'You won, Zoe. The excavation went ahead, and we were refused planning permission on the land. *I* was refused it, rather: the development's going ahead on another field, but Mark won't be involved.'

She nodded. 'I heard that.'

'So you were interested in what happened to me, were you? Even though you've cut Gramps dead, every time he's mentioned my name? Let alone the way you refused to go down to join him for the photo-call or the party.' His eyes narrowed. 'So much for you telling the hospital that you were his granddaughter. You couldn't care less about anyone other than yourself, could you, Zoe?'

It was enough to push her over the edge. 'And how the hell *you* can say that, when you took me to your bed, pretended that you really cared, and all the time, it was a set-up—'

197

'Set-up?' he interrupted. 'What do you mean?'

'Come on. Stop trying to lie your way out of it.'

'I'm not lying about anything, Zoe. I really don't know what you're talking about. What set-up?'

'All right, if you really want to rub salt in it and make me admit how humiliated you made me feel, I'll tell you,' she said angrily. 'I woke up, the next morning, and you were gone. I assumed you were in the farm office, so I dressed and went downstairs, intending to make us both some coffee and toast. I was going to bring it out to you, in the office. Then I heard Mark's answerphone message. You'd even discussed bedding me with him! It was all a way of getting me off your case, as he put it.' She stared at him, hurt and angry. 'I don't like being used.'

'And you couldn't be bothered to face me with that little accusation?'

'What was the point? So you could laugh at me? Or so you could lie your way out of it?' He mouth tightened. 'Get out, Brandon. I don't want you here.

'Zoe, listen to me. What happened between us wasn't a set-up.'

'No?'

'No. Yes, I admit that Mark had suggested to me that I should try seducing you, charming you out of your opposition to the development – but that was after we'd made love, not before, and I told him to stop being ridiculous.'

'Did you, now?' Zoe's tone was hard and disbelieving.

'Yes. You know as well as I do, what happened between us was mutual and had nothing to do with the development. I didn't discuss it with anyone else. And from the look of you, you're in pretty much the same state that I'm in.'

'Go to hell, Brandon.'

'I'm already there,' he said softly. 'And it looks like you are, too.'

'I'm fine. Now, get out.'

'Zoe. Your friends are all worried about you. That's why Steve—'

'Steve? What the hell has he got to do with this?' She suddenly realised why he hadn't needed to break in. 'That's his key you used, isn't it?'

Brandon winced. 'Don't take it out on him. He was only doing what he thought was best. Trying to help.'

'Well, I can do without his help – and I can do without you, too. Just go, will you?'

He nodded. 'If that's what you really want, all right.' He turned, about to go – then spun back to face her. 'Oh, hell, Zoe, why are we fighting? We're on the same side.'

'I don't think so.'

'Oh, yes, we are,' he said softly, pulling her to him. 'And there's only one way to sort this out.' He bent his head to kiss her; she fought him, trying to pull away and twisting her head, but it only made things worse. She could smell his clean fresh scent, and it drove her insane. In the end, she kissed him back, opening her mouth beneath his and giving him the access he wanted. She pushed her hands into his hair, luxuriating in the feel of the clean silky strands beneath her fingers; his hands slid very slowly down her spine, moulding her body to his and finally cupping her buttocks to pull her against him so that she could feel his erection.

He broke the kiss. 'Zoe. I've been going out of my mind, remembering what it was like between us. Right from the first time I kissed you, in the churchyard.'

She shivered. 'You lied to me.'

'I didn't. I honestly didn't know that the survey was bent.'

'I thought you were supposed to be a hot-shot young farmer? The clever young businessman with a university education who was dragging the farm into the twenty-first century?'

'Supposed being the operative word. Everyone makes mistakes, Zoe. Mine was trusting Mark Burroughs. He was my financial adviser. I thought he was on the level: but I was wrong.' He rubbed his thumb against her lower lip, and she couldn't prevent herself opening her mouth and drawing the digit in, sucking on it. His pupils dilated. 'Christ, Zoe, I can't think straight when you do things like that. What I mean is that I made two big mistakes. The first was trusting Mark, but the second one was worse. Much worse. Letting you go – I should never have done it.' He withdrew his hand and bent his head again to kiss her. 'Zoe. I've been dreaming about you, every night. My body's ached to feel your skin against mine.'

'But you didn't call me.'

'What was the point? You made it clear that you weren't interested. You walked out on me without a word – and you ignored the message I left you at The Feathers. You simply went back to London without returning my call.' He licked his lower lip. 'I . . . Zoe, I don't want to think or talk, right now. All I want to do is . . . Oh God. Where's your bedroom?'

'This isn't going to solve—'

'Yes, it is,' he interrupted. 'We can talk later. Right now, there are other things I need to do – and I think you need the same things.' He slid one hand between their bodies, stroking her midriff through her shirt and cupping one breast. Her nipple was hard, and she hissed a sharp intake of breath when he rolled it between his forefinger and thumb, the lace of her bra adding pleasurable friction to the sensation.

He kissed the top of her nose. 'Zoe. Before I start acting like some sex-starved teenager and take you on the floor, right now, will you *please* tell me where your bedroom is?'

'Upstairs,' she breathed unsteadily.

'Show me,' he murmured. 'Take me there, Zoe. Take me to your bed.'

It was more of a plea than a command. She nodded and turned away from him, walking up the stairs; he followed her, catching her at the top and spinning her round to kiss her again. By the time he broke the kiss, Zoe's legs felt weak and her sex was decidedly wet. Whatever her brain thought about this man, however much she hated him for lying to her, her body craved him. Desperately.

She allowed him to take her hand, and finally led him to her bedroom.

He took off her glasses, placing them carefully on her bedside cabinet, then pulled her back into his arms, kissing her hard. When he broke the kiss, she was shaking; he traced her swollen lower lip with the tip of his finger, his eyes darkening. 'God, Zoe. I've missed you. I've missed the way you feel in my arms. I've missed your voice, your scent – everything. I haven't been able to concentrate on anything. I've worked until my eyes couldn't focus any more; but then, the minute I closed my eyes, I saw your face, your smile. It drove me crazy.'

'Oh?'

The disbelief in her tone was obvious to him; he sighed, and kissed the tip of her nose. 'I'll stop talking. I'm only making things worse; maybe I can show you how I feel, instead.'

He let his fingers drift down over her chin, cupping her throat for a second; her eyes narrowed in panic. Surely he wasn't intending to murder her, strangle her and—

The thoughts vanished as his fingers travelled down, and he undid the first button on her shirt. He continued down, undoing the rest of the buttons and brushing the backs of his fingers against her skin; she closed her eyes, arching up towards him, and he bent his head to nuzzle her throat, breathing in her scent.

'Zoe,' he said unsteadily, 'I need to see you.'

She nodded, and he removed her shirt, dropping it on the carpet. Slowly, he undid the clasp of her bra and let it follow suit; he cupped her breasts, pushing them up and together to deepen her cleavage.

'Christ, you're so lovely,' he told her, his voice husky. He bent his head to nuzzle her breasts, and she couldn't help lifting her ribcage, inviting him to use his mouth on her. She felt him smile against her skin, and then trace the curve of her breasts with his lips, exploring her as if committing every inch of her skin to memory.

She shivered as he deliberately ignored her hardening nipples; as if he could read her mind, he stooped to take one hard rosy tip into his mouth, sucking gently.

'Just like the first time,' he murmured against her skin. 'Then, I could hardly wait to touch you, to taste you. Now, I know what you feel like, and it's even harder to hold back.'

'Then don't,' Zoe whispered.

He shook his head. 'I'm not going to rush this. I want to enjoy every second, make it last.' He dropped to his knees, unbuttoning her jeans as he did so, and nuzzled her abdomen; slowly, so very slowly, he drew the denims down over her hips, easing them over her thighs. Zoe kept her eyes closed, remembering how he'd done that before. The first time, in the churchyard, when he'd almost worshipped her body as he uncovered it. Then again, in his office, when

201

he'd used her jeans to hobble her and then spread her, virtually naked, across his desk. And then, that last time, when they'd left a trail of their clothes through the whole house.

She shivered, and he stilled. 'Zoe?'

'I . . .'

He stood up again, placing his finger against her lips; she opened her eyes, meeting his intense gaze.

'Don't say it. Don't think. Just be,' he said softly. 'Just you and me, right here and now. That's what matters. Everything else can wait.'

He bent down again and resumed his task, undoing her boots and balancing her weight against him as he eased her jeans over one foot then the other. He caressed the arch of her foot, kissing the hollow of her ankles, then moved slowly upwards again. Zoe closed her eyes again, revelling in the touch of his lips. Her body remembered this only too well: how it felt when he pushed her knickers to one side, breathing on her quim. How good it was when he parted her labia, breathing on her intimate flesh and teasing her, then bent his head and drew his tongue along the full length of her musky divide.

She could almost feel him tonguing her clitoris, nipping and licking and sucking; when he did nothing of the sort, and she suddenly realised that he wasn't even touching her, she opened her eyes in shock. 'Brandon?'

He smiled, tracing her lower lip with the tip of his finger. 'I was just watching you. The expression on your face, just then – you looked like an angel. A fallen angel, just about to sample your greatest pleasure.'

She flushed deeply. 'I . . .'

He pulled her into his arms, holding her close 'Sh. I know. It's like that for me, too, and I find it hard to come to terms with. No one else has ever made me feel like that.'

She was silent, not knowing what to say; he kissed her lightly on the mouth. 'I think it's your turn,' he murmured huskily.

'My turn?' she echoed, her mind too fuddled with the feelings he aroused in her to think straight.

'To undress me,' he said softly, taking her hands and drawing them to the hem of his sweater.

So he was going to make her wait for fulfilment, was he? A smile curved her lips. Two could play at that game. Slowly, she removed his sweater; he lifted his arms to help her. Then, equally slowly, she undid the zip and button of his jeans. She pushed the garment downwards, revealing his underpants, then curled her fingers round his cock, through the soft cotton. He took a sharp intake of breath as she began to frot him, very gently; he dipped his head to kiss her, his tongue pushing into her mouth and his hands coming up to fondle her breasts, echoing the movements of her fingers on his cock.

She pulled back, giving him a mischievous look, then dropped to her knees. She nuzzled his groin, tracing the outline of his cock with the tip of her nose, and he groaned, 'Zoe. Don't tease me.'

'And who was it who started arousing me, then sat back to watch the look on my face?' she reminded him.

'Okay, we're quits now. But if you don't hurry up, I'm going to have to help you,' he warned her. 'I can't wait much longer.'

'Patience is a virtue.'

'You've told me that before, I think,' he said. 'Or maybe I said it to—' His sentence finished on a gasp as she pulled his underpants down and took the tip of his cock in her mouth. She curled her fingers round his shaft, squeezing gently as she lapped at his glans; his fingers tangled in her hair, urging her on.

She stopped and gave him a lazy grin. 'That's just to be going on with,' she told him, and resumed her previous task of removing his jeans. He leant on her for balance as he lifted first one foot and then the other, allowing her to remove his jeans, underpants, shoes and socks. Finally, she rocked back on her haunches, looking up at him. His body really was beautiful, the muscles all toned and sculpted through sheer hard work on the land, rather than from self-indulgence at the gym. His cock rose from the cloud of hair at his groin, the tip swollen and glistening with a mixture of his arousal and her saliva.

'Zoe.' He reached down to take her hands, pulling her to her feet. 'I can't wait any more. I need you. Now.'

He hooked his thumbs into the waistband of her knickers,

drawing them down; she stepped out of the flimsy garment, then he lifted her and pushed her duvet aside, laying her on the bed. 'I imagined your bedroom to be more austere,' he told her. 'Monochrome.'

She smiled. 'Well, I'm not exactly the frills and flounces type.'

'No. But I didn't expect Victorian sprigged wallpaper.'

'That's a William Morris print you're talking about,' she said. 'Goes with the house.'

'True.' He eyed her wrought-iron headboard. 'Is that original?'

She shook her head. 'A copy. I like it.'

'Me, too.' He picked up one hand, kissing her wrists. 'And if I had the nerve to rummage through your chest of drawers to find a couple of silk scarves, I think it could come in very useful.'

Zoe flushed deeply. 'And who says I play those sort of games?'

'I don't know. I didn't think I did, either, but the way I feel when I'm with you – I want to take you to the limits of pleasure, and beyond.'

She remembered what she'd done with Gareth and Nico, and shivered. 'Brandon . . .'

'Sh.' He dipped his head to kiss her. 'Don't think. Don't talk. Just feel.' He stroked her breasts, teasing the hard rosy tips; then his hand drifted down over her abdomen. Automatically, her legs parted and he cupped her delta, letting his fingers spread along the hot moist fissure of her quim. He pressed down, and she shivered, parting her legs still wider; he used his index and ring fingers to part her labia, then curled his middle finger, stroking her quim as he straightened it again. He repeated the action again and again, lightly brushing her clitoris each time, until she was quivering.

'Just feel,' he repeated, pushing his middle finger into her vagina and using the ball of his thumb to continue stimulating her clitoris. He added a second finger, and a third, moving them rhythmically in and out; Zoe pushed her head back against the pillow, whimpering, as her climax splintered through her, making her whole body shudder.

He smiled, and bent to kiss her quim, exploring her

204

thoroughly with his tongue. Then he raised his head again and knelt between her thighs, fitting the tip of his cock against her sex. Very, very slowly, he eased himself into her; Zoe moaned and wrapped her legs round his waist pushing up to meet him.

'You feel so good,' he murmured. 'So bloody, bloody good.'

'So do you,' she admitted huskily, tightening her internal muscles round him.

He rubbed his nose affectionately against hers, then began to thrust. He moved his lower body in elliptic circles at the same time, constantly changing the angle of his penetration to give her more pleasure. Zoe found herself growing more and more aroused; just when she thought that she was on the brink of climax, he changed his rhythm or his pace, bringing her back from the edge and yet keeping her at a high pitch of pleasure.

Just when she thought that she could take no more, she felt his cock throbbing deep inside her, pushing her to her own release. When she came, she virtually saw stars; the aftershocks continued for what seemed like hours, little ripples of pleasure that ran the full length of her sex and tightened round his hard cock.

Finally, he slipped from her, and rolled onto his back, pulling her into the circle of his arms so that her head rested on his shoulder.

'Brandon—' she began.

He stroked her hair. 'I know. We have to talk.' He sighed. 'Though I think we both needed that, first.'

'Yes,' she admitted wryly.

'And I can't promise not to touch you,' he warned. He ran his fingers through her hair. 'I've been having all sorts of fantasies about this. About . . .' He shivered. 'Never mind.'

'About this?' She shifted so that she could wrap the ends of her hair round his cock, and rubbed him gently.

'Oh, God.' He groaned. 'Zoe, I can't handle this. It turns me on too much. We need to talk. Now.' He swallowed, and gently extricated himself from her. 'My brain's all over the place, now. But if you can bear with me, I'll be honest with you.' He kissed her lightly on the lips. 'Where do we start?'

Chapter Sixteen

'I don't know. You tell me.'

'Okay.' He settled back against the pillows, holding her close. 'I want you to come back to Whiteacres with me.'

She twisted to look at him. 'What? When?'

'Soon. As soon as you possibly can.'

Her eyes narrowed. 'Why?'

He sighed. 'Jack needs you there for the full excavation.'

She shook her head. 'I'm a journalist, not an archaeologist.'

'Exactly. You'd be a bridge between Ed and the rest of us. Ed says that he likes working with you, and so does Ella.'

She regarded him suspiciously. 'And how do you know?'

'Because they're working on my land – and they're staying at Whiteacres. It's easier for them than The Feathers – no travelling – and it's a damn sight more comfortable than a tent. I've spent most evenings talking to them and Gramps, since the full excavation started. When I haven't been torturing myself with thoughts of you in the shower, that is.'

'Oh.'

'I'd like you to chart the progress of the dig, and write a series of articles for the local paper, before we open it to the general public.'

So he didn't want her at Whiteacres for her own sake. He wanted her just because she would be useful. 'Shannon's a good journalist, and she's local. Why not ask her?'

'Because I've met Shannon Lewis, and although she seems okay, she isn't you.' He stroked her face. 'I need you, Zoe. The place isn't the same without you around.'

'Tough. I have a career.'

'A freelance career – so, technically, you can work where you like.'

'It's easier if I'm in London.' Her old mistrust of him surfaced. 'Anyway, you and I are on different sides.'

'No, we're not. We're on exactly the same side.'

'Maybe right now,' she admitted, 'but for how long?'

He sighed, guessing why she was resisting him. 'You're thinking about that bloody answerphone message, aren't you? Look, you won't have to see Mark ever again. He's finished in business – there's no way he can continue as a financial adviser, even if he wins the fraud case, which is highly unlikely. My solicitor tells me that the contract I signed with him over the original development is no longer valid, and I certainly won't be asking him to be part of the new development. I've moved all the farm's business away from him, too.'

'Did you discuss me with him?'

'Only when he asked me to talk to you and stop you stirring up trouble for the development. I said I'd already had a word with you, and he said that he'd try. I told him to be nice to you. He said he'd take you to lunch and talk you round. I didn't tell him to try charming you into bed, believe me.' He sighed. 'If anything, I spent the morning regretting the idea of letting him anywhere near you, because I knew what his reputation was. The idea of him laying a finger on you made me almost insane with jealousy.'

'You seriously thought I'd let Mark Burroughs take me to bed?' She stared at him in disbelief.

'No. That's what kept me sane.' He smiled wryly. 'I guessed that he'd try it on with you, though.'

She snorted. 'Pseudo-sophistication. Saying I was like a Rossetti painting – where the model had completely different colour hair – and playing me the bloody *Four Seasons*.'

Brandon's lips twitched. 'Oh, dear.'

'And you didn't have anything to do with Helena trying to seduce me?'

'*Helena?*'

'Obviously not,' Zoe, registering his surprise, answered her own question.

'Helena tried to seduce you?' he repeated incredulously.

'She told me that the two of you had an arrangement, and that you had similar tastes. That you liked to play games.

I thought maybe you'd told her what happened between us, in the churchyard.'

He shook his head. 'Helena's tried it on with me, a few times. I told her I wasn't interested. And I swear to you, I certainly didn't discuss you with her. Whatever she said, she either made an educated guess or she'd found out from someone you told.'

'I didn't tell anyone, either.'

'Helena tried to seduce you.' He shook his head. 'I wish I'd seen that.'

Zoe scowled. 'What is it about two women together that always turns men on?'

'It wasn't that actually. More like I would have loved to see your face when she turned on the charm – and hers, when you turned her down.' He grinned. 'Did she sulk?'

'Big time.'

'I thought so.' He caressed one breast. 'Though as you brought up the subject, yes, I would like to make love with two women. As long as they were both you.'

'That's incredibly corny.'

'Maybe. But I like the idea of being able to kiss you all over and feel your sex quivering over my mouth, at the same time as my cock was buried deep inside you.' He nuzzled her ear. 'Don't tell me you've never fantasised about making love with two men.'

Zoe flushed darkly. More than fantasised: she'd actually done it, while she was trying to get him out of her system.

'There's nothing to be embarrassed about,' he said. 'It's mildly kinky, but nothing too way out.'

'I'm not embarrassed.'

'What's caused this, then?' he asked, brushing the backs of his fingers against her flushed cheeks.

'Nothing.'

'Tell me.'

She shook her head. 'You won't like it.'

'Tell me anyway.'

'I . . .' Her throat dried.

'Tell me.' He slid his hand between her thighs, and grinned. 'The idea's certainly turned you on. You're wet.'

'All right.' She lifted her chin. 'If you really want to know: I've done it.'

208

'You've made love with two men at the same time?' He pushed his finger into her sex. 'And?'

'And what?'

'Was it good, Zoe? Did they satisfy you?'

'Yes.' Though not in the way that he did: not that she was going to admit that.

'You wanton woman.' His tone was more of admiration than admonishment.

'Yes, well.' She didn't want to go into details. 'We're getting off the subject.'

He continued teasing her sex, arousing her. 'What subject's that?'

'I . . . Look, I can't think straight when you keep doing that.'

He smiled. 'That's the whole point. Come back to Whiteacres with me, Zoe.'

'No.'

He sighed. 'Why?'

'Because it won't work between us. We always end up fighting.'

'Which means that making up will be all the sweeter. Zoe, I think we'd make a good team. I can't promise that it will be perfectly smooth between us – you're just as stroppy and set in your ways as I am – but I think we can work it out.'

'No.'

He changed tactics, rolling her onto her back and kissing his way down her body. 'I remember how it felt to sleep with you in my arms.'

'And I remember how it felt to wake up alone the next morning.'

He jack-knifed up. 'That's what all this is about, isn't it? Look, I know I should have left you a note. I meant to – but I got distracted. I was in the farm office, typing out a fax to the police about Mark Burroughs and what I thought he'd been up to. I said that I'd have the evidence with them later – and you obviously did that for me, as they rang me back, later that afternoon, to say that they'd received the evidence and would like to interview me the following morning.'

'Why should I believe you?'

'You can check with them, if you like. Ask to see their

original copy. You'll see the time I sent it, at the top. And if that bloody answerphone message is still upsetting you, I can assure you that I made love with you because I wanted to, not just to suit one of Mark's schemes. The same reason that I'm in bed with you now – because you do things to me, Zoe. You make me feel like no other woman ever has. I've spent more time masturbating during the past few weeks, than I have in my entire life – and I still can't get you out of my system. I need you.'

She was silent; he sighed. 'I can see why you don't believe me. I was hostile and aggressive towards you, right from the start. At first, it was because I was worried about Gramps. I didn't want the over-excitement making him ill – particularly as I didn't think it would come to anything, and I thought he'd be disappointed. And then it was because I fell for you and I hated you for it because we were on opposite sides. You were forbidden territory, and it was driving me insane.' He shrugged. 'Gramps thinks you feel the same. And that's one of the reasons why I came here today. Steve said you were impossible, and he thought I had something to do with it. He told me I was the only one who could sort it out, and offered me your spare key.'

'I'll murder him for interfering.'

Brandon ignored her. 'Gramps overheard the conversation. He said pretty much the same thing – that I was impossible to live with, too, so I'd better go to London and sort it out with you, then bring you home.'

She lifted her chin. 'I'm not moving in with you for Jack's sake.'

'I'm not asking you to do that. I'm asking you to do it for my sake. Give us both a chance.'

'A chance.' She remembered what she'd said to Dale. *I'm my own woman, and I like it that way. No one to demand things from me, expect me to fit into his way of life.* Brandon wanted her to change all that, for him. 'How do you mean, a chance?'

Unable to help himself, he caressed her breasts. 'It might not work out. If it doesn't, then you can leave and come back to London. At least we'll have tried.'

'And if it does work out?' she tested.

'If it does, then I'd like you to settle down with me and

have lots of little Zoes. With Eileen as our babysitter, or maybe Sam, so you can continue with your career if you want to. Part time, full time – whatever you want. As long as you're with me, and you're happy.'

So he didn't expect her to give up everything for him. Then his comment penetrated her brain. *Lots of little Zoes.* 'Anyway, who says we'd just have daughters? Why not lots of little Brandons?'

'I wouldn't have dared say I wanted lots of sons, as well as lots of daughters. You've already accused me of being a chauvinist. You even said that I'd probably name the development after me.'

She grinned. 'And you will.'

'No. I thought I'd call it Lynton Meadows, actually.' He teased one nipple with his tongue. 'Though I think the place needs to be christened properly, before the development starts.'

'How do you mean?'

'Does Lower Yareham churchyard mean anything to you?' She flushed deeply, and he chuckled. 'Don't say you're going to go all shy on me. I wanted to make love with you in the middle of our land.'

'Our land?'

'Yes. Our land. Marry me, and you get the farm as well.'

'That's what Helena had her eye on.'

He shrugged. 'Tough. I don't want Helena. I want you.'

She narrowed her eyes to hide the teasing glint. 'I'm a journalist. I don't take anything on say-so, without proof.'

'Proof.' He took her hand, guiding it to his erect cock. 'Is that proof enough for you?'

'Possibly. Possibly not.'

'What kind of proof do you want?'

She shrugged. 'They say that actions speak louder than words.'

His eyes darkened. 'They do, indeed. And sometimes, they go even better together.'

He climbed off the bed, and she frowned. 'Brandon?'

'I think I've just found the nerve I lacked earlier.'

Her frown deepened. 'I don't understand.'

He rummaged through her chest of drawers. 'Short memory, hm?'

211

'What the hell – oh.' She suddenly remembered his comment about having the nerve to rummage through her chest of drawers to find a couple of silk scarves.

He returned to the bed, triumphantly holding two long emerald green silk scarves. 'Perfect. They nearly match your eyes.'

'Brandon—'

'Sh.' He kissed her, nibbling at her lower lip and making her open her mouth; she kissed him back, pushing her tongue against his. She was so lost in the kiss that she didn't realise what he was doing, until it was too late and her wrists were tied very firmly to the headboard.

'Brandon!'

He grinned. 'The lady doth protest too much. Particularly as she's admitted to making love to two men at once – which is way, way wilder than what I'm just about to do to her.'

Colour flared hotly in her cheeks. 'That's below the belt.'

'Which is precisely where I'm going to work.' He knelt between her thighs, sliding his hands down her legs until he held her ankles. He positioned her feet flat against the mattress, widening the gap between her legs. 'Have I told you how beautiful your sex is, Zoe? I've been dreaming about it, night after night. Seeing it in my mind's eye, glistening with arousal: and even tasting it. That beautiful mixture of honey and musk and vanilla. It makes me drool just thinking about it.'

'Brandon . . .'

'Sh. Unless you're going to tell me about your two men.' He paused. 'Just how recently was it, Zoe?'

Her skin heated. 'That's none of your business.'

'Yes, it is.' His eyes were teasing. 'Did it happen after you met me?'

'That's none of your business.'

'So it did, then. Otherwise you'd have simply said "no".'

She lifted her chin. 'Let me go.'

'No. Not until you tell me.' He bent his head, drawing his tongue along her sex, teasing her until she was thoroughly aroused. 'Tell me, Zoe. Was it since you met me?'

'Stop teasing me.'

'Tell me,' he insisted.

'All right, then. If you must know, yes. Yes.'

'And would I be right in assuming that it was because you were trying to forget me?'

'That's arrogant.'

'No. I'm just wondering if you tried the same thing that I did – making love with someone else, in an attempt to forget what it was like between us.'

'You slept with someone else?' She stared at him, shocked.

'What's sauce for the goose,' he quipped. 'But I went for a serial approach, rather than a parallel one.'

'You bastard!'

In answer, he dipped his head to work on her clitoris; he'd tied her well enough so that she couldn't free herself, although not tightly enough to hurt her, and his grip on her ankles was firm. Her struggles merely made him tease her more with his mouth, alternately sucking her clitoris and using his tongue to push it hard against her pubic bone.

'Was Steve one of them?' he asked conversationally.

Zoe could barely think straight. 'One of whom?'

'Your two lovers.'

'No.'

He didn't press the point. 'Did you see them more than once?'

'No.'

'So it didn't work, then?'

She refused to answer. He blew on her quim, making her shiver. 'Tell me, Zoe. Unless you want to stay here like this all night. Every time you're about to come, I'll pull back and bring you back down from the plateau, before starting again. I'll tease you all night if I have to, until you're begging me to make you come – and I won't until you tell me the truth. Did it work?'

'No,' she admitted. 'Did it work for you?'

'No. Though, like I said, I didn't try two at once.' At the outrage on her face, he laughed. 'I doubt if it would have worked. Nothing would get you out of my system, Zoe Lynton. And I think it's the same for you. When are you going to admit it?'

'Go to hell.'

'Been there, didn't like it.' He drew his tongue between her labia. 'Whereas I rather like it here . . .'

Zoe groaned as he continued to lap at her; she clenched

her fists, knowing that it was pointless to struggle against her bonds. His skilful manipulations brought her to the point of orgasm; but just as she was about to climax, he lifted his head. 'So are you coming back with me?'

'No.'

'Pity.' He shrugged. 'Never mind.'

'Brandon – this isn't fair.'

'What isn't?'

'I was just on the point of—'

'I know,' he cut in. 'That's why I stopped. I did warn you.'

'That's torture.'

'Tactics,' he corrected. 'Sophisticated ones.' He grinned. 'Unless you want me to try the Mark Burroughs charm method.'

Zoe groaned. 'That's even worse.'

'How about a combination of the two?' Brandon mused. 'Just when you're about to come, I could quote poetry at you. Something really trite and hackneyed. Rudyard Kipling. No – better than that.' He grinned evilly at her. 'Wordsworth. Wordsworth at his most turgid and boring.'

'You're a bastard.'

'Yup.' He resumed tonguing her sex, until she was writhing and pushing her pelvis up towards his face. Just as he judged that she was near her climax, he stopped again. 'Give in?'

'No.'

'Fair enough,' he said equably. Again, he waited until she'd simmered down; this time, as well as paying attention to her sex, he moistened one finger and pressed it against her anus. Zoe moaned loudly as the tight ring of muscle gave way, allowing him access. Nico had taken much more of a liberty with her and, although she'd enjoyed it, she knew that it would have been far more mind-blowing if Brandon had done it.

Not if. *When*, her mind corrected. The thought was nearly enough to make her come: as if he guessed, he stopped again.

'Brandon, I— don't stop. Please, don't stop. Not this time,' she begged. 'I can't take it any more. Let me come. Please.'

'You know what I want you to say.'

She sighed. 'All right, I'll come back with you.'

'Sure?'

'Sure.'

'I love you, Zoe,' he told her quietly. 'You won't regret it. I promise.'

'You *love* me?'

He nodded. 'That's half the problem. I've known it since the minute I met you. Since I saw you with Gramps in our sitting room, making a fuss of the dogs and surreptitiously feeding them bits of Eileen's sponge. I was furious when I realised that you were a journalist and were going to make my life difficult, but . . .' He smiled wryly. 'I had this sudden vision of you.'

'Vision?' she prompted.

'You've already enacted it, believe me,' he said huskily. 'More than once.'

She smiled. 'Then perhaps you could enlighten me, so I can do it again.' She tipped her head on one side. 'Because – hardened cynic though I'm supposed to be – I think I love you, too. That's why I haven't been able to get you out of my mind – and even acting like a slut with two younger men couldn't make up for not having you.'

'No?'

'No,' she confirmed.

He kissed her hard, so that she could taste her own arousal on his mouth, then resumed his tonguing and intimate massage. Zoe's climax, delayed for so long, rippled through her entire body. She yelled out with the sheer pleasure of it, crying out his name hoarsely; Brandon continued licking and caressing her until the aftershocks had died down, then moved up to untie her and drew her into his arms.

'Zoe.' He kissed her gently. 'This is just the start. There are all sorts of things I want to explore with you.'

'Your chamomile lawn.'

He smiled. 'You remembered. Yes, that. And I want to paint your entire body in Belgian chocolate and lick it off. And give you a bath in champagne.'

'It's supposed to be asses' milk.'

'Champagne,' he said firmly. 'And . . . Oh. All sorts of things.'

'Indeed.'

215

'You make me want to run riot.' When he caught the look on her face, he frowned. 'What?'

'I can just imagine you rioting through Lower Yareham,' she giggled, suddenly overcome with laughter.

'Better believe it. Because you'll be right there by my side,' he told her.

Her giggles subsided, and she reached to pull him down to her. 'On this occasion, Brandon Mitchell, I think you might just be right . . .'